Queen of the Zoo 2

Black Migo

Lock Down Publications and Ca$h Presents
Queen of the Zoo 2
A Novel by *Black Migo*

Queen of the Zoo 2

Lock Down Publications
P.O. Box 944
Stockbridge, Ga 30281
www.lockdownpublications.com

Copyright 2022 by Black Migo
Queen of the Zoo 2

All rights reserved. No part of this book may be reproduced in any form or by electronic or mechanical means, including information storage and retrieval systems without permission in writing from the publisher, except by a reviewer who may quote brief passages in review.

First Edition June 2022
Printed in the United States of America

This is a work of fiction. Names, characters, places, and incidents either are products of the author's imagination or are used fictitiously. Any similarity to actual events or locales or persons, living or dead, is entirely coincidental.

Lock Down Publications
Like our page on Facebook: Lock Down Publications @ www.facebook.com/lockdownpublications.ldp

Book interior design by: **Shawn Walker**
Edited by: **Tamira Butler**

Stay Connected with Us!

Text **LOCKDOWN** to 22828 to stay up-to-date with new releases, sneak peaks, contests and more...

Thank you!

Queen of the Zoo 2

Submission Guideline.

Submit the first three chapters of your completed manuscript to ldpsubmissions@gmail.com, subject line: Your book's title. The manuscript must be in a .doc file and sent as an attachment. Document should be in Times New Roman, double spaced and in size 12 font. Also, provide your synopsis and full contact information. If sending multiple submissions, they must each be in a separate email.

Have a story but no way to send it electronically? You can still submit to LDP/Ca$h Presents. Send in the first three chapters, written or typed, of your completed manuscript to:

LDP: Submissions Dept
P.O. Box 944
Stockbridge, Ga 30281

DO NOT send original manuscript. Must be a duplicate.

Provide your synopsis and a cover letter containing your full contact information.

Thanks for considering LDP and Ca$h Presents.

Black Migo

Chapter 1

The hairs on back of Brick's sweaty neck pricked up as he pushed the key into the slot quickly. He fumbled the door open, rushing into the cold darkness of his home as the black Suburban drove past at snail's pace. He slammed the door shut, locking it before peeking out the blinds to catch the red glow of its tail lights as it exited the block.

Through the tiny opening of the curtain, his eyes roamed the quiet street, anticipating the truck's return. After twenty minutes of waiting, it hadn't, and at this point, he couldn't care less if it did.

Noticing it was awfully quiet, he looked around. "Where the fuck this bitch at?" he uttered, moving through the eerie silence in search for his wife, Rucci, whom he'd been trying to reach all day. Dialing her number for the hundredth time, he became furious getting the automatic voice mail, again. "Pussy-ass-hoe, call me when you get this message!" he spat, tossing the phone onto the counter. Removing the dirty blunt of boont from behind his ear, he sparked up, taking two deep pulls of a potent combination of coke, molly, and weed. He erupted in a fitful cough that intensified the high.

Outting the joint, he sensed something wasn't right. Wild things had been happening around Green Street throughout the day. Mail trucks delivering after nightfall? Ice cream trucks parked hours at a time? Drones? He thought maybe everyone around him was overdosing on some trippy making assumptions, but having witnessed the blue suits parked outside one of the five trap houses had him convinced.

It was all bad. And being unable to find his wife had him extremely paranoid. Did the feds have Rucci? He prayed not. Would she crack? He wasn't sure. Considering the threatening evidence that could possibly put him away, he made up his mind. "I gotta kill this hoe."

Or was it the drugs talking?

Removing the .45 from his hip, he clicked off the safety, checking the house once again. "Where the hell is she?"

Suddenly, his stomach rocked up with a grave feeling. He bolted into the bedroom, punching in the pin to the safe. The sight before him was a blow to the gut. He was out of breath. Panting wildly, he rushed to his phone. "This bitch better not be fuckin' wit' me, dawg!" Fury warmed his skin as he called her.

Again, voice mail.

He flopped onto the plush couch, defeated, bursting into sinister laughter. "Ha, ha, ha! This bitch got me! Left me out to fucking dry." He pictured Rucci spending his 400K she took. "My stupid ass!" He laughed some more to keep from crying. Brick relit the blunt, filling his lungs with the toxic haze that altered his demeanor. Swiftly, violence filled his chest, turning his gaze glossy red. His eyes became dark as the midnight sky. "Bitch got me fucked up if she think she gon' take everything."

For a moment, the drugs kept him stuck in place as his mind ran rogue. By the time his high simmered down, he was dressed in all black, gun in hand—fully loaded and ready for war. Taking a quick peek, he saw the black Suburban was back surveilling his home. Every fiber in him said it was 200 and his savage killahs out to get him.

He chuckled at the thought of them catching and torturing him. "Pussy ass niggas can't catch me slipping. Bitch, I'm Brick!" He took out his cell, dialing. "The fuck they think this is?"

"9-1-1 operator, what's your emergency?"

"Yeah, there's a suspicious black truck going up and down the street and is now parked outside my home. I'm afraid they're trying to kill me." He grinned deviously, mimicking the voice of a frightened white woman.

"Ma'am, what's your location?"

"2710 Blossom Street. Send help quick!" He hung up, snickering, "Bitch."

Since he lived in a nice community, police arrived on the street immediately surrounding the suburban. Using the temporary distraction, he snuck out the back door.

At 2:50 a.m., the Uber dropped Brick off outside the one-story brick house deep down Leesburg Road. With caution, he entered

the yard searching for his wife's car. It wasn't there. Angrily, he blended with the shadows.
He knocked on the window since he no longer had his cell phone, having destroyed and dumped it.
Tootsie, Rucci's younger sister, lifted the window after a few knocks. "Boy, what the hell is you doing outside my damn window? Wha'chu want?"
She was the splitting image of his wife and for a moment, he believed it was Rucci until the young woman spoke.
"I need'a come in. Hurry up and open the door."
"Unt-uh! It's three in da mornin', where's Rucci?" She glanced toward the road.
"Shit. I don't know. Let me in so we can figure it out together," he said. "Is you gon' let me in or not?"
She sucked her teeth, curled her lip, and rolled her eyes. "Nigga, don't be rushing me." She pushed the window down. He went to the front door. A second later, she was stepping aside allowing him in. "Don't be lookin' at me eitha." Her soft, childlike voice was flirtatious. She attempted to pull the tiny t-shirt down over her juicy ass and even phatter pussy.
"When's the last you heard from her?"
Tootsie faced him. "Like a week ago. But that's your wife, how come you don't know where she is? Y'all beefin' again, ain't it?"
"She just up and fucking left." He took a look around. There were no signs of his wife anywhere in the one-bedroom house. "Where's your phone?"
The cool room had her nipples probing through the thin fabric as she strained to keep her shirt down. "Mannn," she drawled. "Y'all two stay with some shit going on. Don't put me in nothing."
Brick trailed her into the bedroom, the seventy-inch flat screen on the wall illuminated the room with a porno left on pause. Tootsie called her sister on speaker, putting her eyes on him suspiciously.
On the third ring, she answered, "Hello?"
Tootsi glanced up at him. "What's up, bitch, where you?"
She groggily answered, "You wake me up to ask me where I'm at? I'm home, why?"

"You are not home if your husband just left here lookin' fuh you."

Brick sat on the edge of the bed listening intently to Rucci's background for the slightest hint to where she could be

"How long ago before his ass left?"

"About thirty minutes."

"Put me on speaker... Brick, I know you're there. Don't even worry about lookin' for me, I'm long gone. I love you, but I'm not letting you take me down with you. When all that shit calms down, I got you." She sighed.

He took the phone. "My nigga, don't fuckin' play wit' me. Bring your ass back, and my shit! You took the whole fucking safe, dang. Way they do dat at?"

"Bae, the feds are fucking building a case on you and everybody else dealing with you. I'm not finna let your ass get me trapped off because you can't think past your fuckin' nose. Now, once you get all that mess situated, I'll have everything plus more. Until then, don't bother." The call disconnected.

"Bitch, you—" He glared at the dial pad. "This hoe hung up?"

"The feds lookin' for you, boy? What is you gonna do?"

"Fuck the feds. They ain't comin' for me. They're not even worried 'bout me. They want them niggas moving tons of work. Bricks of shit. Not bust down," he spat with defiance.

"I thought that's what you did, move bricks?"

He tossed her phone back. "Shut the hell up and mind yo' business."

Tootsie sucked her teeth, curled her lip, and rolled her eyes. "Nigga, don't tell me to shut up, ugly ass."

The dilemma of his wife being gone with at least 400K had him beyond furious. He cracked his knuckles, contemplating his next move. One thing for sure, she would answer to the barrel of his .45.

Glaring at his in-law, he said, "I need a few favors."

Face twisted up, she countered with ghettofied attitude, "Nigga, like what?"

Chapter 2

Reminiscing, Zoo dug deep into his memory bank. So much of his past had been buried and over the years, he tried to keep it that way. But as life began to unravel around him, things locked deep in history were summoned to the forefront. He remembered it like yesterday ...

The street lights had kicked on, and all the kids playing dodgeball in the vacant lot—a trap house once stood but had been condemned by the city, burned down, and removed— knew it was time to head home. It didn't matter that shards of glass, used syringes, and empty baggies of dope covered the area. Nor that it was now drizzling with a violent gray sky threatening a severe downpour. The summer was in, and thirteen-year-old Pierre Montana was reluctant as he began his short trek up a pathway that drug addicts occupied frequently. He knew each junky by name. They all knew him. He was the son of a nameless, unidentified father, and Charity, a drunken whore mom with four kids living in section 8 housing.

It began to rain harder. Pierre slowed his feet, in no rush to get home. He did so hoping the lightning cracking through the sky would either strike him down dead or give him special abilities like no other. His imagination was wild. Instead, the rain raised away dirt and sweat from his soiled clothes after a long day of playing outdoors. Climbing the steps to the front door, Mike, one of his mother's many male friends, stopped him.

"Aye, yo, Pierre, my man. Do me a favor, youngin', give this bag to your mother for me. Tell'er I can't stay 'cause the wife is on my tail, but that I'll come through tomorrow afternoon to get what she owes me," he said.

Frankly, he asked, "Why you can't just go in there and tell'er that?"

"Well, I can, but, you know your mother is something else. Tell you what ... you give it to her for me, and tomorrow when I come over, I'll have a couple dollars for you," Mike charmed. "How that sound?"

At the sound of money, Pierre grabbed the grocery bag from him. "Better have my money too." He turned and marched inside, drenching wet. He wished he could've stashed the bag but knew he was damned if he did or didn't. Liquor brought demons out of Charity, and he was in no form of wanting to deal with her. Before he could shut and lock the door behind him, his mother boomed from her bedroom.

"Pierre!"

"Ma'am?" He kicked my shoes off at the door.

"Did you see Mike out there?" she asked angrily, ready to explode if he hadn't. She may even send him on a search for the man who made her a promise.

"Yeah, he gave me this for you." He extended the bag.

Charity glared at him like he was crazy. "Well, why the fuck is you still standing there with my shit? Give it to me." She snatched it from him then smacked spit from his face. "The next time a muthafucka give you something to give to me, you break your damn neck trying to get it to me!"

Sucking up tears, he replied, "Yes, ma'am."

"Now get the fuck out my room. And next time, come in this house late and soaking wet, I'ma fuck yo' ass up, bitch!" she spat, twisting open the bottle top to the malt liquor, chugging it. "Playin' wit' my damn shit," she mumbled on his way out.

In the second bedroom he shared with his three sisters, he undressed. Rema, seventeen, was the oldest. Tati was sixteen, and his baby sister, Maya, was only two years old. Each had different fathers that neither knew. Though all lived under the same roof of the cramped two-bedroom apartment, it was as if they didn't exist to Charity, who kept herself locked in her room drinking liquor with random men, day and night.

Rema asked heatedly, "She hit you?"

He nodded his head.

"Don't cry, okay. You're a big boy. Take the rest of your clothes off. I'll run you a bath and heat your food back up."

***

Queen of the Zoo 2

That night, well into his deep slumber somewhere in the wee hours of the morning, Charity entered her kids' room extremely drunk and angry. The extension cord was wrapped around her hand, and suddenly, with rage, she began to whip Pierre in his sleep. He bolted upright, confused, attempting to shield himself from the excruciating pains. Tangled in the sheets, he was unable to fight away the assault. Each time the cord struck his skin, welts formed, blood spilled, and his hatred for the woman he thought he loved grew.

Unleashing her violent temper on him, Charity was bent over panting wildly. "Now get your ass in that damn hallway closet, and you better not come out!"

"Mama, noo!" his sisters yelled.

"Y'all bitches shut the fuck up! Say sum'n else'n, both you whores can get the fuck out my shit."

Silently, the girls fumed. Pierre sniffled and whimpered, fighting hard to keep from sobbing as his mother forced him into the dark, cluttered closet. The wooden kitchen chair could be heard as she pent it beneath the door handle so he couldn't come out.

"Sick of yo' shit," she uttered. "Dumb ass little nigga ain't gon' be shit. Just like your motherfucken daddy!"

Snapping out the reverie, Zoo opened the steel-reinforced door, allowing the group of five young boys to descend the flight of stairs from the third level of his mansion. It was an intense six hours and a secret to what went on behind the scenes. It was necessary, mandatory, and pivotal to his operation.

The woman who carried the ambience of a God-like force nodded to him reassuringly as he closed the door behind them. Without her, he would not reign, king of the zoo.

In a single-file line, the youngins stopped outside his second-level office awaiting Shooter. His blood homie and goon was being escorted in. Zoo led them into the office that reeked of nature. Poisonous insects lined one side of the large room, while hostile reptiles occupied another. It was his sanctuary, a place he felt at home and adventurous. However, he needed the moment to test his new young prodigy. It was a test no one could avoid, and as he proceeded, Shooter's body language was interrupting him.

Anxiously, he spoke, "Bruh, I got some really bad news."

Zoo held up a finger to silence him. "Taylor, come up here," he called the first of five while he slowly opened the glass case to one of the world's deadliest spiders. The six-ounce Brazilian furrow spider was equipped with one-inch fangs strong enough to penetrate shoes and toenails. He grinned maliciously. A test used to detect fear he utilized. "Put your hand in."

He did so, fearless.

Each of the new goons passed the test as well. Satisfied, he rounded his desk and took a seat. Shooter's demeanor bothered him.

"Bruh, we need'a speak. It's important."

"What is it?"

"It's the lil' homie, our cousin ... Gary."

"What about 'em?"

With a grim expression, Shooter answered, "Some police killed 'em in the hood not long ago this morning. Got the jungle on fire."

"You better be jokin', homez," he gritted.

"G50 just messaged me. He said you weren't answering your phone."

Devastated and hurt, Zoo replied, "Damn! This shit ain't needed."

Zoo cleared them all out his office, needing a minute to think. Knowing the mentality of his blood homies, he was certain retaliation was inevitable. It was also a possibility it would disrupt the game of monopoly, bringing down the pressure of law enforcement.

Fifteen minutes later, he joined his company out on the back patio. Shooter had left Zippy, one of his trusted young killahs, who had returned from a task. Summoning all his youngins from around the property of his mansion, they gathered about.

"I did like you asked," Zippy began. "And I found this on one of the fiends on Green Street. I don't know what it means, but it looks offensive."

Queen of the Zoo 2

Zoo examined the stamped wax paper. "Fck PHP." fuck Pine Hurst Posse. Whoever designed it intended to send a message. Zoo didn't voice his thoughts but knew a group of ambitious gangstas had kicked off a beef.

"I tried to located that nigga Brick too. Somebody called police on us last night when we almost had 'em. Luckily, we weren't strapped. What I do know is they're pushing products out of five houses. Two spots on both ends of the block with a major trap house in the middle. We tortured the junky behind the house. She said Brick must've robbed somebody and mixed the dopes because it's the best in the city," Zippy reported.

Zoo spat, "Best my ass. I'll have somebody test this shit later. What else you found out?"

"The feds watching him," Zippy answered. "We seen 'em. We seen Brick too, but we was warned if we made a move on 'em the feds would've gotten to us before we could ever get away."

He took a seat, further examining the powder substance. Though the bricks of dope, guns, and money were a loss, it was nothing compared to losing two loyal goons and their mother. Now that he knew who was responsible, he had to act quickly in delivering street justice before police could solve the case.

"You say it was five houses they're pushing my shit out of?"

"Yes, sir," he answered. "Took pictures of every spot too." He handed over the cell phone with dozens of photos. Zoo took his time studying every house and its address. This young goon did good.

Removing his phone, Zoo made a call to his uncle Jerry, who was highly ranked in the Marines special forces.

"Nephew, talk to me, boy," Jerry answered.

"I need you immediately."

"10-4. We'll meet. Three hours."

Black Migo

Chapter 3

"Just behind me is where seventeen-year-old Gary Jackson was fatally gunned down after being shot numerous times in the back while attempting to flee. Witnesses say Mr. Gary took off running when he spotted Officer Matthew Wilks attempting to stop him. Officer Wilks maintains that Gary Jackson reached for what he assumed to be a firearm. Fearing for his life, Wilks responded with deadly force. At this point, it is unclear whether the officer will be charged. However, an investigation is surely underway," the seasoned news reporter spoke nervously into the microphone, sensing the thickening tensions escalating around them. The Pine Hurst community was growing hostile as word spread like wildfire of another young black man being gunned down by white cop.

The white female news reporter, Sara Gene, forty-one years old, swallowed hard as she received the atrocious glares from folks that tightened her throat with fear, making it difficult to breath as crowds gathered. "I think it's time for us to wrap up and get out of here."

The cameraman, white, thirty-four years of age, brought the camera down. "We have to at least get two more shots. Locals are going to want to see these developments."

Sara Gene surveyed the notorious Pine Hurst Park community. It was no place to be caught after dark for any outsiders. But her job, career, and reputation in giving the rawest of stories was most important. She couldn't cheat her viewers, and knew it was her obligation to collect more footage.

As the evening came to a close, Sara Gene checked her watch. "Fine. We go live in ten minutes."

***

Lala shook her head, sad and hurt. "That was so messed up. They know they ain't have to do 'em like that. For real. I'm willing to bet you Gary brother, G50 dem, finna raise hell out this bitch."

"They betta," Mena, her best friend, replied. Both were in the upstairs apartment of Four Seasons watching the spectacle down below in the parking lot as police left the apartments. The crowd was growing. Despite the pandemic and regulations, angry residents gathered around the chalked concrete Gary last laid sprawled. His blood stains were the only remnants along with teddy bears, burning candles, smoking incense, and red bandannas scattered about.

"'Cause if they don't, I'm never ever claiming Pine Hurst Park anymore."

"They gon' do somethin', I know it." LaLa stood, pulling up her pants. At sixteen, she was curvy, well developed, and fast beyond her age. Having grown up in the Pine Hurst projects, she was nothing new to the streets. Having lost her virginity years ago, she was ratchet as hell.

Mena was no different, being the same age as her best friend with a birthday only days apart from each other. The two fast asses both lost their innocence at thirteen. Big Ray, a man Zoo had murdered weeks ago in the parking lot for all to see, had paid them both $500 apiece for the pussy. To them, it was all a part of the struggle.

Standing, Mena jumped and wiggled her pants back up over the voluptuous backside inherited from her mother. LaLa and Mena were inseparable, and many around the hood considered them siblings. The two did everything under the sun together. Some would even say they were churchgoing good girls with prosperous futures ahead of them. What they didn't know was that the two girls were far more in tuned than their mothers knew. They didn't know their fathers, like most of the other girls around the way. Both of their mothers hung out tight and were always in the street together, so the two girls lacked all guidance and leadership.

"What's wrong? You acting like you're tryna have some fun," Mena asked.

LaLa presented her devious grin. "Bitch, them pigs killed Gary, that was my mothafucken dawg."

"Mine too."

"Okay?" She craned her neck. "So, what's up? We both know them blood niggas finna do some stupid shit. I wanna have some fun too. We should go over to G50's apartment and ask'em to let us participate"

Mena gave her a silly look. "You're bein' stupid. Them niggas not gonna let us do nothing wit' dem. They already think we some nappy head thots. We might as well shoot ourselves asking some shit like dat. Don't forget them niggas don't respect bitches at all unless—"

"We show 'em something."

"Exactly."

LaLa sucked her teeth. "Fuck dat, and fuck dem stupid, stank ass niggas. We can do our own shit." She went to the window, recognizing all the familiar faces gathering out to mourn Gary's life. Though he was troublesome and most of the hood was afraid of his violent behavior, he was still loved. A real Pine Hurst goon.

Mena joined her at the window sill, listening to the music as the sun descended in the sky. "Look at all them niggas goin' in G50's apartment. They're mounting up."

"And look at Lil' Monkey dem bad asses, like they're finna do something stupid."

Mena rushed to the closet, pulling on a sweater and baseball hat while LaLa pulled on a dark purple hoodie. "Bitch, come on, hurry, we gotta join the action." They bolted out the back door.

***

"We gotta do it quick. If Zoo hears we doing some shit like this and it don't work, we'll never walk through Pine Hurst again," Lil' Monkey said with aggression, emphasizing the severity of their grand scheme if it went wrong. "We can't fuck up at all. Everything has to be perfect."

Dex asked, "You really think we can pull this off, bruh?"

"Fucken right, nigga! It gotta work. You tryna make it out the hood too, ain't it? So am I." Lil' Monkey scowled, glaring at the group of childhood friends before him. It was a rare moment. One that showed it was serious and unlike anything they'd ever done. "Too much is invested. We waited long enough. The time is now. On blood, if this shit don't work, we're all fucked." The fifteen-year-old's tone was menacing.

Dex, also fifteen, and his right-hand man checked the time before peeking around the building. "Let's make this shit happen then."
Suddenly, they were confronted. "What y'all stupid asses finna do?" LaLa asked. The crowd where Gary had died was growing by the minute.
Mena added, "Yeah, what y'all 'bouta do?"
"Why?" Lil' Monkey glared.
"'Cause ... we want in."
Dex looked to his friend. Lil' Monkey grinned. "I'ght, fuck it. Check it out…"

***

With two large drink cups apiece, LaLa and Mena snuck out the back door of the apartment discreetly, while keeping the fluids from spilling as they rounded the van, out of view.
LaLa cracked up. "This is sooo craaaazyy."
"I know, bitch, don't make me laugh. I might drop this shit on my shoes'n clothes," Mena said. "You doin' too much."
"Okay, okay, okay, get ready, 'cause it's going down."
One cue, both girls excitedly doused the news van with gasoline.
"Hurry up and light it."
When LaLa lit the fuel, the vehicle burst into a scorching ball of fire before racing off into the night.

***

The moment the camera's red light cut on, Sara Gene began.
"This is News 19 live, here with a follow-up to the fatal shooting of a teenage male, Gary Jackson, who was gunned down earlier by Richland County Sheriff Matthew Wilks, who maintains he reacted in self-defense. The case is under investigation at this point. We are not sure if the state will bring forth any criminal charges against the officer who assumed Mr. Gary Jackson reached for a

weapon. Behind us, you can see the community rallying into a large—wait, is our news van on fire?" she asked openly, astonished. "Our van is ... is a ball of fire. Are you getting this on camera?"

The cameraman replied with a frightened yes. Just as the news crew was heading to the burning van, two assault rifles came into view.

"Bitch, get on the ground!" Lil' Monkey set the barrel of the gun on her face. "Now!"

Another barked, "Nigga, you too!"

"Sara Gene, do as they say," the cameraman instructed, scared beyond anything he'd ever been, pissing his pants as he laid down as well, keeping the camera rolling.

"Oh my—good Lord. Don't hurt us," Sara cried in terror. Quickly, she and the cameraman were zip tied. She knew staying after dark was a bad mistake. "Please, don't hurt us, we're not racists."

***

Lil' Monkey gripped the News 19 microphone. Aware the camera was running live footage, Lil' Trip worked the camera as he learned on YouTube months ago. Dex made sure the instrumental made by Zaytovan months ago came blaring crystal clear from the club speakers for the whole hood to hear before rushing back to his friends.

At least a dozen young boys hid their faces behind Halloween masks with customized shirts to represent Pine Hurst Park, wielding assault rifles with drums and red bandannas. One young boy held two cell phones steady streaming live on both YouTube and Instagram.

When the beat dropped, Lil' Monkey zoned out, rapping.

Neva too much ice, murda game stone cold/Like Miami got heat, kill'em for a bank roll/make this Gucci look good, 'cause the choppa rose gold/Got blood on the diamonds, he dead 'cause he told/Now the streets gettin' scary, rest in peace Gary/Zoo give da green light, erbody got buried/Gang-gang-gang-gang! Pop a nigga cherry/I'm da first killa to shoot, 'cause I'm already ready/Lil' Monkey go bananas, ape shit wit' a stick/For a brick, a whole family get hit wit' dis bitch/Blood gang, bandanna redder than a hoe lip stick/Pine Hurst Posse forever! I swear, neva switch.

As Lil' Monkey was finishing up his live spectacle, sure to have the burning truck in the picture as well as the two news crew personnel tied on the ground, the spotlight from above shined down on them, marking the area with its bright beam. The bull horn blared. "This is Columbia Police Department. Lay on the ground!"

A second helicopter came into view overhead with its spotlight, filming.

"Shit!" Lil' Monkey panicked from the unexpected visit. Wielding the rose gold Draco, he aimed at the bright light above. Fearing the police sirens closing in around them, his trigger finger jerked happily.

Kraat! Kraat! Kraaaat!

His young friends, Pine Hurst goons, joined the action, taking aim. The assault rifles opened fire ruthlessly on the two birds in the sky. The choppers went sailing to elude the hail storm of automatic weapons with rapid fire. The thunderous cracks of bullets hitting metal sent mourners fleeing with fear.

"Lil' Monkey, let's go!" Dex shouted. Lil' Trip tossed the camera aside, taking off as squad cars filled the street.

As he turned to flee, the reporter, Sara Gene, tried to prevent him from escape by tripping him up. Enraged, he turned.

Dex yelled from behind the building, "Let's fucking go!"

But Lil' Monkey was mad. He glared at the red light on the camera. His face was visible. Gritting his teeth, he aimed the rose gold AR-47. His trigger finger tightened. A burst of flames followed by hot lead ripped through Sara Gene like wet paper. *Kraaat!*

"Monkey, let's go!" Dex yelled desperately. "They're coming."

Smirking, he aimed at the police cars in the street, giving them the whole clip before he disappeared with his friends into the projects.

Queen of the Zoo 2

***

Reluctantly, G50 answered the phone. "Yo, fam, where you at?" Zoo's voice boomed through the truck's speakers. He had his cell phone's Bluetooth connected to the system. The hostility in Zoo's voice meant he was livid. "We need'a get up immediately." G50 looked back. In attendance, Shooter, Swine, Kash, and the driver, 5th, each wore the faces of murder and violence.

"I'm leaving the hood," he half-lied.

"How far away are you? You hearing this shit with the Lil' homies out there right now, thuggin'?" Zoo asked angrily. "Them niggas shooting at the helicopters and news reporters!"

Astonished, G50 answered, "We just left the hood."

"And that bullshit just went down!" Zoo shrieked. "Get that shit under fucking control!"

The call disconnected. G50 looked at the phone, confused. He hadn't expected the hood to spaz out. He knew the youngins Gary's age were burned out due to being under Zoo, but to go against police? Hearing the news encouraged them.

Shooter's phone vibrated with notifications. "Shit, Instagram on fire right now! These stupid mufuckas is rapping? Ahh, hell nah!"

"In six minutes, four million views. This shit going viral," Kash blurted with disbelief.

G50 sat back, thinking. The loss of his brother tarnished the effort to think clearly. His heart was heavy. Dark. Crushed entirely. Having part of him gunned down in broad daylight by a white supremacist dressed in police uniform angered him greatly. The streets would suffer. Anybody related to the cop would suffer!

"So what the lick read? We doin' this shit or what?" 5th asked.

He shifted his violent gaze. "Fuck you think we came all the way down town to be playin?" He jacked the slide on the carbon nine machine gun. "Period. Bitch, when you pull up, they gets it!"

The mob pulled down their masks, clicking off the safety to their guns. The mission was dangerous. Stupid.

23

5th rounded police headquarters. The parking lot was fairly empty except for the dozen squad cars scattered about.

"Stop this bitch right here!"

The mob spilled onto the concrete, instantly taking aim at cars and the front doors of the precinct. The rifles exploded in a violent fusillade, battering concert, shattering glass, and shredding metal. Tires exploded, furious waves of rounds sparked fires inside cars as police ran to the front of the building, taken completely by surprise.

Police were unable to counter the barrage of shots sending them ducking for safety. Hot balls crashed into the building frantically.

By the time they were satisfied, nearly three hundred wasted shells covered the grounds. They vanished from the scenes, leaving behind a fog of gun smoke and two wounded officers.

It was only the beginning.

Chapter 4

The brutal drive-by shooting that fatally took his mother's life touched Cloud's soul on a deeper level. Mentally, he was at war. His sanity was fighting a losing battle. Filled with grief, he thirsted for blood and murder. The anguish he felt kept him up at night, seeking, lurking for his enemies. Searching for his children, he became desperate. With every drop of life in him, he vowed to keep looking for his kids and the man responsible for taking them... Zoo!

However, as he and a few of his trusted, ruthless crip soldiers exited the National Guard armory, gun, and knife show after purchasing a tremendous amount of clips, ammo, and weapons, fear suddenly overwhelmed them.

Two clean-cut men approached from thin air. The goons tensed, clutching their weapons, ready.

"Cloud, right?" a short white male, mid-thirties, asked. He wore New Balance track sneakers, blue Wrangler jeans, and a red, plaid button-up shirt that hugged the bulletproof vest beneath.

"Why, who the fuck is you niggas, homie?"

In a swift manner, the badge flipped down exposing its gold shield. "FBI, Jason Bryson. This is my partner, Vincent Taylor," he introduced his partner. A black man, stocky and slightly taller than him, who had a more friendly appearance.

Cloud glared down at the extended hand intended for a shake then turned to see the curious faces of his friends. The moment was tense, turning deadly.

"We're not here to arrest you," Jason Bryson said. "And we're going to pretend we didn't watch you and your friends spend at least five thousand dollars on weapons and ammunition."

"So what you want, cuz?" Cloud asked, knowing there was enough to send him and his goonz back to prison for life.

Vincent Taylor said, "To speak with you ... alone ... in private maybe."

"I can't do that." He was tempted to reach for the 9mm on his waist and start thumping.

Black Migo

Jason Bryson told him, "It's about your daughter. You'll want to hear this."

In the presence of the feds, they began shaking like a dice game of craps. C'Lo urged, "Handle your business, cuz." They walked away, leaving him alone.

"What is it about my daughter?"

"We found her ... dead. She drowned. We're sorry for your loss."

Jason added, "For the loss of your mother as well. Though it's a tragedy, we do believe you know who is responsible for both their deaths."

Tears welled in his cold black eyes. He had his hopes up, hoping God would deliver his children from evil, only to be let down and devastated. The news hurt, destroyed what little faith he had managed to hold onto. He wanted to explode, the rage within melting away at his self-control. He didn't have to be told that his junior was somewhere dead as well, he could only imagine. "And who will that be since I'm 'pose to know? Tell me?"

"Does the name Pierre Montana or Zoo ring a bell?"

"What about my son?" He ignored the question.

"A fisherman pulled your daughter from the Broad River this morning. She was cuffed behind her back, ankles bound to cement blocks. We're waiting on an autopsy. We do believe she was thrown over alive. There was no luck with the bridge cameras. Both are old and busted. At this moment ... your son hasn't been found, but local authorities are searching," Vincent said.

Nose flared and teeth gritting, he asked, "So what's up?"

"We'd like to know why there wasn't any police report filed for your children's disappearance yet. They were last seen with you, their mother, Veronica, says. There's witnesses saying two juveniles were taken from your home in Apple Valley during a home invasion. Your mother's house has been riddled with high-caliber rounds as well. Why so? Is it retaliation for something you've done to this man, Zoo? If so, you're in deep shit with this guy," Jason said pensively.

Queen of the Zoo 2

Vincent backed him up. "This man's a gangster and very rich and powerful. Unlike any gang member we've ever investigated. Actually, we're even surprised that a man of his success, intelligence, and stature is even involved with such. To make it sound worse, he's after you. Why?"

"Shit, nigga, I don't know." Cloud swallowed the lump of fear.

"What about your children, did he take them? What did you do to piss off this titan?" Jason asked, hoping for any form of confession. "He's coming for you. Your whole crew possibly. This is a fact," he half-lied, saying what sounded good. "That is, unless you can get rid of him first."

"What you mean by that? Kill 'em?"

"Nope. A written statement. He's a suspect, but we can't act on him unless you break your street code of silence. Give us evidence against him, and I can assure you he'll come falling to his knees, out of you and your men's way. All we want is him, Zoo. We'll even fix the paperwork so your name is nowhere on black and white," Vincent said.

They were serious. He could see the thirst in their eyes, the drive to knock down a major figure from the ranks. They'd do anything to take him down.

"Dawg, I don't know no, Zoo," he said. "And right now, I'm grieving, so if you'll excuse me, I got shit to handle." He backed away.

"You're going to regret this!"

"Fuck y'all crab ass niggas," he mumbled.

In the running car, C'Lo asked, "What they crab ass on?"

He sat back in the seat, telling them the news of his children.

"We gotta slide on them niggas." The car grew deadly thick with tension. "We gotta slide on them niggas immediately," C'Lo spat aggressively. "Each one of them slimy, grimy slob niggas gotta get hit with this blue flames, cuz. All of 'em!"

As the car filled with gangsta crips eased through traffic, Cloud could only plot his murderous revenge.

***

Black Migo

Brick flicked the joint from the passenger side window after blazing the dirty up to calm his nerves. "You not finna have me driving around all day with your hot ass over there smoking that stank ass shit! Boy, what I look like?" Tootsie complained. "I got you the rental car and a motel room in my name. You ain't even pay me yet, and now you're talkin' 'bout drive you around all over the place? Hell no, boy bye. You better pay me something." She held her hand out. With a sassy attitude, she told him, "Dig in dem pockets and get me-me, 'cause I know they're deep. You ain't foolin' me with that I'm broke shit."

He exhaled sharply, exasperated. He wasn't broke but was damn near. "My nigga, I just need you to slide with me over to the hood so I can pick up my money and drop off some work." Desperation had him going. He was agitated that his wife was gone. With the feds lurking, it had him both paranoid and frustrated, keeping him from doing what he needed to do. "Soon as we make this happen, I'll gladly give your ass a stack."

"Mannn ..." she whined.

"Head back to the city. You ain't finna do shit but watch that same boring ass porn flick all day anyway."

"Nigga so, fuck you," she retorted. "You better be lucky I need that stack, 'cause I swear, I would not be with your ass. And you better not let nothing happen to me either."

"Whatever, dawg." He closed the knapsack loaded with drugs. "Take me to Millwood Drive, the orange panty shop."

As instructed, Tootsie backed into the parking spot, giving them a quick getaway if needed.

"So how long we're gonna have to wait here?" she asked, looking around suspiciously.

Brick sent a text. "Not long, few minutes tops."

"So ..." She turned to him nosily. "What's in the bag?"

"All that your punk ass sister left me with."

As they waited, she continued with her nosy questions. Brick would've been shut her up, but considering he had so much going on in his mind, he needed the distraction.

"You ain't got no homeboys for me? I need a man who can get money and fuck me good all day."

"That ain't gon' happen, Tiger, 'cause if he fuckin' all day, he ain't gettin' no mufucken money. And all my homeboys more for the money over hoes. And they damn sure can't keep up with your nympho ass."

"Nigga, don't judge me." She frowned. "I'm just—"

"Hold that thought, Lil' Freak." He cut her short as the familiar Jeep Cherokee pulled into the empty space beside them. His friend Red climbed out and entered the laundry mat casually with a clothes hamper. A short while later, he was coming out emptyhanded, approaching the Dodge Challenger passenger side. Brick downed the window, and they dapped. "What the lick read?"

"Dryer number four," Red answered. Brick signaled for Tootsie to retrieve the load. "Yo, you and Rucci should fall back for a while. I think the feds is trying to build a case on you. There's no telling what they got so far, but if I was you, I'd fall back to make sure them bitches ain't got nothing."

Grimacing, he replied, "Fuck the feds, nigga. They ain't stoppin' shit. Green Street forever and a day ours!"

"You already know. We in this together. So, have you figured out what you're gonna do when shit gets low? Ain't nothing else in the city like the dope we pushing. If it runs out, it's over," Red warned. "That is, if you can make something happen before then to keep the million-dollar block pumpin'."

Brick handed over the knapsack. "Don't even trip, dawg. Whoever got what we need, I'm going for it."

"Be careful, homez. Don't let these niggas live." They dapped up.

"Trust me, they won't."

Tootsie returned as Red got into his ride and left. "I got it. It's heavy." She placed the loaded pillowcase in his lap.

He opened the bag, inspecting the money as she pulled into traffic. Thick bundles of fives, tens, twenties, and larger bills stuffed the bag. Doing the math, it was an estimate of a hundred thousand. He handed her a thousand.

"We even, Lil' Freak."

She sucked her teeth. "No we ain't. I'm tryna make some more money. I do have bills."

"Of course, not happening. Hell no. You just gon' slow me down. Drop yo' self off."

"Hmph. Nigga, your ass 'bout broke, huh? Rucci said the feds is checkin' for you, so there ain't much you can do to get your bag up."

"Bitch, do I look like I'm worried 'bout some fucken feds? And if I was, what can your little ass do for me?"

"You jack niggas for their shit, ain't it?"

"How the fuck you hear that?" He glared.

Tootsie cut her eyes his way. "My sister tells me everything."

"Stupid ass hoe," he mumbled. "You're a lame. Who you got that I can rob?"

"Nigga, who you got to rob?" she countered all jazzy like. "'Cause if you gonna pay me, I know a few people."

Chapter 5

The city of Columbia was chaotic. Local authorities were in the streets full force head hunting for any and all involved with the reckless murder of a news reporter and string of shootings. Zoo couldn't risk being anywhere close to Pine Hurst Park, so he decided to call a top-secret meeting deep in the country outside the city.

Babygirl gazed at him in the rearview mirror. She sat in the front seat, afraid and nervous. "Are you okay, Zoo?"

Ignoring her question, he stepped out the BMW truck clad in Jordans, sweatpants, and a tank top. "Lil' Zippy, let's go." He cracked his knuckles, standing in front of the truck as the rest of the dozen or so vehicles unloaded around him. A total of sixty-plus blood homies. Everyone met in the open field away from the rides. Watching his back just in case, Lil' Zippy stood off by the truck, both hands clutching the twin .40 cals on his waist, ready to work.

Shifting his murderous gaze to each of the high-ranking men in his litter, he finally spoke with aggression, "Where the fuck is Lil' Monkey and them stupid niggas rapping with him?"

"We've been looking for all of 'em and can't find not one dem little muthafuckas," G50 spoke up. "The task force has hit damn near everybody crib looking for 'em too."

He gritted, "All of a sudden, none of y'all niggas can't find any of them?"

"Me and Jrock been everywhere in the hood looking," Star Chain said. "Them fuckers in hiding somewhere."

Shaking his head in disbelief, he was two seconds away from exploding. He locked sights with his cousin, needing to address a second issue. "Ight, so fuck dat. Maybe I'm trippin, maybe I'm not. Which one of y'all niggas had a hand in shooting up the police headquarters downtown?" It sounded like a trick question. He was so mad that his body was drenched with sweat. G50's gaze fell to the ground, guilty. "Bitch. On da five, I wanna know everybody involved with that stupid ass shit."

There was a long, tense pause. Everyone exchanged looks. Some surprised, some angry.

Truth be told, he already knew exactly who was involved but wanted to test the loyalty and integrity of his soldiers.

None came forth. This made him angrier. With a devious grin, he spoke, "So I'm trippin' now, huh?" He chuckled. "It's all good. Hustle, Blood, 5th, Kash, and G50 ... up front."

Nervously, they stepped forward with apprehension. The remaining homies glared, suspecting them of violating codes. To violate orders and regulations came with severe punishments. Each of them were vicious and took the gang very serious.

Hustle spoke heatedly, "What is all this shit about? What, you think we had something to do with that shit?"

"Nah, I know the answer to that already," he said. "This crab nigga Cloud still living?"

There was no answer.

Since they were so anxious to be activated when he insisted they stay low and out the way, he had to get back on his bullshit. "Shooter, up front, dawg."

He was in hot water.

"It was your responsibility to handle that nigga. You failed, so take the 031 like a G," Zoo said, maliciously. "Y'all five, fat 'em. I'll keep count. One ..."

Shooter took his violation for a slow, grueling thirty-one! Shooter was sprawled across the grass, knocked unconscious. G50 stood his friend up, feeling bad for doing his right-hand man dirty.

"Fuck this shit!" Zoo stormed back to his ride. "Take me to my condo."

As Babygirl mashed the gas, kicking up gravel, Zoo could only think of the current situation he was in. Being blood with the high status was a burden. He felt cornered being surrounded by flaw and fake niggas who cared nothing about the overall well-being and only themselves. A sour taste was left on his tongue along with an eerie, chilling feeling in his bones.

They had all watched how the 5'9 brims were taken down by the feds. It was easily obtained evidence due to the numerous amounts of deadly shootings stemming from senseless beefs that could've been avoided if someone in leadership had the ability to strategize, think, and conquer. He wasn't a fool and took everything around him as a learning lesson. The homies were careless, and before he fell victim to their recklessness, he'd sever all ties.

"Fuck all them niggas," he sighed, exasperated. "Every last one of 'em." He drifted off.

Marvin was Pierre's first best friend growing up together. Every day for the entire summer, they played dodgeball and manhunt. Marvin was the brother he wished he had. Many took Pierre as the weakest among the neighborhood kids due to his sisters always running to his rescue, fighting his battles, whether it was against girls or boys. He suffered from being bullied about his mother's whoresome reputation. He got beat up every time he defended her name despite the hatred he had rooted deep for her. At home, she took her anger out on him, so he was tough, and nothing the kids around the projects did could hurt him. Marvin was the only friend he had that actually understood him.

Together, Pierre and Marvin sat on the bottom steps to his mother's apartment enjoying frozen cups of Kool-Aid. The summer July sun sat high in the sky, its rays beaming down, scorching without mercy. It wasn't until they finished the summer treat when Marvin spoke.

"Wanna see something?"

"What?"

Marvin took off his backpack, sitting it between his legs. He looked around cautiously before pulling the pistol out. "I snuck it out the house today." He smiled proudly.

Pierre gawked with astonishment. "Whose is it? Does it work?"

"It works. My mom's boyfriend got locked up last night for selling dope to an undercover. She didn't know he had it stashed, so I got it. It's nice, ain't it?"

"Why you bring it out the house?"

"'Cause, I'ma gangsta. And in a few months, I'ma get down with blood."

Pierre looked at him crazily. "That's stupid. You're not a gangsta yet. You ain't kill nobody, and all those boys got bodies. If you don't have one too, you can't join."

"I don't have a body right now, but I will. Watch." And who you going to kill, he started to ask, but the moment he noticed Kema speed walking up the street toward them, he hurriedly shifted his attention. "There's my sister. Hurry and put that shit up."

Marvin put it away as Kema entered the gated yard. The coochie-cutting boy shorts had her young camel toe on full display as well as her cheeks jiggling with each step. It was no wonder all the dope boys were hollering cat calls, cars slowing in the streets to get her attention. Marvin had his mouth wide open with drool easing off his lip.

"Boy, close your mouth." Kema twisted her face up. "Lookin' at me like you wanna get knocked the fuck out." She stopped before them. "Pierre, what you doin' wit' dis pervert?"

"Uh ..."

"Bitch, I ain't no perv'. I'm a gangsta. You got me fucked up."

"Little boy, you got me fucked up. I got your bitch when I beat the gangsta outta your soft ass," she started. "Better watch yo' mouth 'fore I make my brother beat yo' ass!"

"Kema, chill. He was just—"

Marvin spat, "Your brother ain't gon' do a fuckin' thang."

Please, don't make me fight 'em, Pierre thought. He didn't want to be pitted against his friend.

Kema wiped the forming beads of sweat from her forehead. "You know what, it's too hot out here. I ain't going back and forth with you." She climbed the steps.

Playfully, Marvin squeezed her ass. "Soft ass!"

"Boy!" She punched him in the arm. "Knock your ass out next time."

"No you ain't," he laughed. When the screen door slammed behind her, he said, "I love your sister, bruh. And when I get older, that's gon' be my bitch."

"Not happening. That's my sister." He was boiling inside.

"Bros over hoes," he laughed. Pierre didn't find anything funny. He chose to bite his tongue to keep from self-destructing. "You goin' wit' me to see if this thing really works?"

"Let's do it."

As the sun began to set and the street lights kicked on, Pierre became anxious to get back home. He could not take another ass whooping. The old scars had not yet healed. And as he kneeled low behind trees and bushes in the empty short out behind the projects, his patience was wearing thin as Marvin crouched low to fill the Colt .45 automatic with bullets. He was still upset about his friend disrespecting his sister.

"Aye, Marv, we should just do this tomorrow. The street lights are on and I have to get home before my mother starts tripping."

"Stop bein' a scared bitch, nigga! Just watch my back while I finish loading the bullets," he spat. "The street lights are on and I have to get home before my mother starts tripping," he mocked.

Spotting the red brick off to the side, Pierre lifted it from the ground. He had enough. *This nigga think I'ma bitch, I'ma show 'em.*

Marvin cocked the .45. "Scary nigga, you wanna go first?" He turned.

The brick came crashing through the air, making a swooshing sound before it connected with Marvin's forehead. The loud crack echoing into the trees. His face went numb. Then he went to sleep with his eyes open immediately. In slow motion, the gun slid from his grip as he fell on his back.

Heart racing rapidly, Pierre pounced on Marvin's chest, smashing his face viciously. "Now who's the scared bitch?"

Panting wildly, he picked the pistol up, aiming its barrel at his friend's chest, unsure if Marvin was dead or not.

Clah! Clah! Clah! He wiped blood splatter from his face. "Get that nigga," he mumbled, tossing the brick away. Frantically, he rushed home, mad he was late and would be getting his ass whooped when he got home.

***

"Brick, wake up, hurry." Tootsie shook him woke with urgency. The fear in her voice snapped him awake.

He clicked the safety off, aiming at the front door. Morning light seeped through the window blinds. *I ain't goin' to prison*, he told himself, ready to squeeze first, suffer the consequences later.

"Who at the door?"

"Boy, nobody. Chill." She touched him. He shifted his gaze to her nakedness. "Come in the room, you got to see the news."

Rushing into the bedroom, he said, "Ain't this 'bout'a bitch." He gripped his forehead in despair. "This shit can't be happening."

"Maybe I'm trippin', but that's the guy you met yesterday, right?"

"It's Red, what you heard?"

"Him and his girlfriend was fighting, she cut his ass and called the police. When they got there and searched the house and found a bag filled with drugs, they locked both dem up."

He sat on the bed, devastated.

"Don't let it get to you, bruh. Was that all you had?"

He couldn't answer, he was crushed. Everything left to his name was in Red's possession, and now it was all gone. With no more product, he had to figure something out. Green Street, a million-dollar strip from years of hard work, could be snatched away. His pride wouldn't let that happen.

"I need one of those licks you got." He stood.

"Krissy and her man, Dirty?"

"Already shitted him. Who else?"

"Zoo or Krock?" she suggested. "I know Krock is super up. His wife Venice and her sister, Shay, be flexing on Instagram. I don't like either. And Zoo—well, you gotta go through hell to reach him."

"Get dressed, I need you to drive me somewhere."

That night, Tootsie cut her view his way as she stopped at a red light. "What's wrong? There's something crazy goin' through your head."

"I need to get high. And I'm goin' to kill your sister."

Queen of the Zoo 2

"No the hell you ain't either. Matter fact, I'm done driving your crazy ass around."

He grinned wickedly. "Pull over into this gas station."

On the corner of Two Notch Road and Taylor Street, Tootsie pulled into the College Corner gas station. She was both tired and nervous having driven around with the hottest man in Columbia. She was not trying to get caught up in his web of chaos. Parking at a pump, she kept a close eye on him surveying his surroundings. His paranoia was contagious. Brick climbed out slowly and cautiously. His face was behind a medical mask and Ray Bans.

A teenager sat on a crate between two ice machines a few feet away from the entrance. In three large strides, he was up on the youngin' gun out. "Bitch ass nigga, way it at? All of it?"

"Yo! M-my man. What, is you crazy?" the shocked teen asked.

"Give it all up or your little ass'll get the whole clip!" he growled.

Frightened, the boy said, "It's all in the store, dawg. I only have a little bit on me. I can't give it up though. Zoo'll kill us both!"

Brick jacked the slide again dramatically. The .45 round jumped out. "The next one'll push yo' top back, no cap. Where it at?!"

The teen shoved the brown paper bag into his stomach. Brick then shoved it into his pocket, jacking the boy up by the shirt collar and forcing him into the store. "The rest is in the Bud Light beer box beside the cooler." He pointed.

Brick retrieved the bag, making the mistake of turning his back to the young boy. Suddenly and forcefully, he was pushed from behind and off balance before the teen bolted off, yelling in distress.

Klum! Klum! Klum! Three rounds erupted after him, shattering glass. When the boy hadn't dropped, Brick panicked, getting to his feet in a hurry, giving chase.

Tootsie saw Brick's every move. Trouble was inevitable. She couldn't believe she was seeing him in public, snapping. Noticing the fear on the boy's face as he tripped and stumbled out the store followed by the thunderous explosions that blew the store's front glass into a mist, she shifted the car into reverse. The teen reached his stashed pistol in time to defend himself.

Brick spilled from the store, greeted with a barrage of rounds. Tootsie burned rubber out the parking lot in a frenzy to reach safety, leaving him to slug his way out the shootout. She'd rather take her sister's advice to get far away Brick or end up ... dead. Brick looked around. Realization hit him in the face. His ride was gone and police sirens were on the way. The teenager was squatting behind a gas pump dumpin'! Relentless, making his exit when an opening came.

As he ran full speed through the Benedict College parking lot, thoughts of murdering Tootsie for leaving him stranded fueled his drive to reach safety.

Ducking between two dumpsters on the college campus, he panted as his phone rang. "Kenny ... where you at, bruh! I need you to come pick me up. I'm in trouble."

"Homie, you hotter than fish grease right now. Ain't no way I'm getting caught up in that shit. I can't come, bruh, hell no!"

"Bitch ass nigga if you don't—"

"You ain't gon' do a fuck shit!"

Brick hung up. First chance he got, his cousin was dead. Peeking from around the dumpsters, he called an Uber. Once in the back seat slouched down, he could finally think clear enough. Tootsie would suffer a gruesome death.

Paying the driver, his heart fluttered with panic and fear. There was no sign of the Dodge Challenger. A grave feeling surged through him. Brick dashed to the back door knocking, banging. The inside was completely pitch black. He purposely left the front light on in the house before they left, so seeing it off worried him. Stepping back, he kicked the door off its hinges, rushing inside like a speed devil.

"Fuck!" he snarled.

Tootsie was gone. And so were much of her personal items.

Brick had been swiped clean, twice, and this time it hurt worse, ripping his heart out his chest. Sweating profusely, he sat the bag on the coffee table, dumping the baggies of dope, at least a hundred bundles. He recognized the red wax paper stamped black with PHP (Pine Hurst Park), along with several balls of coke.

Queen of the Zoo 2

Hungrily, he burst a bag of coke, snorting it all up until the bag was cleared. His head tilted back to stop the drain, ecstasy gushing through his veins. The euphoric drug amplified his feelings and mind state, making him angrier. Violent.

As he sat back trying to enjoy his high, blue lights flashed through the front blinds, stealing his attention. With haste, he jumped to peek out the window. Two Richland County Sheriff Tahoes were parked. Three officers spilled onto the lawn, guns drawn, approaching with caution.

"Shit!" he gritted. Out of bullets and unable to put up a fight, he dashed back to the table, scooping up everything in a frenzy. With the drugs in his pocket and empty gun in hand, he bolted out the back door before police could corner him.

Black Migo

Chapter 6

"Wake up, Queenie, wake up." The familiar voice was music to her ears, pulling her from the deep, dark slumber. "Queenie, wake up!"

Groggily, she fought to open her eyes. The light was blinding. Squinting, her blurred vision became clear. She could barely move her entire right side. Her left wrist ached.

Batting away tears, her heart fluttered. "Precious?"

"It's me, wake up. Are you tired?" The smile on her sister's face was rejuvenating.

"How'd you get here? Where am I? Where's Dad?"

Precious giggled. "Slow down. You're in the hospital. You've been here for a few days now." She touched Queenie's forearm gently. "Dad brought me. Everything is fine, we're here to take you home with us."

"No! You can't. We can't go back, Precious." She panicked, struggling to sit upright. "I can't let'em hurt you anymore. He's a monster, he doesn't love us! He killed Mom. Uncle Drew. Miranda." She began to hyperventilate. "He-he killed … Gary," she murmured sadly. The tears welled thick. Reality was like a ton of concrete weighing down on her chest.

"He didn't kill anyone," Precious defended. "Don't say that, Queenie."

"But he touched and raped you. You told me you ran away from home, that you're pregnant."

"But I'm not pregnant."

"Help me out this bed, Precious. Hurry."

Suddenly, her father, Matthew, emerged from the doorway. "Hi, Queen. You're awake, I see. Are you ready to go home?" The sinister grin on his face made her flesh crawl. She tensed when he touched her bare foot. "You're still so pretty when you wake up."

"Don't fucking touch me!"

Evil glistened in his icy gray eyes. "That's not a nice way to talk to your father, now is it?"

"Don't be mean to Dad, Queenie. He loves us both."

When he touched her again, she screamed as loud as she could. "Get off me. Don't fucking touch me! Stop!" She kicked and fought the new faces running into the room as her father and Precious vanished before her eyes. She continued to fight harder. Soon, doctors ordered her to be restrained as the needle filled with tranquilizer eased into her buttocks.

"No ... Get ... Awa ..." She struggled weakly, until she was knocked out snoring.

"Good morning, feeling better today, Miss Wilkes?" The nurse opened the room curtains, allowing the warm sun beam to glow up the room.

Exhausted, she opened her eyes completely. Was it a dream? She tried to roll out of the hospital bed, only to learn she was still bound. "Why am I still cuffed? What's going on?"

Nurse Brittany, brown skinned, slim thick chick, standing 5'3, and at least a buck-thirty, was no older than twenty-one years old. Her friendly smile was welcoming. "I'm not really sure why you're handcuffed. I was told to come in and clean you up. Someone will more than likely come see you."

"How long have I been here?"

"Two days almost. This the first time you've really spoken."

"My sister, she's ..."

"You haven't received any visitors." Brittany unwrapped her bandaged wrist. "Your wounds are starting to heal."

"Gary?" She fought back tears as grief filled her chest. She'd been under so much medication lately that she hadn't had the chance to dwell on the situation. Now that it was flooding her memory, it felt as if she was reliving it all over again. "Did I miss his funeral?"

"Who?"

"My boyfriend. He was killed by police."

Wrapping her wrist, Brittany replied, "Yeah, I heard about something like that in Pine Hurst. Honestly, it's so much going on out there, it's always on the news. Those guys out there are somethin' else."

Queenie sat up as much as her cuffed wrist would allow. "I need to get out of here, Brittany. My sister, Precious, is out there in the streets in danger. I have to find her."

"Relax. Calm down. I can't help you if you're acting out."

"My sister, Precious, she's twelve. She ran away from home. My dad raped her." She started hyperventilating. "He raped us both. Now my sister is pregnant and I have to help her. Will you help me? Please?" she asked, desperate.

"Okay, slow down. I'm sorry you had to go through that. Does she have a number? Maybe I can call her. Tell her where you are."

"Where's my clothes? My phone? Shit ... my money? The ... the gun?" Panic set in. "My stuff, where is it?"

"I'm not sure."

"You have to help me get out of here."

Soft taps came from the half-cracked door. "Knock, knock," a female voice announced, entering. "Is she up now?"

Queenie noticed Nurse Brittany's sour demeanor, disgusted as the woman and her male company followed. The nurse left.

"Who are you? What do you want?"

"I'm Officer Nicholes," the woman answered. "This is my escort. I'm here to serve you a warrant." She grinned.

"For what?"

"Assault and battery. Intent to kill."

"What?! I didn't try to kill anybody," she bellowed, vexed. "I don't even know what you're talking about."

"Here's your copy of the warrant. You'll be given a preliminary hearing after you complete a mental evaluation. Your bond will be set by the jail's magistrate court."

"Wait. Who did I try to kill?" She took the paper.

"Read it and see," the officer said with a nasty tone that irked her nerves as they exited the room.

And she did.

"On the above date and time, approximately 2 p.m. on the block of Waverly Street, 'Tempest Darby' was assaulted with an unknown weapon and then thrown from a window by the alleged suspect, Queenie Wilks ..."

She remembered the day she beat Tempest's ass. Flopping her head down on the pillow, she yelled, "This some bullshit!"

Hours later, she was awakened by two females. One nurse, the other an officer.

"Miss Wilks, if you will get up for me and get dressed," the nurse instructed.

The cop removed her cuff.

"What's going on?"

The nurse gave her a hospital undergarment to put on beneath the gown. "You're leaving today."

"But where's my clothes and shoes? All my money? Where's my fuckin' phone?"

"You didn't have any property when you came."

What about the gun Krissy gave me? she thought to herself, needing answers.

Quietly, she sat on the back seat of the squad car, enjoying the ride to a mental health institution where she would spend the next thirty days going crazy.

***

At thirteen years old, Krissy was a runaway. It wasn't until then when she learned the power of sex and everything it could provide if utilized properly. By fourteen, she found herself searching for a man with the qualities of a father figure to fill the emptiness of love and attention. Instead, she was pregnant by a forty-year-old preacher. She been sexing for funds. Lots of it. Sex was nothing new around the way. It was almost taboo for young girls to be broken in as early as eleven or twelve by men in their thirties, forties. Men took it as sport to break the young tenders in before the streets took hold.

Krissy was one of them. So young, sitting in abortion clinics year in and out, even health centers. It was then on her fifth abortion she realized she'd have to change her hustle up quick or risk being completely ruined.

Queen of the Zoo 2

At sixteen, she was bait. Black Mane was her twenty-four-year-old boyfriend. He stashed her away at his mother's house while living at home with his wife. Krissy didn't mind as long as she had a place to live. He always made sure she had what she needed and wanted. In return, he'd sicc her on other drug dealers, setting them up. For a year, she did this and made her own profits. But as her slim figure filled out more into a curvaceous figure that made niggas go crazy when she took a walk to the store, Black Mane tried to control her freedom by abusing her mentally, physically, and emotionally. After a few black eyes and busted lips, she was gone back to the streets, living pillow to post, maintaining her independence as a self-made boss bitch.

Living on her own wasn't cheap. So, to feed herself she learned to sell drugs and shoplift merchandise. The hood offered plenty opportunity. She wasn't afraid to jump off the porch, head first. After a while she had a name. Each time, she gave them exactly what they hadn't expected. Drama found its way onto her plate with the more money she made, and she couldn't care less as long as the money kept flowing.

Krissy shook the rain water from her Chanel umbrella as the front door opened. "Thanks for letting me come over for a few days, girl. Shit is crazy on my end."

Venice closed and locked the door behind them. "I know, boo, I heard. It's good to see you, though. I could use some company right now myself anyway."

"Keep it real wit' me, girl, what you heard?"

"The same thing you heard. Your ass got a body."

"Bitch, I swear that's a damn lie. Swear to God it is. Mufuckas keep saying that shit and now everybody believing it." She took a seat on the end of the white leather sectional couch. "That shit done got all kinds of shit started too."

"Hoe ... I know you. If anything, you ain't kill that shiesty nigga Ta'maine for nothing. For whatever reason, he dead and now you're to blame."

"Yeah, they're blaming me, but I know the real story," she said. "But you know I ain't no fuckin' snitch, feel me?"

45

"Bitch, you got ta tell me." Venice was thirsty for the tea. "Hold on, let me get us something to drink. What you want, wine or Hennessy?"

"Hennessy."

"Be right back." Venice rushed off.

Krissy sat back on the couch, massaging her throbbing temples. It'd been weeks since her man Dirty got ambushed for something planned for her, shot up, nearly murdered. She had an idea behind the hit. It kept her up late at night, afraid that at any moment someone would appear to kill her. Stressed, she had to outmaneuver police. A street bitch, she knew what came with the territory. It angered her that instead of allowing police to solve Ta'maine's murder, the streets was doing all the heavy lifting, making their jobs easy. Still, she refused to be bested.

Vernice returned, handing over the drink, sitting on the couch beside her like old besties. "So ... what the hell happened, Krissy? Tell me."

"Where's Krock and Shay?"

"Shay's in the city. Krock's in Memphis. I can't wait 'til he comes back home." She sighed.

"Promise me you won't tell nobody nothin' I'm finna tell you?"

"Bitch, I promise."

Krissy started. "I met this lil' chick name Queenie. We went to club Top Floor. Zoo shit, together. Some dude tried to rob us, people was shooting, running, and screaming. Ta'maine ran up, I ran, and the chick Queenie shot 'em like three times." She felt better confessing a lie than the truth.

Venice now understood her pain. "Now I can see why you're mad everybody's trying to make Ta'maine seem like the victim and you the villain."

"That ain't even the half of it. Them PineHurst niggas tried to kill me, bitch. They shot up my car and fucked up Dirty."

"What? You're playin'," Venice exclaimed, shocked.

"I'm dead ass serious. I'm scared to even go home, afraid they'll find out where I live. I ain't tryna die."

"You're good out here in the country. Ain't nobody gon' fuck wit' you."

Krissy took a sip of her drink. "I hope so," she said, smirking behind the glass. She was there for one reason and one reason only, and catching up as friends wasn't it.

***

With Krissy settled in the guest bedroom asleep, Venice eased beneath the silk sheets, pulling her phone out. Her heart went out to Krissy. She was going through a crisis. Although they were friends, Venice couldn't help being messy. Being tucked away, deprived her of everyday drama that came with the city life, she was unable to do normal things since she was the wife of Krock, a Sumpter king pin. So, having opportunity, she jumped at it.

Everyone was aware of the rumor that Krissy was suspected of murdering a known gang member. Though it was merely speculation, hearing the truth from the horse's mouth had her anxious to spill tea. She pressed the play button on her phone's recording, listening back to Krissy's confession. Her heart thudded in her chest cavity as she listened to all the juicy details. Saving it to her iCloud account, she dialed her husband's number after midnight.

"What it do, sexy?" His deep, smooth voice filled her gut with butterflies.

"Hey, big daddy. I miss you, how's everything?"

"It's perfect. What you doin' up callin' me this late?"

She bit her lip seductively "I'm a little tipsy, and I got something I wanna tell you."

"Baby, that's gonna have to wait 'til morning, ight?"

"But—"

"Venice. Call me when you wake up, baby. I love you. Gotta go."

"Love you too, big daddy." She hung up, depressed. She continued to scroll down her call log.

"Bitch, what you want?" her sister Shay's groggy voice answered.

"You sleep?"
Shay whined, "What it sound like?"
"I got something you ain't gonna believe. Krissy here sleep in the guest room."
Uninterested, she replied, "So, what that gotta do with me?"
"This stupid bitch told me everything about that Ta'maine situation," she whispered.
"No she didn't."
"I'ma send you the recording. Don't tell nobody shit, though."
"I'm not."
Venice didn't believe her messy sister would keep tight lip, but her own messiness wouldn't take heed. So, she sent the recording anyway. "Call me in the morning."
"I will." Shay disconnected.
Venice snuggled into her bed, unaware of the game she played into.

***

The instant Zoo entered his attorney's office, he knew there was bad news in the midst. He sensed it, felt it too.
"Todd, what's hannin', baby boy?" They slapped hands.
Todd Rutherwood, a black man in his mid-40s, was equipped with a strong long list of victories and responsible for all of Zoo's criminal run-ins. He even taught him law as well as keeping his record untouched.
"Not all good," the attorney answered. Zoo took a seat. Todd sat as well. "Listen to me. I always give you the real, and this is what's going on. You're coming up on the feds' radar. You escaped them last round up. You're doing well, keeping a low profile, what is happening?"
"Shit, nothin' really."
"Pierre, I'm your friend. If you're in that water, then I'm in hot water. You do know that I can't protect you if I don't know what's going on."
Curious, Zoo asked, "What the feds for?"

Todd sighed. "You've seen the video, right? Young fella, Lil' Monkey ass?"

"A few times." He frowned, heart pounding with rage. At first when he saw it, he was proud of his little homies making a low-budget video appear extremely real, only to realize from hundreds of calls that everything was shot live on camera and aired across the world. If he could get to Lil' Monkey before the police, his young goon would perish. "What about it?"

"Two hundred thirty-one million views as of today. That means at least half of this number are witnesses to a foolish, brutal murdering of a damn news reporter. In your neighborhood. Not only that, he mentioned your name, Zoo. Everybody knows you. Catch my drift?" Todd said.

"We can fight that though, right? I don't know dem niggas type shit?"

"As long as you don't give them any more than this, you're good. Tread lightly, move smart. You're one of the smartest I've ever dealt with, stay ahead," Todd spoke from the heart, and he could understand why he felt strongly about the law not having anything against him.

"How'd it go?" Babygirl asked once Zoo eased into the backseat of the BMW. Lil' Zippy slid into the front passenger seat. Zoo couldn't help but to notice as each day passed, Babygirl was becoming more and more attached to him. If only he could get his dick out her highly addictive box. Being around the young tender day in and out made sex convenient. He smirked at the idea of her being on anyone else's team but his. She was loyal.

When she came to him she was fourteen. Drawn to him by the glitz, glamour, and reputation. For a while the streets called her his daughter. Zoo was beginning to believe so too, until she was eighteen and ripe. She gave herself to him. He accepted, and for a while it was something they did periodically. Now, he could see she wanted more. Maybe more than he was willing to give. He made eye contact that said not to question him.

"Okay, where to then?"

He laid his head back. "Harbison Mall."

No matter the circumstances, Zoo always made time to hang out and support his family. He had to show love to his three sisters, three nieces, and two nephews. Sadly, when Zoo was sixteen years old, his mother committed suicide. She had discovered his hidden pistol used to kill his best friend, Marvin. When they found her, her brains were splattered all over the wall. Life had been hard. She couldn't take it anymore and left him, the only man of the family, to carry the burden of taking care his family.

At thirty-four years old, Zoo was truly a sole survivor. Because his mother had no heart nor will to fight for her kids, Zoo vowed to always provide.

Entering the mall with Lil' Zippy and Babygirl strapped and flanking him, the familiar squeals of happiness caught his attention.

"Zoooo!" his youngest sister shouted excitedly, rushing and pouncing on him. She kissed all over his face lovingly. "I miss youuu!"

Bursting into laughter, he said, "Damn girl, I just spoke to you on the phone yesterday."

"Sooo. Still, I miss you." She didn't want to let her big brother, hero, and best friend go.

Kema, the oldest sister, pried, "Let us hug'em too, Maya. Dang. You always trying to hog him up."

Maya snapped, extremely territorial, "So! I'm the baby."

"Y'all chill out, it's a lot of me."

"Hey, Babygirl, hey, Lil' Zippy," his sister spoke nicely. "Y'all not tired of killing people yet?"

The two burst into laughter. "No comment."

"On some bullshit already. Where my nieces and nephews?"

They all walked over to the mall's playground area where he was stampeded by toddlers. "Uncle Zooo!" They surrounded him, latching onto his legs and waist. "W-where-where you been, Uncle Zooo," his three-year-old niece asked adorably.

"Uncle Zoo been working, y'all miss me?"

"Yeeesss!" they yelled, overwhelmed with excitement.

He smiled, cherishing every second. "You better. So, who's ready to go shopping?"

The kids screamed, "Meee!"

"Good, let's go fuck up a check."

Three hours later, everyone was tired of walking and hauling bags. Together they occupied a large section of the food court. Babygirl blushed, rolling her eyes. He chuckled.

Maya kept her playful tone hushed. "Why that girl keeps looking at you like that? Let me find out."

"Who, Babygirl?"

"No, I already know why she stares at you, stupid. Putting your thang-thang in her. I'm talking 'bout that pretty chick walking away from the Subway place. Lookin' like she know you."

Zoo scanned the floor until he saw her strutting away wearing six-inch red pumps, low-rider designer jeans that clung to her shapely figure, and a half-shirt that showed off her flat stomach and supported her B-cups. He knew exactly who the Instagram model was and who she belonged to.

"Maya, I'll be back. Lil' Zippy, come on." He walked across the food court, following the woman into the Michael Kors boutique. She was oblivious to his presence until he was wrapping his arms around her tiny waist so she couldn't escape while he pressed the print of his dick in her ass crack.

"Who the—what the fuck?"

He grinned. "You feel all dis meat I'm workin' with, girl?"

"Oh my god, Zoo? Get the fuck off me, nigga!"

Zoo kissed her neck then sucked on her sweet skin passionately. Moans escaped her lips unintentionally as she tried to fight out his hold. 'When you gonna give me some of this pussy, girl?"

"I'll fuckin' scream right now if you don't get off me!"

He gripped her fat pussy print, pinching her nipple as well before letting her go. She was livid and seeing red, charging him. He gripped her wrist before she could fire away.

"Chill, girl."

"Ain't no fucking chill!" Venice spat bitterly. "The fuck you think this is, Zoo? You tryin' me? If I tell my husband what you just did, he gon'—"

"Not do a damn thing," he finished her sentence.

Venice glared. "My husband ain't scared of you, nigga."

"Fuck your husband. Your sister Shay couldn't handle the dick, but maybe you can."

"Muthafucka, you think this shit a game, huh?"

"What you gon' do?" He pressed up, she pushed, but he didn't budge.

"Everybody else scared of you, not me, bitch. I got you." She pushed past him, storming out the store.

If it hadn't been for Shay throwing herself at men he was turf warring with in order to get back at him, he wouldn't have done what he did. He also wanted to get Krock out the picture. The dope from Sumpter was second best to his and his only competition.

"Everything good, big bruh?" Lil' Zippy asked, snapping him out his daze.

Zoo grinned. "Yeah, let's get the fuck outta here. I got shit to handle."

***

Cloud jacked the slide on his brand-new Smith and Wesson .9mm. "You sure it was that nigga, Zoo?" He needed assurance as C'Lo circled the mall parking lot a second time, hoping not to lose sight of the BMW.

"I'll never forget that fuck boy's face. He was with a group of kids and women. Maybe his family. If you ain't gon' smack that nigga boots, I'll pull over right now and od 'em myself."

Cloud snapped, "Shut the fuck up, bitch, and drive!"

In the back seat, two crips sat anxiously strapped to the tee.

C'Lo kept his eyes on the BMW as it broke away from traffic flow into a median, preparing to turn at a red light.

He couldn't risk not getting his man at point-blank range. Cloud had never been a drive-by shooting type, and always would be a walk down, get up close type to ensure he hit his target.

Without indication, he jumped out the gold Cadillac CTS, gun extended, beam bright as he crept between cars toward the BMW.

His mouth was salivating, murder sweet on his tongue. This was his moment to kill another enemy.

Witnesses watched astonished and in horror. The face mask hid his identity, though he couldn't care less who saw him.

Just as he was about to squeeze ...

Blaaa! The explosion erupted from within the BMW, making a quarter-size hole out the back window. The round whizzed over his shoulder. Cloud ducked, his element of surprise ruined.

He stood fingering the trigger to his .9mm like a bitch's wet pussy. Bullets spat rapidly. The deafening sounds of his gun pierced through the air. Shells tumbled away, dancing across the warm concrete as its hot balls slammed into the BMW's rear, ripping it apart.

He tried to get closer, but a barrage of return fire spazzed his way outrageously, nearly wetting up his face.

The BMW burned rubber, fishtailing before lurching into traffic. The front passenger hung out the window, clapping recklessly.

Innocent bystanders and car passengers got out and took off screaming in different directions, feeling like sitting ducks.

Cloud kept it hot, his crips behind him backing the move.

Blah! Blah! Blah! Blah!

The dare devil teen hanging out the car answered back with his own thunderous wave of shots, yelling, "Bitch, what's up?"

"Pussy ass slobs!" Cloud retorted, angry the enemy was getting away. Still, he continued to empty his clip, rushing back to the cap with haste. C'Lo U-turned in traffic, fleeing.

"I almost had them muthafuckas!" He growled, "Fuck!"

C'Lo gazed at his leader. "Don't even trip, cuz. Next time we catch'em, it's on and crackin' all over again."

Black Migo

Chapter 7

The fresh scent of strained citrus tingled her nose while the aroma of fried bacon, scrambled eggs, and french toast activated her stomach into a growling fit, waking her up completely. Krissy checked the time on her phone, 9:38 a.m.

Sighing and stretching, she sat up the moment she heard the front door slam. Climbing out of bed, she headed into the kitchen to find Venice standing on her tippy toes wearing only a lace pantie and bra set, kissing Krock, who was ready to get nasty. That was ... until she cleared her throat, getting both the love birds' attention.

"Y'all is sooo nasty."

Krock squeezed his wife's ass roughly, unashamed. "You can stand right there and watch us if you want to."

"Stop, baby. We is not fucking in front my friend." She hit him playfully.

He grinned deviously. "We'll be back then, Krissy. Finish cookin' breakfast," he said as Venice pulled him away.

"Go get that nut." She giggled. Thirty minutes later, Krock was back. "Damn, y'all done already?"

"Pussy good as a mufucka," he laughed. "So what the hell is you doin' at my crib, in my city? We don't want no bullshit."

"No drama. I promise."

"I hear you. How ya man doin'? Heard niggas tried to off 'em."

"I have to go pick him up from his granny mama house later. He doesn't really fuck with me right now. But he'll be ight. Shit is so crazy."

"If anything, let's get to the money. Dirty still owes me that 130 bands. I need that. I know he got hit up, but he's still alive, so he still owes me."

Krissy frowned. "Cold hearted, ain't you."

"That's me bein' warm."

"I'll make sure you get your money like I always do. But now I need a favor. Just one. I need a shooter, a little mufucka that'll kill anything for me, protect me, and do as I say. Can you help me?"

"I got contract killahs, not do-boys." He chewed on bacon. "Can't help ya."

***

Leaving Krock's emptyhanded and without a killah had Krissy on edge. The longer she existed in Columbia with a bullseye on her back, she'd get no peace.

Pulling into the yard, she inhaled and exhaled sharply, making sure the shades covered her face entirely. Climbing the flight of stairs, she was let in through the side door. "Hey, Mrs. Avery."

Dirty's grandmother hugged her tightly. "It's good to see you, baby. How you been?"

"Stressing, missing my man."

"I know. Are the police still looking for you?"

"Unfortunately, but I'm not worried."

"Remember, anytime you need me, just call. Now, your man is very upset about something, but he won't say. I'm sure he'll tell you. He doesn't want any of his friends to see him like this."

Krissy followed into the den. "Hey, gubby." She forced a smile, unable to recognize him. There was no smile. His eyes were dark and murderous. He'd lost 100 pounds. The moment he laid eyes on her, his jaws clenched off/on. "You don't seem happy to see me."

"Take me home," he gritted dryly.

"Be nice, baby," Mrs. Avery said. "This woman loves you."

The red in his eyes meant he felt differently.

"Where you want me to sit you?" she asked as she helped him inside their home.

He chose the bedroom.

Setting him on the bed's edge, she hurried away, making sure the back doors were locked and alarm armed. Re-entering the bedroom, Dirty had begun to undress. She rushed away, starting his bath water. She let out a deep sigh. His presence made her extremely nervous. The relationship, the love, the bond they once shared was destroyed.

"Your water is ready," she said.

Dirty said nothing. Instead, he limped, deeply pained, into the bathroom, slamming the door shut behind him. Krissy stood there staring at the door.

"Damn. Did he see the stuff?" she whispered. She couldn't risk it, so she scurried over to the bedside dresser, removing the grocery bag stuffed with items, before rushing out into the back yard, digging a shallow hole behind the shed and setting the bag in. Covering the hole back, she dashed back inside. She then stripped down.

Dirty emerged from a steamy hot shower. His icy gaze made her uncomfortable. "What's up?" He glared.

"I'm six weeks pregnant."

"Fuck you telling me for? It ain't by me."

"Don't play with me, Dirty. Or I swear to God."

"Swear what?" He scowled.

"I didn't do shit to you! What are you mad at me for?"

Dirty spat violently, "Bitch, you got me shot the fuck up! This shit wasn't no accident, it was an ambush. Over fifty rounds, and if I hadn't ducked when I did, niggas would've killed me. So I blame all this shit on you."

Tears welled in her eyes, the guilt heavy. "But it's not my fault, bae."

"So why the fuck was the law coming to my hospital bed questioning me about you killing Ta'maine?"

"But I didn't shoot nobody."

"That ain't what them folks believe."

"Fuck dem! All of 'em. And when I get a few things together, I'm gonna turn myself in and clear my name."

"Whatever you do, bitch, get an abortion."

His words crushed her chest.

***

Dex snuck back into the abandoned house filled with fright. His friends looked at him, afraid he had bad news. "My nigga, Pine-Hurst is on fire right now! The feds snatched up Tony Baby and his brother dem. Mark Man and Rut. My girl called me on my way back

here saying the feds have been to all our houses, bruh. We hit!" he murmured in defeat.
 Nobody wanted to hear that.
 Paranoid, Lil' Monkey asked, "You already cut your phone off, right?"
 "I did that three blocks away."
 He lit another cigarette, taking a deep, satisfying pull to calm his frazzled nerves. His head was trapped in a fog. Everything had changed for the worst. He hadn't even thought for one moment they would be pent down in hiding, unable to enjoy their newfound fortune and fame. "What all did you see out there?"
 "I checked the IG. We got like 246 million views. That video broke the internet. A check should be going to your aunt since we shot the video on her phones. That check should be enough for all us to get a lawyer and get out. I seen an ass of rappers on the page too. Da baby, Lil' Baby, Yo Gottie, Quality Control, so many more. I was moving so fast I couldn't remember all of 'em. We're definitely lit as a bitch."
 Hearing the clout he now had put a smile on Lil' Monkey's face. What he wanted, he accomplished. Now Lil' Monkey was trying to put it all together.
 "Oh, and I forgot to tell you, them two chicks from Four Seasons' apartments, LaLa and Mena, both of them got caught up in some shit. I couldn't reach 'em."
 He scowled. "Man, fuck dem pussy ass thots. Them bitches ain't wit' us. This is what we're finna do, though." He put out the cigarette butt. "We have to change locations. I know another bando over on McAllister Street. If we can get there, we can stay low for another day or two."
 "Then what? My nigga, we got everybody on our line. We'll never be able to stay in hiding. Look at us, hungry, tired, scared as a bitch. Nigga, this shit already driving me crazy. I'm ready to go to jail and get this pussy ass shit over with."
 Lil' Monkey was tempted to kill his cousin, Dex. His trigger finger itched feeling he would fold.

"Shhhuush … Y'all heard that?" Rut asked. The room instantly went silent. No one moved nor flinched.

Nothing.

"The fuck is you trippin' about?" Lil' Monkey's tone was low and harsh.

Rut snapped back, "Bitch, I thought I fucking heard something."

"Nigga, you ain't heard a fuck thang."

Dex held his finger up to silence them completely. "Nah, I just heard something."

They all heard it just then.

Before anyone could move to inspect, the police K-9 came rushing into the room with lightning speed, latching on to the closest thug. Lil' Monkey shrilled in agony as the dog sank its razor-sharp teeth deep into his forearm and started shaking him.

"Arrghh!" His ear-piercing cries ricocheted off the walls. He dropped his pistol and terror filled the room. No one knew what to do and only watched in horror.

Dex couldn't take it. Seeing his cousin in pain, he emptied the clip on the dog, killing it.

Lil' Monkey was in pain. "That bitch tried to take off my fucking arm."

A tactical canister crashed through the window, followed by another one. The deafening explosion of a concussion grenade bent them over in confusion. The second explosion filled the room with gas.

Another explosion followed by another rocked the abandoned house on its foundation. The front and back doors were blown off.

"Police! Get down on the ground!"

"Get the fuck down!"

The house was raided with such violent force they were taken by surprise. Soon, they all would be arrested and hauled to a juvenile detention center, neither sure of their future.

***

Four days later, Lil' Monkey walked to the visiting room, anxious to hear some good news. He had been separated from all his friends and unable to make any phone calls. He was losing his mind. He hoped the sudden visit would shed light, and he hoped his aunt had cashed his check to get them an attorney.

He watched the two men standing off to the side as he sat in the cold seat.

"Lil' Monkey." The white man smiled warmly, playing with his name. "Get very comfortable. We can be here for a while."

"And who the fuck is y'all?" He shifted his gaze between the two, one black, the other white.

"Little fella, we're the big boys. The FBI, and with us here it means you're in some very deep shit. And I do mean VERY DEEP SHIT. I'm Jason Bryson and this is my partner, Vincent Taylor. By the way, you're looking really famous these days." The agent gazed down at the file. "Two hundred million-plus views. You broke the internet. You and all your friends are famous. Must be nice. What're you gonna spend all that money on?" he asked sarcastically. "Of course, commissary. Maybe some shoes and that's it." He laughed.

Lil' Monkey clenched his jaw. The agent was pushing a button.

Vincent settled down. "It won't matter what you spend it on. Where you're going, you will never get out. I mean NEVER! That is unless, well … you start rappin' those lips. Then I can help you. We're actually not that hard to please. We got so much power you can snitch and no one will ever know. We'll let you out and say someone else did it. All you have to do is give us one thing."

He swallowed dry and hard. "What's that?"

"For you to tell us everything about one man, one man only. The man you kids worship. Zoo."

Lil' Monkey hung his head.

Chapter 8

The broad day attempt to assassinate Zoo had his nerves frazzled. It had been a while since anyone had the guts to make a move on him. Though it had also happened many years ago, the incident was vivid in his mind. He remembered it like it was yesterday.

It was the first day of the year 2009. The elected president was Black, a recession was hitting hard, and all over the city, streets were suffering from the most vicious drought it had seen since the early '90s. For him, it was the best head start he could ask for. While every drug dealer was scrambling to find a connect with product available for a reasonable price, he had the plug. His very own friend, Black Elmo, was in charge of Allen Benedict Court and currently, he refused to supply anyone but Pierre. Without leadership, the flow of money from around the entire city was pooling into the infamous PineHurst Park.

Being connected brought along the envy and jealousy. Pierre was not sharing his product with anyone, wanting School House Road to be the number one location. A few of his selected men assisted in pushing the highly addictive heroin, cocaine, and ecstasy pills. And as he stood on the corner of Edgewood and School House Road, keeping a close eye on the overflow of traffic stopping for his products, a smile spread across his face. Money was pouring in.

Out the corner of his eye, he noticed a bad ass youngin' coming his way, cat walking the dirt bike. He cracked a smile. "What you want today, Black Migo? I ain't got no money or no guns."

The seventeen-year-old sat the bike on its kickstand, playfully tapping his pockets. "What you got for me, Big Lil' Homie?"

"Lil' Nigga." Pierre threw a quick jab, and Black Migo weaved it perfectly. "What I told you 'bout doin' that shit, boy? Make a nigga whoop yo' lil' ass one of these days."

They both laughed.

"Nigga put they hands on me, his ass goin' to heaven."

Pierre knew the youngin' was deadly serious. It was no secret the teen was released nearly a year ago after serving five years in a juvenile facility for manslaughter. At seventeen, the cold look in the youngin's eyes and emotionless facial expressions were a sign he was nothing to take lightly. Being playful made him likable, but still, that didn't shake the goose bumps once in his presence.

"I already know, killah. What you up to?"

"I'm tryna get on, bruh. See, I fucks with you, but everybody else you got working, I'ma rob them just 'cause. So you gon' put me on?"

Chuckling. "Homie, you crazy. Tell you what, you strapped?"

Black Migo lifted the sweater, exposing the handle of his Glock. "Ready, set, bitch I'm on go!"

Pierre laughed. He was going to give his friend the task of scaring the hell out someone but changed his mind when he spotted the black Trailblazer circling the block for the fourth time that evening. Danger was closing in. "Yo, Migo, do me a favor. Go over to that church, I'll call you over in a few."

The teen hauled the dirt bike out of sight. The Trailblazer neared, its passenger side doors opening up. Before Pierre could signal his distress, two assault rifles were aimed at his face. The first assailant smacked him with the butt of the weapon. While he was dizzy, the second figure tossed him into the back seat, jumping in beside him as the third man, the driver, stomped on the gas before anyone could rescue him.

Pierre winced, saying, "What the fuck, mane?"

Holding the gun barrel on Pierre's jaw, the masked gunman glared. He would die and no one would ever know who got him.

"Nigga, don't cry now. Where the fuck dem birds at?"

"I don't know what you talkin' 'bout."

"Bitch, we gon' see 'bout dat!"

The Trailblazer came to a jerking stop. The driver then barreled the van up a steep driveway and around the abandoned house, out of sight. Parking the truck, the sliding door snatched open. Pierre was yanked out onto the ground. "Nigga, you better tell us where them fuckin' birds at or you dead!"

"I ain't got no birds." He wasn't going down without a fight. The most anyone could do was kill him, and he wasn't afraid.

"You think this shit a game?"

Bang! The punch rocked his jaw, rattling his brain. "Shoot this nigga fucking nuts off, he'll start talkin' then."

As the second assailant aimed the rifle, ready to get paid, the sudden whine of a dirt bike's engine came revving up the driveway, bending the house's corner in fluid fashion, kicking up gravel, stopping abruptly. Black Migo had the Glock out, screaming.

Doo Doom! Doo Doom! Doo Doom! "What's up, bitches!" *Doo Doom! Doo Doom! Doo Doom!*

The kidnappers scurried behind the truck as bullets whizzed through the chilly air, burying hot lead into the vehicle. Pierre was on his stomach watching the scene unfold, astonished.

The youngin' was smiling bright. Wildfire danced in his deep browns. He stood without cover or shield, letting his trigger finger squeeze happily. *Doo Doom! Doo Doom! Doo Doom!* "Fuck. Bitch, let's go!"

The assailants had been taken by surprise and were unable to get a shot off, feeling overwhelmed and outnumbered. Pierre saw his opportunity. As Black Migo turned up the heat, he took off running toward the street at the bottom of the hill.

"Shit. He's getting away!" one shouted. Pierre hauled ass. "He's fucking getting away!"

Black Migo teased, "Bitch, do sum'n 'bout it!" He emptied the clip before revving the dirt bike, spinning off into a wheelie. Shots erupted after him.

Pierre ran nearly a mile up the street when the dirt bike pulled alongside him. The broad smile and crazed eyes greeted him. "Get yo' scary ass on," he cracked up.

But Pierre wasn't scared, just bested. He climbed on. "How you know where I was, bruh?"

"How else? I followed you, nigga."

"I owe you, Lil' Homie, I owe you my life," he yelled over the wind.

"Yeah, you do. And you gon' start by putting me the fuck on."

Thinking of his homie, Black Migo, who was locked away in Coleman One United States Penitentiary, Zoo made a mental note to send him a bag.

Zoo received the iPad, trying to understand what he was seeing. "What am I looking at?"

Lil' Zippy proceeded with showing him. Babygirl kept her eyes peeled, index finger toying with the baby blue .380. Having been shot at and nearly killed the other day had her anxious to catch a body. She wanted to show her boss that she was worthy of more than spreading her legs and driving him around.

The park was quiet except for the lawn care service going about 9 a.m. duties. Zoo was fed up with being passive. He had taken his thumb off the streets when the 5-9 brims got indicted, afraid he'd get caught up in the RICO. However, he managed to escape and figured instead of being traditional, being the loudest, most violent, even largest gang in Kill'umbia, he had dimmed down the G-shine to protect them from further unnecessary attention. Unexpectedly, the blood homies were growing rebellious to his tactics and leadership. He feared sooner than later he'd be forced to make a decision. One he was preparing to make.

"What this is, is a drone. What you see is coming from the drone's camera. Live. I can control everything from the drone right here." Lil' Zippy demonstrated, having the top hover outside the truck's window. Zoo rolled the window down. Their faces became crystal clear on the pad. "This thing can record visuals and audio, with long-lasting battery life."

"There's a lot of traffic on Green Street today. All five of the trap houses booming."

Yeah, not for long, Zoo thought.

"Uncle Jerry, how we lookin'?" he asked once he pulled into the massive yard, deep in the country.

"Looking really good, nephew. In my opinion, you got some good material to work with. These young boys are tougher than I expected." Uncle Jerry slapped hands with his favorite nephew.

"They come out the trenches, that's why. Where are they?"

Uncle Jerry cracked a toothy smile. "Hunting, come, let me show you."

Entering the backyard of the enormous property made Zoo envious. "This mufucker got me in my feelings, Unk. Damn." He admired the plush green grass surrounded by hundreds of miles of forest.

"I love the space. It's peaceful, prolific, and ... mine."

Blooom! The shotgun explosion sent birds flopping into the air in panic, followed by a second explosion.

"The hell was that? What, they hunting?"

"Yep, deer. And that shot means they got 'em one. Give 'em a while, they'll be hauling fresh kill in."

Zoo laughed, humored. "You got my youngins on some wild cowboy shit. I need them to be war ready, not hunting deer."

"What's the difference? Regardless, these boys are being taught to get their hands bloody. When it's time to kill, they'll perform. And that's why you called me. Besides, these boys gotta eat. They're gonna get you far in life."

He nodded his head. That was the plan.

Suddenly, the group of boys emerged from the tree line hauling deer covered with fresh blood across the vibrant grass. Zoo was excited to see them, though he hid it well.

"Surprise the hell outta me." Jerry examined the boys.

Booby, Cloud's son, laid the small doe on the concrete. "Killed the mama deer and her baby too."

Zoo studied him closely. A great prospect. Trickled, the young boy's father, almost succeeded with killing him. Anything less than effort was unacceptable.

Jerry putted Booby on the back. "That's right. Ain't no need to let 'em both live. Somebody get the water hose so we can clean mama up. We'll skin'er and cut'er up. Zoo, crank up that grill."

***

Before day break, the hand-picked band of boys moved down Green Street trailing a minute apart from the other. Through heavy foot traffic of junkies racing up and down the street, no one paid any of the boys dressed in school uniforms and backpacks any attention. As instructed, Lil' Zippy led by example.

Walking to the end of the street, he passed fiends hopping in and out of cars, some scurrying up porch steps to buy their arm candy, others retreating to a dark corner to enjoy the high. Sneaky like a ghost, he dipped into the yard of the first trap house doing numbers. Rushing to the back, he removed the large Super Soaker water gun filled to its max with gasoline. Pumping, he sprayed each window then the back door. He then soaked the front porch and door, emptying the fuel all over the sides of the house. With the trap house drenched, he used a grill lighter to ignite the gums on the front door then back. In a matter of seconds, the entire house was engulfed in flames, trapping those inside. The ear-piercing cries and screams echoed onto the streets. Lil' Zippy jogged away.

When he and his friends reached the bottom of the strip, they turned to see four of the trap houses were burning to the ground, its flames ascending high into the sky as the heat warmed their drilled hearts. Green Street was raging with chaos.

Behind them, they hear, "You there, freeze, FBI!"

"Shit!" Lil' Zippy flinched as two agents sprang from an unmarked surveillance vehicle that neither of them thought twice about.

Booby, trigger happy, had the .9mm raising hell instantly. Shots rang out utterly. *LAH-LAH-LAH-LAH!* "FBI this dick, bitch!"

The feds fell to the ground, giving them enough time to vanish.

***

Vincent Taylor shouted into the walkie talkie, frightened, traumatized, "Shots fired! Agent down. I repeat, agent down, shots fired!"

Jason Bryson grunted. "Ugh … I'm okay, I'm okay." He winced in excruciating pain. He ran his shaking palm beneath the vest. No blood. Sighing, he took shallow breaths. "That litter motherfucker shot me, almost killed me!" he said with disbelief. "We didn't even see it coming."

"I know, it sucks, but you're okay," Vincent said. Soon the entire neighborhood was swarming with every branch of law enforcement. Firefighters battled the blazing fires unsuccessfully. It was pandemonium.

Hours later, the remains of eight bodies in total were counted, dead. A sharp exhale of exasperation came from Jason's frustration, climbing out the car back at the job. "Willing to bet you each of those bodies were a part of the indictment. This investigation could very well go up in flames as well."

Vincent assured. "It won't. The grand jury has already granted arrest warrants. Regardless, Brick and everyone rolling with him will perish. That's a slam dunk case, so no worries. Their main concern is, Zoo. A few pieces to this jigsaw puzzle."

"Sounds good." Jason winced.

"You don't seem optimistic."

"Those kids earlier... They weren't ordinary. They came, focused, fearless. They moved too synchronized. Four of the five houses, down? Each of the spots under surveillance. Those fires were well plotted, planned, executed perfectly. I mean, Jason ... those little bastards had water guns filled with fuel for Christ's sake!" Vincent ranted, replaying it over in his head. "The funny part ... There was no respect for nothing, the look in their eyes ... empty."

Vincent dug out his iPhone as it chimed. "Check it out, this picture just came in. Looks familiar, doesn't it?"

"That's the missing boy. Cloud's son. What's he doing with these boys?"

"And that's what we need to find out."

Black Migo

Queen of the Zoo 2

Chapter 9

Queenie was thrilled for her time on Bull Street to finally be over. The mental evaluation had proved one thing for sure. She had issues. Bottled up anger and pain kept her raging on others. She was unpredictable. The fact that she was unable to protect her sister, Precious, crushed her on all levels, giving her an attitude of sour bitterness that kept her in trouble with staff and patients. No one wanted to believe she had been raped and abused by a sick, twisted father. This drove her crazy. Along with the idea of her father forcing himself onto Precious. The medication helped some, but thoughts of suicide were still there. She would never forget what she endured. It triggered her, causing this sweet young girl to use anything with a sharp edge to cut her wrist.

She looked around, instantly disgusted as the police squad car eased into Alving S. Glenn Detention Center. The female officer parked and climbed out, opening the back door for her.

Officer Brownlee, a tall Amazonian white woman, said, "I hope that you're going to behave yourself, Ms. Wilks."

Hands cuffed in front her, she stepped out onto the concrete. Even if she wanted to be nice, she couldn't. The natural disgust, mistrust, and pure hatred for police was so deeply embedded in her soul. She couldn't hide it. "Know what, bitch? Fuck you and all your friends, your family, your kids, if you got a pet, fuck dat too and everything you love. Fuck all the police!" she snarled, yanking her arm from the woman's touch.

"Little bitch, this ain't what you want." Brownlee snatched her up. "You might've shown your ass out there and got away with it, but here you'll get your ass handed back to you starting with me." She dragged Queenie across the garage. "I was going to be nice, but since you want to desire—"

"Fuck YOU! Stank hoe," Queenie taunted. "Want me to spell it? I will, 'cause I know your stupid ass can't."

"Ma'am, shut the hell up before I—"

"You ain't gonna shoot me," she cut the cop off. Her makeup was beginning to moisten due to her rising temperature. "Soo smart but not smart enough to see you're a ugly-pussy bitch." She cracked up, amused.

Brownlee jerked her off balance, wishing she could rough the young chick up off camera. She shoved her into the sliding door of the sally port. "Do you wanna get tazed?"

Queenie laughed. "Do you wanna eat my ass?" She laughed.

The officer was having a hard time keeping her composure. Her face was flushed red. The tip of her ears were beet red.

"That's what I thought, ol' ugly, pussy ass, police bitch!"

The second the sliding door opened, she went back to being professional, escorting Queenie into central booking proudly. As the cop processed her into the system, she looked around with utter disgust. Jail was not where she wanted to be. An hour later she was in, the cop grinning wickedly as she removed the cuffs.

"There you go, Ms. Wilks, congratulations. You're officially an inmate."

"And you're still a pussy-eating bitch!"

Dressed down in blue jail attire, Queenie went to the nurses office where she was asked various questions.

"It says here you take psych meds morning and evening?" A black heavyset nurse peeked over the pink frames of her Prada glasses.

Blankly, she answered, "I don't want it. You take it."

"Why not take something that can potentially help you?"

"Because it doesn't help. It only makes it worse."

"Makes what worse?"

"Nothing. It's not your problem, it's mine, and I don't want meds."

The nurse checked off boxes on her clipboard, peeking over the rim of her glasses to see her wrists. "Are you contemplating suicide?"

"Is you?" She self-consciously covered her left wrist, revealing a dozen slits that resembled a bar code. Each line was personal. A moment she felt like giving up. Being locked inside rooms without anyone to speak with left her alone with her thoughts and memories. The trauma was so vivid she couldn't focus on anything but that.

"Do you have any STDs or anything we should know about?"

"Do you have anything we should know about?" she spazzed, irritated.

The nurse kept her cool. "Thank you, Ms. Wilks. We're done. You can go out and be seated in the waiting area. An officer will get with you."

As soon as she stepped out, she was thrust into a holding cell crowded with other females. The overpowering stench of fish and ass attacked her nose with hostile force, nearly choking her. A dozen faces watched her enter the can. "Oh my god, it stinks in here so bad!" She gagged, teary eyed.

"Bend out!" The CO slammed the door shut.

Queenie was livid the judge set her bond at 25K. She knew she'd never get out. A new correctional officer came and retrieved her from the holding cell. She was then escorted through a maze of hallways. The woman said nothing. Instead, she pressed a button that soon opened a hydraulic door. Entering the closed quarters, the moment the doors shut, the boisterous noise of females kicking, screaming, and banging was deafening. The sour stench of urine, feces, and fish punched her nose again.

The officer led her to a suicide watch cell. "Step in, strip down, squat, and cough."

"Bitch, I'm not goin' in there, you go in there."

CO James twisted her face up. "Who the fuck is you talking to?" She removed the can of riot spray, shaking the canister. "Gon' get your bad ass up in there now, or it's gonna get ugly."

"You ain't gon' do shi—"

Schh! Thick orange mist blurred her vision. "Into the cell, ma'am," CO James shouted, hitting the distress button.

"Arrgggh! Shit. You fuckin' bitch!" Queenie yelled. "You sprayed me."

The dorm was suddenly crawling with COs wrestling her to the ground.

"It burns!" She resisted. "Get the fuck off me."

"Strap her in the restraint chair in the cell," a sergeant ordered.

Queenie continued to kick and scream as the orange goo burned across her skin. An hour later, a nurse finally came and wheeled her to medical, strapped to the seat.

"Ms. Wilks, I don't know what you're trying to prove, but here in this detention center, these folks don't care who you think you are or what you think you're going to prove. I suggest you get it together before you find yourself hurt really bad."

Queenie glared at the woman crazily. "Fuck you and the police."

"If you say so." The nurse stood, leaving her untreated. "She good and ready to go. Take her back to the hole."

"Nooo, wait!" she bellowed. "This shit burns, get it off me."

"You'll get a shower sometime next week." The female officer snickered, pushing the physical restraint chair into the filthy suicide cell.

She tried to free herself from the chair to no avail.

CO James slammed the door shut. "That's what yo' ass get."

Tears and snot ran down her orange-foam-stained face. Unable to see, she shuddered with violent rage. "God ... whoever the hell sprayed me, I'm gonna kill 'em for this ... oohh .. it hurts!"

***

Krissy entered the downtown Starbucks dressed heavily to hide her identity behind a face mask and shades. She headed to the back, noticing the woman from the phone book instantly. "Mrs. Kanna Johnson?"

The attorney stood. "Krissy Burress?"

She shook the woman's hand, surveying the business operating at 50 percent capacity, making it easy to spot any undercovers pretending to be civilians. "Yes, it's me. I 'preciate you for meeting me, even though I'm late."

"You're welcome, and no problem. I understand you're being cautious."

"Right. So here's the retainment. Were you able to find information on my case?"

Kanna Johnson removed the file. "You're wanted for second degree murder, and from what I'm also hearing from my private investigators, not only are the local authorities searching for you, but a gang is pushing to have you murdered as retaliation, am I right?"

Her face said it all.

"Don't worry. As your attorney, what we discuss is solely between us. I can assure you everything we speak will stay between us."

Krissy didn't trust nobody but knew this was one of those times she had to. "So ... about the murder ... what am I looking at if I don't beat this charge?"

"Normally, I'm the trial approach type. So, in my opinion, based on what police have in their report, I'd say trial is a good bargaining tool since there's no witnesses from the scene, at least that's what we know so far. They have a way of digging up witnesses and in these circumstances, witnesses are critical."

Her stomach tightened when she thought of Queenie. Now she regretted letting the young girl live. "What if I don't want a trial? What can you do? I'm pregnant, I can't go to jail."

Kanna touched her hand for comfort. "I'm going to fight for you. And I fight hard. My record shows that. Considering the victim was a known gang member with an extensive criminal record, I may argue for a lesser offense, something with probation. However, you'll have to tell me everything from that night, leave out no details, even a speck is vital, understand?"

Krissy nodded, handing the envelope of money over. She desperately needed to get the law off her tail. The streets she could maneuver better without having to run from two enemies and was willing to pay her way out. "That's 17K. I'll give you the rest when we have the tangles sorted out. If you get me a sweet deal, I'll give you a bonus 5K."

The attorney secured the money in her bag. "I'll see what I can do. So, tell me what happened that night."

Krissy settled, coming clean about the entire shooting. The attorney nodded, deep in thought, formulating a defense. She went as far as explaining that she wasn't the shooter but that her friend Queenie was. When she was done, she asked, "So ... what do you think?"

"That you can beat this. I'll see what I can do about the fugitive task force hunting you down. I'll let the city of police know that I'm representing you and that you're arranging to turn yourself in."

"But—"

"Hear me out, turning yourself in will be a good look. I'll get you out the same exact day, on bond. It'll show you're not a flight risk. From what you're telling me, we can beat this thing completely."

Music to her ears. She was pregnant and confused. Having a baby in jail, she never imagined. She was raised in the streets where bitches had to be cut different and made stronger in order to be respected. She learned early that sucking dick and laying on her back for coins in exchange for a man's nut, misinterpreted love, and affection was all but a little girl's mindset. When she knew she could do just about anything a man did, she took those chances.

"Trust me, I know jail for a second sounds bad but in the end, it's worth it."

"I'm going to trust you."

"So I'll get an investigator to do some digging in the streets. In the meantime, you stay low and avoid police until we get this sorted. I'll be in touch. You have my number. Call me if anything happens."

Krissy shook her hand before leaving. "I will."

Chapter 10

In a hurry, Brick tied the long-sleeved shirt around his face before snatching up the gun and drugs off the kitchen counter. He swore up and down he was hallucinating when the familiar young boys sprinted past his trap house. Green Street morning rush was a few minutes away and he was hoping to make a quick come up. He desperately needed the money. Paranoia kicked in, sobering him up. The feds were supposed to be posted at the end of the block. He was glad for their presence, needing to keep Zoo and his goons at bay. Realizing danger and that the devil had come to collect his soul, he prepared to put up a fight.

Cracking the back door slightly, he took a long peek out. The strong scent of fumes and smoke hit his brain. The sun was rising about the tree line in the distance. The shadows gave him the creeps. Too afraid to sit, anticipating a raid, he finally decided it was time to change locations.

Heart thumping like bass drums in his chest, Brick gripped the pistol tight, taking a peek around the house. No one was there. Yet, he felt cornered, so he crawled hands and knees up under the humid house, being swallowed by darkness until reaching the front of the house so he could see the street. He sucked in fresh air greedily. Shots rang out. Within minutes, the entire area was crawling with authorities. Massive fires sealed off both ends of the street, and Brick felt as if the world was ending. The very own strip he and his crew fought so hard to establish was burning away. Screams and cries crackled in the flames, longtime friends dying a gruesome death. Brick could smell the stench of charred flesh, turning his stomach.

It wasn't until hours later when he was finally able to sneak away.

Being his parents only child raised in a very decent home with both parents, he often wondered where did his life go wrong. His mother, a middle school teacher for nearly twenty years, was strict, caring, and loving. His father, a lifelong mechanic, was always present in his life. For a young man whose parents would give him everything he wanted if they could afford it, he chose the bloody route. Living in a nice home outside the 'hood couldn't protect him from the curiosity of discovering uncharted territory. Hearing the intense gun battles urged him to seek out what he didn't know. Getting caught up in the hype of the streets was swift, fluid. He adopted the name Brick after robbing so many drug dealers outside his neighborhood.

Selling drugs wasn't always his thing. It wasn't until he met his wife, Rucci, who at the time was running her own hair salon on the northeast side of town. She planted the seed into his head to really hustle. All his friends trapped on Green Street, which at the time was a barely capable strip. Rucci taught him the ins and outs of distribution, which led to Green Street becoming a million-dollar spot and his crew into paid men.

And now, after all their history, Rucci had abandoned him at the first sign of danger. Her actions crushed him deeply.

Apprehensive, he cut the headlights off on his rental car while taking a very keen survey of his surroundings. It was his father's mechanic and detail shop, established since the mid- 80s. Farrow Road had been good to them. Brick was undecided on what he should do. But with money scarce and his source of income cut off, he had to do something to survive. The sun was setting, making him comfortable though extremely paranoid. Stuffing the few ounces of blow into his briefs, gun snug on his waist, he checked his surroundings one more time for good measure and climbed out.

Brick entered his dad's shop unnoticed.

"What's good, old man?" He startled Denise.

His father clutched the monkey wrench, ready to pounce. "Boy! What the hell have I told you about goddamn sneaking up on me while I'm working?" The old man glared, visibly upset.

"I called your name a few times," he lied. "You ain't answer me, so I came in."

"Stop that damn lying, boy." Denise pointed the oil-black finger at him. The decades of hard labor on cars and tools buried deep in the cracked skin.

"You're always damn lying. What are you doing here anyway?"

"You act like you're not happy to see me, Pops, your son."

Denise threw down the red handcloth, fury burning in his gaze. "I'm not! And you should know why."

"I can explain."

"There ain't no need to explain, son. The four-count indictment does say it all, so don't waste your breath."

Brick instantly felt nauseous and queasy.

"I'm guessing you didn't know them damn FBI people came two days ago to our home busting the door down searching for you and your friends. Damn near gave your mother a heart attack!"

"Damn," he sighed. "How is she?"

"Embarrassed. Hurt. Her only goddamn son is a fugitive to the law. How else is she 'pose to feel?"

Brick rubbed the back of his neck, stressed. Tired. Fatigued. He could not see himself wearing chains and shackles for the rest of his life. "I can't believe this shi—"

"Believe it, son. The damn paper said it's you versus the United States of America. The WHOLE god damn America. And don't even dare ask me to help you with nothing, 'cause I can't. There ain't a goddamn thing I can do to help. Matter of fact, you needa get on up outta here. I don't need dem white folks snooping around mine," he said disdainfully.

"It's like dat, Pop? After all I've done for you and Ma?"

"I still love ya, son. But it is what it is."

Disgusted, he replied, "Hell nah! I gave you sixty racks to hold down for me. I need it."

"Son, it's gone. I had to keep the lights on in here and help your mother out with a few things. It ain't much left, if any." Denise turned away.

He couldn't believe his ears. The knife went through his back and out his chest. The pain of betrayal ached deep in his heart, nearly making him grip the pistol and fire away. "Come on, Pop. I need that money. Don't cross me out like this. You're better than that. We're family. I'm on the run."

"Son, I love you ... so does your mother. But you're a grown man and wanted by the feds. I can't risk losing my business, my wife, my freedom with you here. I'm sorry, son, but you have to go." Denise pointed to the exit.

"I need something, anything toward my lawyer fee at least. Don't play me fucked up, that ain't you, Pops. I'm your son!"

His father removed the cell phone from his breast pocket. "You're a man, and if I have to call the cops in order to protect my wife and this business, I will. Don't make me, son."

"You're gonna call the cops on me?"

Denise pressed the dial button. "I love ya, son, but I'm not playin' ..."

***

Sixteen Years Ago ...

Pierre knew someday soon the police would come bursting through the front door of his mother's house to lock him away for what he did to his friend Marvin. It had been weeks since then, and still no one came. Did they even know? He wasn't sure. Part of him craved to tell someone, maybe his older sisters, Kema and Tati. He even considered expressing what he did to his one-year-old sister, Maya, who was smart. That idea was quickly dismissed the moment she started babbling words. The thought of her growing up and repeating his words kept him tight lipped.

It was eating him up inside. It wasn't like he was having nightmares or hearing voices, it was irking him not to expose the fact he's now a cold-blooded killah.

Trusting no one with his secret, Pierre stayed in the house, refusing to play with his friends or talk much with any of his sisters. Most of his time went toward reading newspapers and watching squirrels run and play on the power lines. Over time, he'd become genuinely fascinated with all animals, loving that they, too, had a mind of their own.

Queen of the Zoo 2

Pierre devised a plan to capture one. He collected enough pecans, nuts, and seeds, anything he figured squirrels liked to eat, placing it all in a bowl beside the window. It wasn't long before he got the attention of a sneaky little one. For days he would do this without interruption, until one day when the squirrels came to the window and slid down. The trap he set had worked, securing the baby squirrel in the room. Having previously already sealed all possible escape routes, he got the squirrel and introduced himself.

Weeks after capturing it, Pierre had it trained, earning the squirrel's trust while teaching it to enter the bedroom through the cracked open window to find the hidden nuts he had stashed around. His sisters had met "Sneaky." Maya was still afraid of it, running and crying. Eventually, she, too, came around and started playing with it as well.

However, one day after making a store run for his mother, Pierre returned to find his mother screaming at the top of her lungs, slapping the broom across the floor. "It's a goddamn RAT in my house!"

Kema yelled, "Ma, stop. It's Pierre's squirrel. You're goin' to kill it."

"I don't give a fuck!" She chased the squirrel frantically.

Pierre came to his friend's defense. "Don't hurt it, Ma. I'll make it leave."

She ignored his plea, slapping the broom around. They tried to calm her down, but she continued. Tears welled in Pierre's eyes. Anger swelled in his chest. He wanted to dig up the colt .45 automatic and end his mother's day with a bang, but was too afraid to turn his attention away from his pet, Sneaky. Charity was relentless. Evil burning on her glossy eyes, she wouldn't stop until the animal was dead. And Sneaky had made the fatal mistake of squeezing into the oven.

"Ma, nooo. Leave it alone!" he bellowed.

But Charity turned the oven up to its max, smiling with victory. "Kill this disgusting motherfucking RAT!"

Pierre watched with hatred. Deep in his soul, Charity was dead to him. The smell of burning flesh filled the small kitchen with smoke when she opened the oven door to find a black, charred squirreled. She giggled, taunting Pierre. "Now clean this damn shit the hell up!" She stormed away, slamming her bedroom door behind her.

Zoo got the chills every time he thought of that incident. Such cold history made him the gangsta he was. And because he was always himself, he never shied away from his love and admiration for animals.

"Sheba! Solomon!" He whistled loudly. Suddenly, the two wolves came dashing from the woods at top speed toward him. "That's right, did y'all miss Daddy?" He rubbed their coats, missing his animals. For an hour, he bonded with them. There was nothing like the power of control. Zoo understood it well. Giving his pets a good wash, he gave them both a large portion of Uncle Jerry's deer meat.

Entering the mansion, he called out, "TiTi! Boo-Boo?" The pet parrot and monkey emerged from the sound of his voice. The two made animalistic sounds of excitement. Zoo fed them fruits and vegetables. Showed them both attention, love, and affection. Being around his pets put him at ease. Temporarily, he forgot about the world and everything around him. He treated his pets like babies, handling them carefully, respecting them. It was there, in his mansion where his sanctuary existed, giving him the calm space to strategize against the streets, his opponents.

"Go watch TV," he told them. In a playroom, cartoons played on a screen, keeping them entertained.

In the living room, Zoo flopped onto the couch, turning the television to CNN. The world was going up in flames. A smile spread across his lips. *That's right, tear this shit up. Burn everything*, he thought, amused seeing protesters fight back against systemic racism and police brutality. He felt good inside.

Again, Lil' Monkey's video was being played. "Stupid niggas always fuck up a million-dollar operation," he mumbled, disturbed.

Turning off the television, he checked the time on his phone. A few hours to burn. Standing, he headed up to the third floor, knocking on the steel door softly. She wouldn't have to say anything nor make a sound for him to know she was at the door. Her energy was strong, special. So was his. Needing no verification, the heavy bolts could be heard unlocking. As the door cracked open, the vibrant, hypnotic glow from her flawless skin greeted him warmly.

He swore she had to be a goddess.

"Can I come in ?" he asked, smoothly.

She stepped aside, allowing him to enter her realm once again.

***

Three Hours Later ...

Zoo emerged from the haven mentally, emotionally restored. As he descended the stairs, his phone vibrated.

"Yolo," he answered and heard laughter.

"That's not a true saying."

"What's good, nigga?" He recognized the voice.

"You sound happy to hear from me."

"I am," he addressed his longtime drug connect. "Thought you'd never call."

"Well, I did. And as much as I would like to chop it up, you know I don't do cell phones."

"Where to, I'm on the way."

"Chuck town. Four hours, I'll call you back then." The call disconnected.

Sighing deeply, Zoo went about preparing for a mandatory trip out of town.

In Charleston, South Carolina, Chucktown, the sun was fading from the sky. Zoo made the trip safely, meeting his friend and connect in a downtown restaurant. As he entered, so did his shooters, Babygirl and Taylor. One would easily mistake the trio for a family. They moved through the fairly lit dining room to a secluded privacy booth in the far back.

Babygirl and Taylor took a seat at the last table, creating a barrier between the entire room and the booth Zoo had a meeting in. Armed with a baby .380 loaded with a 50-round drum and hand grenade, Babygirl began to order. Taylor, strapped with a Mac-10 beneath his Carolina Panthers windbreaker, sat pissed, pretending to be having a nice time while also keeping an eye on everything around them. Both teens were anxious for some heated excitement.

When Zoo entered the booth shutting the curtain behind him for privacy, he thought maybe he was in the wrong spot. The woman stood, smiling. If he didn't have an important meeting to attend, he would've entertained the dark-skinned chick. But time was money. He had to get to it. "My bad, I'm in the wrong booth."

As he turned to leave, he heard, "Got damn, my nigga. What the fuck is good?"

The familiar voice made him turn around quickly. "Black Elmo?"

The dark skin chick was smiling, nodding her head. "Damn right, nigga. It's me. What's good, glad you could make it."

Zoo slapped hands with him, shocked and confused. He was truly at a loss for words. His mind was struggling to process what he was seeing and hearing.

"Black Elmo?"

The chick nodded. "It's me, nigga."

"Damn, dawg, a lot has changed, huh?" He tried not to be rude to his friend. Though they'd done business periodically, yet consistently, they hadn't met face to face in years since Black Elmo went on the run. He still couldn't believe what his eyes were seeing.

Levi "Black Elmo" Fuller stood 5'8, his name given for his charcoal complexion and commercial laughter identical to Sesame Street's Red Elmo. From Charlotte, North Carolina, he, his mother, and four sisters moved to Columbia, South Carolina for his fifteenth birthday. The Allen Benedict Court (ABC) projects swallowed him alive, regurgitating a murderous gangsta.

Black Elmo was rumored to be responsible for over a dozen homicides, including the deaths of two city cops, an investigator, as well as a bondsman. It was also rumored that Levi was the offspring of a notorious legend, Mr. Black, who eluded the government for decades.

Zoo and Black Elmo became friends at seventeen. Levi was being supplied by drug kingpin Ryno, who had taken a special liking to the kid. What had started as a murder-for-hire deal transformed into a business relationship, which eventually led to him and Zoo doing business since they were extremely respected and close, though from two different communities.

Now sitting across each other, Zoo was adjusting.

"A lot has changed." Black Elmo admired his body.

"I mean, I heard, but didn't really ... you know ... think it was true." He took a seat.

"You feel some kinda way 'bout me looking like this?"

"Nah, homie. You're still Black Elmo to me, bruh."

Levi got comfortable. "Then that's all that matters."

Safe in his sexuality as a straight man, it was still hard seeing Black Elmo, his good friend and connect, sitting across from him wearing form-fitting jeans, a shirt that clung to real breasts, weave, makeup, piercings. Everything about him was feminine. Zoo could only imagine how much money it cost to get a model look. "So ... what that shit run you?"

Levi palmed his B-cups. "What ... these? Not much when you're rich as fuck. I'm a transgender. I know it's crazy you had to find out this way, but I've been this way, mentally, my whole life. I just finally said fuck it and came out. A lot has changed, but at the end of the day, I'm still a gangsta. You knew about it then and respected it. It ain't like I'm hiding it."

"Honestly, I ain't even trippin' homie. Just caught by surprise."

"I know, I seen it. Anyways, let's get down to business. I asked you to meet me because I know it's that time. There's twenty bricks of coke and ten keys of raw heroin still good as ever, on the way to your storage."

"I'm guessing the ticket is the same as well?"

Levi chuckled, "Ya already know."

"Say less. So what is this meet about? To show off your new rack to me?" He cracked up.

"Nigga, you still funny as hell. But nah, homie, this meet is about you."

Zoo noticed the killah in Levi's eyes. No matter what, he wouldn't sleep on no man, no bitch, no ... tranny. "What about me?"

"Your whole neighborhood is on CNN and every other news station these days. Your goons even mentioning your name, that's not a good look. I'm on the run and on the prowl. I still got connections, and right now it would be stupid on my behalf to keep any connection between us going. Until you cool down, this is our last meet, our last exchange. Everything is on hold."

Zoo nodded his head. He could understand his connect's decision. He had every right to protect his liberty. There was nothing he could do about it.

"I ain't got to tell you how to move, but we both know you have to get rid of every problem you have before those problems make more problems. Hate to see you on the run, like me."

Zoo stood, slapping hands with Levi. "I'll shoot that bag to you as soon as I check the storage. Same as usual."

And with that, they parted.

On the ride back to Columbia, Zoo had to shake Black Elmo from his head. He whispered in disbelief, "This nigga a cold-blooded bitch now."

Babygirl locked eyes with him in the rearview mirror. He quickly shifted his gaze out the window. A lot of thoughts flooded his mind all at once.

Entering the storage unit, as promised, he noticed the television box in the corner of the space. The strong stench of high-potency drugs punched his nose. Opening the box, he saw thirty blocks. He owed 800K for the load.

He thought about what came of Black Elmo. His stomach hurt, disgusted. "Fuck that faggot ass nigga, fuck this storage, fuck paying." He set the box into the back seat. He nodded to Babygirl, who stepped on the gas.

Chapter 11

Being locked inside the house with Dirty night and day was torture. At times, the tension was getting so thick one word could start a fire. The mental warfare of silence and paranoia was eating Krissy up so bad inside she cried at night. Something she rarely did. She had no one to talk to, no one to trust her secret with. The heavy burden of truth weighed down on her guilty conscience. Seeing her man, Dirty, struggle to stand, groaning in agony as bullets lodged in his hip and shoulder ached tremendously. Never had she witnessed so much pain that someone as tough as him shed tears. For the first time, Krissy felt wrong for not keeping it real with her man about the incident.

"Are you hungry, baby?"

"The fuck it look like?" he grunted, shifting his weight in bed. She felt stupid, knowing he hadn't eaten all day. It wasn't her fault. Dirty hated her so much at this point that he couldn't stand the sight of her let alone eat from her hand.

Krissy went to the kitchen, swiping away a lone tear. The drum beat rapidly in her heart, and she sighed deeply. It wasn't like she needed Dirty for anything. She had her own bag. Even contributed her hustle ethics to increase his financial gains. She needed him because being pregnant, she didn't want to throw away the opportunity to raise a child in a household where the father was present. She never forgot coming up without love, support, or parents at least pretending to care. The streets provided her with false hopes, promises, dreams. To raise a baby in a home better than she had was retribution. To make it happen, Dirty had to be on board.

Preparing his meal, two grilled chicken sandwiches on garlic buttered Texas toast, topped with turkey bacon and honey sliced cheese, with seasoned fries and sweet iced tea, Krissy carried it to him on a tray, setting it across his lap.

The frown on his face made her nervous. "You trying to kill me?"

"Huh? What? No! Why would you think that?"

"Take the first bite."

Black Migo

Doing so, she chewed and swallowed. "Don't play me, Dirty." When she didn't die, he ate into his food while she rubbed his feet. This was the closest she'd been to him and wanted to enjoy it.

"I know you hate me right now and don't want to see or be around me, but I promise I love you and want to make this work. Whatever I need to do to make you feel better, let me know, and I promise I'm gonna try to make it right." Her voice was pleading.

Dirty ate in silence. His gaze made her uneasy. She wondered what was going through his mind. When he finished, he swallowed two pain pills, wincing. She took his dishes away, coming back to find him watching the news, amazed at the protests taking place around the globe.

Krissy sat on the edge of the bed. "I spoke to my attorney. I'm going to beat this charge."

"Of course, you're gonna beat it. You're innocent." His words dripped with sarcasm.

"I'm going to turn myself in soon so I can get a bond and get back out. It won't be no longer than a few hours."

"And that's supposed to change the fact I got shot the fuck up?"

"It wasn't my fault though."

"And you're still lying? Honestly, I don't even give a fuck. I got hit up behind yo' fuck shit. What you're gonna do is get me close to that nigga, Zoo. You was fuckin' that nigga behind my back. He got me shot, I want my lick back."

She lied, "I wasn't fucking Zoo. Who told you that?"

He chuckled. "Still lying, huh? Cool … Get me close to that nigga or this shit with me and you is a wrap, bruh. Get the fuck away from me." The malice in his tone struck her with fear. If that's what he wanted, that's what he'd get. Still, she had no clue where to start.

***

"Kanna Johnson speaking?"

"Hi, Mrs. Johnson, it's Krissy, any news yet?" She sat still in the quietness of the rental car, a Chevy Malibu with tinted windows.

She couldn't risk being caught slipping by police or bloods, so she was paying close attention to her surroundings.

"So far, the district attorney is going to work with us. In return, you're going to have to tell them what happened. They want to hear it from you. Not me."

Butterflies filled her stomach. Snitching was not how she was raised. She wanted to squeeze the most lenient sentence she could possibly receive. However, she had to confess. She was ready if it meant she wouldn't have to spend a day in jail. "What about my bond, will you be able to get me something reasonable?"

"The investigator will make the recommendation to the bond court judge. You'll get released immediately."

"I'm going to my bondsman sometime today to have it all situated beforehand. I also have another payment. Are you at your office? I'm close by."

"I'm not actually. I won't be back until later. If you want, Krissy, I'll call my assistant and tell her you're coming."

"Do that."

"Great, head on over." She hung up.

Krissy took a deep breath. She was timid going anywhere downtown due to the rioting. Swamped with paranoia, she parked outside the law firm. The chanting for justice carried with the breeze. After dropping off the money to the assistant, she headed to EZ Out Bail Bonding.

"How can I help?" a tall, Dog the Bounty hunter lookalike asked once she entered.

A young guy stood from the desk where he had been seated waiting for a receipt. As he left, he licked his lips.

"I called earlier." She shook his hand. "Kristen Burress."

"Oh yes, you spoke to me, Marvin Riley." He gestured to a seat. "How can I help you?"

"I called to pay my bond before me and my attorney arrange a self-surrender."

Marvin grinned. "Thinking about fucking your boyfriend?"

"No," she answered, bashfully.

"I'm just goofing around. So, what would you like to place as insurance?"

"Five thousand."

"What we'll get you to do is some paperwork. In any case, if you withdraw this down payment on a bond, you'll have to pay a 10 percent withdrawal fee, agreed?"

"Agreed."

"Good. Now, how this works is if you do go to jail for whatever reason, we'll come get you. Period."

Smiling. "That's what I need to hear." She handed over the money. Ten minutes later, she was done with the paperwork and feeling better.

Two miles away, Krissy pulled into a gas station, parking at a pump. Climbing out, she went inside, purchasing a ginger ale and powdered donuts.

The cashier asked, "Will this be all?"

She handed over a ten-dollar bill. Waiting for her change, she pondered. She had been so focused on spending money to save her ass that she forgot to replace it in order to keep her level up. Being broke and pregnant wouldn't cut it, and relying on Dirty was a liability. She wanted hard cash and planned to get back on track, formulating a scheme.

The gray Nissan Maxima easing past filled her with fear. The driver made eye contact. Something wasn't right. It was the same teen from the bonding company, the wild savage glint of murderous intentions pranced in his sights.

Krissy shifted the rental into drive. "Oh hell the fuck no!" She punched the gas. "Y'all bitches won't catch me." She whipped into the street, punching the accelerator.

Gripping the wheel tightly with her left hand, the right felt around the purse for the nigga that would get ignorant on her behalf. The XD .45 with its heavy weight secured firmly in her pal, she thumbed off the safety.

***

G50 jacked the slide on his Springfield .9mm, chambering a hollow tip. He had been so engrossed in his phone texting with Shooter's girlfriend letting her know his bond was paid, that he hadn't seen Krissy enter the bonding company.

"Moe Moe, you sure it was that hoe?"

The teen cocked his pistol as well, focusing on the entrance. "It was her, I'm sure. Ain't no room for mistakes. You know that."

He sat up in the seat, glancing around the parking lot. There were no cops in sight, but he was no fool. 48 Bluff Road was a long stretch, and police could be anywhere close.

"You wanna let her come outside?" 5th asked with attitude. "I say run up in there and crush that bitch and er-body else!"

Kash interjected, "Stupid nigga, how you sound?"

G50 took another glance at the entrance. The grief of losing his baby brother had him emotional. A few tears here and there did little to take off his bottled up rage. Unreleased anger made him feel two seconds away from exploding. In front of the homies he had to stay tough, calm. His violent actions and deadly eruption could influence them to follow suit. Taking a deep breath, he shifted his gaze to Moe Moe, giving instructions.

Moe Moe doubled back, the Malibu was gone. He stomped the gas.

5th pointed. "That's her car right there."

"Circle the parking lot. Whether she killed my cousin Ta'maine or not, this bitch gets dropped." G5 covered his face.

Moe Moe circled the store slowly, his gaze locked with hers. He was going to pull up beside her but had to circle the store once more.

G50 exploded with anger. "Nigga, this hoe finna get away!"

The Maxima burned rubber, lurching into the street chasing the Malibu. With skill he gained on her. 5th and Kash rolled their windows down, completely following G50's lead. Krissy took them on a high-speed chase, zipping through Shop Road, Kilbourne, and Beltline. It wasn't until she tried to lose them within Midlands Technical College that she got blocked in.

BLAH-BLAH-BLAH-BLAH! Shots erupted, bullets ripped through the black fiberglass with vengeance. Hot lead traveled through the Malibu's interior before burying itself into the dash, the floorboard ripped to shreds. Seats exploded with holes. Krissy screamed, balling up on the floorboard. She was unable to go anywhere. Cringing in fear, she was unable to find her pistol. The impact from heavy rounds vibrated and shook the car violently.

"Please God, don't let 'em kill me dead," she sobbed, overwhelmed.

BLAH-BLAH-BLAH-BLAH!

The fusillade of multiple weapons being fired all at once filled the air with rancid gun smoke. She popped up from hiding once the shooting stopped. The car was smoking. Frantically, she checked herself for any shots. She had went unscathed. Tears stained her face. She was trembling uncontrollably with the windows shot out and engine rattling. She looked around frightened.

Hyperventilating as she sat upright in the seat, she came face to face with one of Pine Hurst's deadliest. G50.

"You thought we was gon' let you live?" he snarled. The tone of his icy voice paralyzed her. The same voice to call her phone when Dirty was ambushed.

He aimed the smoking gun at her face. "For my blood, Ta'maine ..."

She squeezed her eyes shut, anticipating the burst of flames. Life flashed before her eyes. It was the end.

Click!

Her heart sank! He had no bullets.

And in another desperate attempt, Krissy punched the gas.

Chapter 12

Brick couldn't believe his father. If he didn't have love for his mother, there was a strong chance he might've filled Denise up with slugs. The drugs had taken control of his mind. After robbing one of Zoo's dealers, he was using the product to feed his own cravings. The dope was highly addictive. Mixing it all into a potent concoction sent him to a very dark place.

And so he sat outside the vacant house as the sun set. The dark Ray Bans hid his rabid eyes as he inhaled a deep pull of toxic smoke from the dirty blunt. Inside the car reeked of burning coke. Out of his mind, he put out the blunt, shifting the car into drive. His action was slow motion, circling the block once more, stalking his prey.

Parking the rental outside the house, he slid out heading to the front door. Ringing the doorbell, he wiped the thick white foam forming in the corners of his mouth. *This hoe got me fucked up*, he thought. Suddenly, the door made a noise, and Brick was so high he had to calm his brain.

The feminine voice answered, "Who is it?"

"It's me, Peaches."

"Me who?"

"Brick."

Quickly, the locks unbolted and the door swung open. "Boy, hurry up and come in. What the hell is you doing here?" Peaches asked. "You do know dem damn feds is searching for you, right?"

He nodded, looking around the room.

"Then what the hell is you doing here at my house? They've already kicked my doors in two days ago looking for you and my damn daughter. I don't need them doubling back."

Brick ignored his mother-in-law's concerns. Instead, he went through the two-story house searching.

"Hold up, Brick, what's wrong?"

Gritting, he asked, "Where the fuck is Rucci and Tootsie?"

"I'm not sure," she replied truthfully. Both sisters were the spitting image of their mother, Peaches. The strong physical attraction he had with his wife was crazy, and seeing his mother-in-law gave him an instant sexual reaction.

He removed the .45 from his waistband. "I don't fuckin' believe you! None of y'all bitches." He snatched the shades off.

"Br-Brick ... wh-what are you doing? Put that gun away."

"Both your daughters will die if they don't bring me my shit."

Peaches had her hands up. "O-Okay, baby ... wh-what did they take? Whatever they took, I'll help you get it back."

Snatching the blouse off her, he exposed her breasts. In a violent manner, he gripped the back of her neck with his free hand, planting the pistol on her jaw before forcing her into the living room. At 5'2, 125 pounds, Peaches could not match him.

"I asked you for that bitch's hand in marriage. You said yes. You poisoned me, giving me that snake hoe." He slung her onto the couch, aiming the gun at her face.

In shock, Brick's violent temper struck her with terror, her heart threatening to explode. The atrocity on his face made her bladder leak. "I-I don't ... know what she did, but I-I'm sorry. Talk to me, you don't have to kill me, we're family," she pled.

He spat, "Fuck family!"

"What do you want me to do? I don't even know what she did." She shivered.

"She ran off with 400 stacks. Tootsie took a hundred, and I want it all the fuck back!" He snatched the phone up and tossed it to her. "Call Rucci, tell 'er bring me my shit!"

Peaches trembled, dialing her daughter's new number on speaker.

"Hey, Mommy, what's up?"

"Where you at, baby?"

"Ma, I already told you I wasn't sayin', not over no phone, anyways. Why you ask?" Rucci sounded like she was having the time of her life while he was down on his dick. He hated it.

Peaches, exasperated, asked, "Rucci, you know better. Why would you take your husband's money?"

"I don't feel like hearing that, Ma." She sucked her teeth.

"And I don't give a fuck what you don't feel like hearing. Why would you take that man's damn money?"

"You know what ... Is Brick there? Put 'em on the phone."

He gripped the strap firmly. "We ain't got nothin' to talk about. Bring back my shit. That's it!"

"I've been doing some thinking. I want a divorce."

"Bring me my shit!" He ate the heavy blow to the gut.

"You don't even care. Just like you don't care who you drag down with you. The feds are going to hide your ass in prison, but not me. I'm not ever coming back to you. So fuck it, and fuck you!" she spat, disgusted.

"Better hope that money hold you over forever, 'cause bitch. if I go down, you going down with me."

"Brick, don't fucking play with—"

He disconnected the call.

Peaches started crying. "This is some crazy shit. I can't believe her."

Snarling, he said, "Get up, now. Get the fuck up."

She stood. He snatched her by the arm, dragging her through the house and down the hall into the basement. Having spent so many holidays over, he knew the home like it was his. Descending the flight of stairs, he pulled the string, and a light bulb clicked on.

"Brick, wait, don't kill me. I had nothing to do with my daughter's bullshit. Please, don't take it out on me. I don't deserve it."

He took the bundle of Christmas lights off a box, shoving her further into the room. His silence was destroying her.

"Don't do this. Please don't kill me."

As he pushed the pistol into his waistband, Peaches reached for it out of desperation. Brick was quick, punching her in the jaw, knocking her out instantly. Her small body tumbled to the floor.

"Stupid hoe. Now I got to kill you."

Taking the Christmas lights, he hogtied Peaches's hands behind her back then ankles before tying them into a tight knot. Glancing over, he drug her across the floor to the deep freezer. Carefully, he removed frozen packages of meat, and when the bottom of the freezer was visible, he lifted Peaches effortlessly, setting her down inside. Slowly, she began to stir awake. It was too late. She had been covered with layers of packaged meat, unable to fight herself free.

When the lid closed, she was trapped in darkness, freezing cold.

Brick wiped down his prints before leaving. As he lit the blunt of boont, he felt no remorse as he pulled out the hood. "Bitches that flock together, die together."

***

Rucci stepped out of Club Follies Atlanta after hanging up with Brick. Her heart broke knowing he was in Columbia going through the motions. She took everything he had stashed. At the time, she didn't care about his own well-being and wanted to escape the chaos before the heat came down on them. Brick was hard headed and wouldn't listen.

"Better hope that money hold you over, 'cause if I go down, you going down with me."

His words echoed in her mind. *Fuck does he mean by that?* Fear filled her chest.

"He better not play wit' me." She strolled through her call log. She knew her mother loved her son-in-law dearly, and now that she knew Rucci had ran off with his money, she'd be blowing her up any minute to give her a good cursing out. Peaches hated drama and would be trying to get her to return the money. To prevent the aggravation, she blocked her mother's house number.

She didn't know what to do, too afraid to call anyone associated with Brick, in fear her new phone would get tapped. To avoid detection, she kept a low profile in the city of Black Dreams. Getting out the hotel room for a few hours was the only reason for hitting a strip club.

"Damn, shawdy, I thought you was ditching me." Her new friend, Rocko, emerged from inside.

Discreetly, she swiped away the moisture forming on her lids, brandishing a gorgeous smile. "Nah, I'm good, just getting some fresh air. All that ass and titties in there can suffocate a bitch." She giggled.

Rocko palmed her phat ass. "You wanna go back in or you ready to go?" He studied her with lust. They had met a few days ago at Lenox Mall. The attraction was immediate and just what she needed to distract her from the chaos back home.

"We can go back inside, boo." She replied coyly, "Later, you can take me to your room."

He flashed a quarter-million-dollar smile.

"'Cause if I go down, you going down with me," was all she could think about as the night carried on.

***

Tootsie used her spare key to let herself in to her mother Peaches's house. She checked over her shoulder. A haunting, eerie feeling came over her skin like goosebumps. She was scared for her life, knowing she had run off with her brother-in-law's re-up money. Listening to her sister, she felt was a bad idea. But since the pandemic struck and the job laying off, with no real money saved up, made times extremely hard. Desperation made her follow through with her sister's idea, despite the fact she knew he was a cold-hearted killah. And now, until the feds arrested him on charges that could lock him in prison forever, she would have to live in fear.

Closing and locking the front door behind her, she called out, "Mommy, where you at?" She called out again, again, and again.

Silence.

"Mommy?!"

Tootsie stepped into the living room, picking up the cell phone off the couch. It was her mother's, battery dead. She sat the phone on the table before heading into the kitchen. There was no sign of Peaches anywhere. She ventured through the house, calling for her mother to get no answer.

"She must've snuck away with her new boyfriend." Tootsie grinned, taking a seat on the couch.

Thinking about all the money in the trunk of her car, she felt bad. The only reason she stopped by was to check on her mother and drop off some cash. She had a hotel reserved in Miami she couldn't wait to reach. For two hours she sat, dozing off waiting for Peaches.

"Damn, she ain't back yet?" she murmured impatiently.

Sitting up, she decided giving Peaches money would have to wait.

"I'll be back next week." She left out.

***

Cautious, Brick parked his rental at the end of the street just in case. Gun on his waist, he stepped out into the morning. He had been drinking, smoking, and snorting, so it was no wonder his eyes had a deranged gloss to them. There was a tremendous amount of guilt he felt for Peaches but easily dismissed it every time he thought of his treacherous wife, Rucci.

It was a little after 10 a.m. The smell of smoke, burning cars, buildings, and trees filled the sky. Briskly, he rushed into his attorney's law firm unannounced, taking the elevator up to the third floor. He stepped off, entering the receptionist area. Each stride screamed hostility. The paralegal, Cindy, greeted him.

"Hi ... um, do you have an appointment?" Cindy, a beautiful petite blonde woman, stood.

"Is ... Mr. Lii in? I need'a speak wit'em. Tell'em it's Brick."

Cindy made the call.

"He says come on back."

Following her lead, he entered the attorney's office. Victor stood to shake his hand, flashing a bright and friendly smile that warmed the room. "Brick, I've been trying to reach you. How's everything been?"

"I got a new number." He took a seat. "What's going on though?"

"I spoke with your wife some weeks ago when she came to make a payment on your behalf. Did she tell you the news?"

"About the feds? Yeah, she told me after she ran off with all my shit," he gritted bitterly. "What they want anyway? What about my state cases?"

Victor loosened his tie, taking a deep sigh. Tensions grew thick. "This is what's happening. The feds are taking over your state cases as well. I have to say, it's not looking good for you."

"Fuck!" he barked, irate. "This some bullshit. Can you arrange a meeting? Can't I become an informant or something so they can't lock me up?" He thought about being locked away without pussy or drugs.

Victor thought about it. "I can't. They'll lock you up since I'm not your federal attorney. It's not my jurisdiction and … I can't mingle with those guys. They play dirty."

Brick sat up straight. "Then I'ma need that money back my wife dropped off to you. That whole twenty stacks."

"I can't do that."

He stood slowly. "I wasn't asking." He drew the pistol. "Run me that safe!"

"Woah, woah, woah, wait a minute." His hands went up. "Brick, listen … I know you're upset, but don't make matters worse on yourself. Take it easy."

A soft tap sounded from the door. Cindy stuck her head in "Mr. Lii, I—"

Brick snatched her in by the hair, stuffing the barrel of the .45 deep into her mouth, knocking out teeth. Her eyes watered. Brick kicked the door shut. "Lii, run that safe, bruh. You're a lawyer, I know you got money in this bitch. Run that! Don't make matters worse for you or this white hoe. I'll put her fucking scalp all over this mufuckin' office, homes. Now run that safe!"

As he stuffed the barrel deeper, the paralegal gagged violently.

Victor was wide eyed and paralyzed with horror. Seeing his partner suffer, he turned and shoved the shelf of law books aside, revealing a small wall safe. Quickly, he punched in the code. Snatching it open, three stacks of money he had received only yesterday were visible.

Brick's heart fluttered at the sight of it. "Put all that shit in that McDonald's bag." He was fiending to get high. "Hurry the fuck up, Victor. You're making me nervous moving all slow'n shit. I ain't got all damn day!"

Victor moved rapidly. "Don't kill us, Brick. Take the money. Flee. I'll chalk this as a loss. Just go." The Asian handed over the bag, hands shaking.

He removed the pistol from Cindy's beet-red face. Tears and snot were everywhere. She was petrified. With brutal viciousness, Brick pistol whipped the woman until she was knocked out unconscious.

Brick then turned the weapon on Lii. "On your knees. The only reason I'ma spare your Japanese, Chinese, Korean, whatever you are, is 'cause you got me off a shit load of charges." He took the heavy bag of money. "Now lie face down, fingers locked behind your head. Count to 100. It's sad shit came to this, Lii, but it is what it is. I'll holla." He left.

Victor struggled to breath, having almost had a panic attack. He listened to the elevator close before rushing to Cindy. She was out cold but breathing. Immediately, he dialed 9-1-1, requesting assistance, all the while locking the door in case Brick returned.

It wasn't until he parked his car at one end of the street that he felt at ease. At a motel room outside West Columbia, he headed inside to count up his riches. From the weight of the bag, he knew he hit the mother load. After he dumped the bag, the money stared back at him. A sinister chuckle filled the room as he began to inspect the money.

He couldn't believe it.

"Dirty bitches!" His chuckle escalated into a fitful laughter as he continued to ravish through the money.

Instead of a come up, he was stuck with two thousand dollars of single bills. This only way to keep from crying was to laugh it off.

Chapter 13

Strapped in the physical restraint chair for the fifth time since her transfer from a mental hospital, Queenie continued to fight against the bonds, determined to free herself. Hearing a muffled rip of thread tearing encouraged her to keep going. Harder and harder. Every few minutes she heard the tearing again, until finally the strap holding her head firmly in place loosened. Able to rock back and forth, she worked the strap across her chest until it loosened as well, giving her enough slack to use her razor-sharp teeth to bite through the wrist straps. With her hands finally free, she snatched her leg straps away excitedly. Adrenaline pumping, she felt free.

Wet tissue paper was slapped across the camera glass so no one in the central control center could see her. She rushed around the disgusting room, caged in. Taking a spoiled carton of milk, she poured half the lumpy white fluid into the toilet before squatting over the toilet, filling it with feces and piss. Satisfied with her handy work, she stashed the carton out of sight, sure to have quick, easy access. She then pushed the chair further into the cell before peeking out the blurry square window of the suicide cell. The CO hadn't started her rounds yet to end the 6 p.m. shift. Figuring she had a few minutes to spare, she studied the chair closely for anything she could use to make a weapon later.

She was miserable and wanted out the closed quarters. There was too much time to reminisce, mourn, think. She was tired of it all.

"Count time! Count time! IDs on the doors, ladies!" CO James announced loudly with her shift relief in tow.

Queenie smiled broadly. She sat in the chair punching herself in the nose, causing blood to trickle. She hurriedly placed the torn straps around her ankles, chest, and wrist to make it seem as if she was safely secured. As the noisy jingle of keys came closer and closer, she pretended to be slumped, chin resting on her chest as blood spilled over her naked flesh.

Tap-Tap-Tap! CO James hit the window for a reaction.

Queenie didn't move or flinch. Listening, waiting.

"Shit! She's non-responsive." CO James pulled on some gloves before opening the cell. The second officer was right on her hip, entering. "Ms. Wilks, can you hear me?" James stepped in closer, horrified at the sight of blood. Panic in her trembling voice. She had purposely neglected to check on Queenie, and now she could possibly lose her job, everything, if an inmate died on her watch. It scared her. She didn't know what to do or what signs to look for. For a split second, she dropped her guard as tears welled in her eyes.

Before she could press the panic button to summon help, Queenie lurched from the seat like a dead monster from a horror film, traumatizing both officers with fear.

"Bitch! You thought I forgot?" She attacked, punching the woman once in the nose and twice in the jaw, sending James crashing to the ground. The second guard was new and taken aback as well as too slow to duck the hailstorm of blows Queenie unleashed. The guard tripped over the toilet, falling onto James.

Queenie doused James in the mouth and face with the horrendous concoction of waste and spoiled milk. The second officer received the end of the mix.

"Fuck the police! Bitch!" Queenie yelled, snatching up both cans of mace and James's door keys. The officers were frantic, trying to get to her.

Queenie then busted the sprinkler, sending the fire alarm blaring and murky black water spraying from the ceiling before locking the COs in to get soaked. She laughed, thoroughly entertained.

Erratic officers stormed into the door. The entire mass of chicks locked behind steel doors erupted with kicking, screaming, and banging, cheering Queenie on. The moment was exhilarating. Lock up exploded with chaos. She was going to open every cell but had no idea which key did what.

Ass naked, she ran around, dashing up the stairs to the second tier. The madness was so loud that it was impossible to hear anything.

"Ms. Wilks, get back here!" one black male sergeant roared in utter disbelief. In all his years, he'd never seen anything this wild.

Every officer within Alvin S. Glenn DC had become awfully familiar with her as every other day of her stay had caused major disruption. "Do not make me chase you!" His big, burly frame bolted up the stairs.

Caged inmates encouraged her to go even harder. She ran to the opposite end of the dorm. "I'm not going back in that cell!" she screamed boisterously. She ran to the end only to be met by a large pack of officers. Behind her, officers were closing in. More officers rushed the dorm. Shaking both cans of mace, she popped the tops, aiming in both directions. A standoff.

"Put it down!" one yelled.

Schhh! She unleashed the burning chemical on the sergeant, hitting him directly in the eyes. He dropped his can then let out a gut-wrenching shrill. She emptied the second can on the entourage of COs rushing up the stairs.

"Bitch ass police. Fuck all y'all motherfuckas!"

Queenie took off past the blind, burly man. More officers entered the door dressed in riot gear. She ran until she was exhausted, winded. In a desperate attempt to end her life, she jumped from the second-tier rail.

***

Four days later, Capt. Thomas, a white female, and Lt. Griffen, a black man, escorted Queenie into an office. Lt. Griffen remained standing by the door. Queenie took a seat.

Thomas combed her fingers through her blond hair, visibly frustrated. "Ms. Wilks, what's the problem?"

"I don't know what you're talking about. You tell me."

"Seriously? Four days ago you assaulted twelve of my staff. You've destroyed three restraint chairs, a camera, a toilet, uniforms, an institutional phone, the list goes on. Not including you jumped from a second tier and would have broken your neck if not for an officer catching you."

"It wasn't me. I didn't do anything."

Thomas looked as if Queenie lost her mind. "Why haven't you been taking your medication?"

Lt. Griffen cut in, astonished. "Do you even see how much trouble you're in? You're burying yourself. In a month you've accumulated nineteen new charges. You can't keep doing this."

"I'ma get out. And when I do, I'm gon' sue all y'all. Your officers abuse me and get away with it. When I react y'all charge me and lock me in the cell by myself for no reason. I've been here a month and your staff has only let me use a shower twice. I have to clean up in a sink. That's violation to my rights and when my attorney comes, we'll push for an investigation that'll tear into all the fuck shit your STAFF is doing. Lots of jobs will be lost, I'll be rich and home, charges dismissed due to a corrupt jail. Who wants smoke?"

Capt. Thomas was shaken. "How can we get this behavior to stop? I understand you're going through a lot of issues, but you can't continue to take it out on this institution."

"Y'all got me in lock up for no reason!"

"After all this chaos, you don't expect to be in the box?"

"No, 'cause y'all got me in there with no clothes, no roommate, and nothing to do. It's driving me crazy. Fuck y'all!"

"No, fuck you," Lt. Griffen countered.

"I would but you're fucking Officer Whitely. The nightshift guy with the big muscles and blond mohawk … the white dude." She struck a nerve.

Capt. Thomas was taken aback. Lt. Griffen was speechless.

"Mrs. Capt. Thomas, if you put me in a regular dorm, I won't act up, I promise."

The two high-ranking officials exchanged gazes. Thomas sighed, sitting back in her chair. "I don't normally negotiate with prisoners. I'll make an exception. This is my terms. Give me thirty days of clear conduct in the box, and I'll have you placed in general population. Mess up one time, though, I'll do everything in my power to keep you in the hole. This time you won't have the opportunity to hurt anyone. Do we have an agreement?"

"I guess."

"Good, because if you ever pull something like that again, you'll get the worst end of the stick."

***

Agent Jason Bryson and Vincent Taylor sat around (SAC) Special Agent in Charge Robert Morgan, a pale white man in his late 40s. They ran down to him everything they could about Pierre 'Zoo' Montana, and the fact that they'd had little success. Each of his businesses were legit with no trace of or link to drugs. Besides his name being mentioned by informants, he was clean as a whistle.

No one being willing to offer information on him made their investigation difficult to move forward. It was a stalemate, and at this point they were drawing up any strategy to get what they needed to bring the weight of the federal government down on the G-shine.

Morgan scratched his beard, deep in thought. "There has got to be a way to get this guy. All of them. The last blood organization was a success, so I see no reason for us to be struggling. I suggest you two find something strong. Evidence that'll hold up in front of the grand jury. Whatever it is you gotta do. Lie if you have to, then find some evidence and snitches around the bureau of prisons to support the false evidence. We cannot allow these freakin' imbeciles to run free, making all this money. Stop them."

"We'll keep you updated."

***

Keisha sighed deeply. More so out of frustration and stress than exhaustion. She passed through security clearance. She wasn't sure how to feel. The last few weeks had been an emotional rollercoaster. Knowing that her little boy was in jail facing a murder charge was heart breaking. The only relief was that at least she knew where he was. He was safe, protected, and being fed. As a single mom in the projects, she had seen too many black boys die at the hands of officers and gang violence. There wasn't a day passing when she answered her phone, afraid it was a call from someone explaining her son had been murdered.

It was all over the news every day. Cover of the state paper, replayed over the radio constantly. Lil' Monkey had sacrificed his freedom for fame. Livid, she wanted to cut him off and let him suffer the consequences, but love wouldn't allow it.

"Ms. Durham, you can have a seat anywhere in one of these sections," an officer instructed. Keisha took a seat at the last table on the end. Discreetly, she ran her palm over her breast to ensure she hadn't dropped her money.

Shortly, Lil' Monkey was entering the visiting room shackled. "Ma, what is you doin' here?" he grimaced.

Keisha stood, inspecting him head to toe as a mother should. "I had to come see you, baby. To make sure you're alive and alright. How are they treating you?"

The escort guard removed his cuffs, leaving them alone. "Keisha, I told you on the phone not to come see me in here. I don't need you coming down here trying to bother me."

She hugged him tightly. "Boy, shut the hell up. I'm yo' mama. If your ass would've listened to me and obeyed my damn rules, you wouldn't be in this damn predicament. Now would you?"

"C'mon, bruh. I ain't tryna hear dat fuck shit."

"I ain't cha damn, bruh," she asserted. "I told you, I'm your damn mother and you're going to respect me. Now, how have you been holding up?"

"It ain't that bad, like a daycare. Better than being in PineHurst right now." He cracked up.

"Wipe that damn smile off your face, 'cause ain't shit funny."

He kept his smile, knowing it would irk the hell out her. "How many views my video got on the Gram?"

"Bitch. Your stupid ass is in here looking at a fucking life sentence and you're more concerned about a damn view on social media? I should slap the dog piss out your clout chasin' ass!"

Lil' Monkey laughed hard like it was a joke. "And I'm a slap fire back." Keisha was astonished. She couldn't believe her ears.

"So is you gon' tell me how many views I got?"

Silence.

"So you finna cry?"

"No." Her voice cracked, saddened.

"Yes you is, Ma. What you come up here cryin' for?"

"Because it's sad. If you ever wanna get out of jail to enjoy your fame, you're gonna have to help yourself. You can walk right up outta here today if you tell the FBI exactly what they want to know. They already know you work for Zoo. They know everything. All you have to do is give them enough to lock him up. They'll let you go. And your friends."

"Hell no, Ma. I ain't doing that, you sound crazy as hell."

"Sound crazy? Little boy, your ass will be in prison for the rest of your life."

"So!"

"So? Bitch, don't make me fuck you up in here. They're threatening to lock me up too just 'cause I'm your mother."

"If I can do the time, Ma, you can do it too. You're a grown up." He smirked. "No matter how much time they give me, or what you or anybody else say, I'm not going to snitch on Zoo. He's innocent, like a father to me, and you know that. I don't even know how you even sit here on some fuck shit and try to make me tell shit on him. After all he's done for us. He bought us furniture, kept the rent paid, lights on, even got you a car. If they're waitin' on me to say something, then I'ma tell you like I told them last time they came: to suck my lil' dick. How 'bout dat? I'll stay in here." He sat back in the chair, folding his arms across his chest defiantly.

Keisha was trembling with anger and fear. "If you don't tell on Zoo to get you and your friends out, when they do get him, there won't be any way for you to get out from prison. As bad as I hate to see you here, I'm never, ever coming to see you again." She wiped away tears. "And I have my sister's phone. I'll erase that same IG account and say fuck your stupid clout and spend that check."

Lil' Monkey stared into her eyes for a long minute. She was dead serious, trying to force him to snitch, and he hated it. "Fuck you, Ma. Your ass is the fuckin' feds, swear on God. You're tryna help dem crackas, fuck you, stank bitch!" He jumped to his feet and started banging on the door for an officer's attention.

Keisha was sweating, moments away from breaking his face.

The officer removed him from the room. Tears flooded down her cheeks. She couldn't believe what had transpired. She was a mother who'd do anything for her baby, but the streets were so deeply rooted within him that she could see in his eyes, he was doomed. Standing, she got herself together and was then greeted by FBI.

"Ms. Durham, you done what you could, we appreciate your assistance." Vincent Taylor touched her shoulder.

Jason Bryson said, "We'll have you try again some other time."

"Can I keep the thousand dollars?"

Vincent Taylor nodded. "It's yours. Have a blessed evening." As Keisha left out the jail, he and his partner began removing the hidden microphone and camera from the visiting booth. "What the hell. I've never seen anything like that."

"It's going to take a lot of hours and resources to bring down this Zoo character." Jason was amused. "We have to cheat this one."

Vincent nodded his head in agreement. Playing dirty was the feds' specialty.

Chapter 14

Knock-Knock-Knock!

The band of boys looked around to each other, going silent as someone knocked on the apartment door. After wreaking havoc on Green Street, Zoo made it clear for them to get to the condo and lay low. There was to be no company allowed, so hearing someone outside the door had them each on high alert. Simultaneously, pistols cocked.

"Stop being scary, that's my girlfriend, Deja." Milli went to the door, checked the peephole, then opened the door, smiling.

Deja, sixteen, 5'1, and very light weight, entered. Her dark chocolate complexion and deep dimples made her something gorgeous to see. She wore a strapless sundress with cute flats on her feet to show off her toes. She stood on her tiptoes to kiss Milli in the mouth.

"Hey, y'all." She waved.

Lil' Zippy looked over to Booby, MuMu, and Toni, confused.

"We gon' be in the room." Milli grabbed her by the hand, taking Deja into the bedroom. The door closed behind them. Silence filled the room, and Zippy wanted to know why Milli had invited a chick from the projects to their safe haven without first running it by them all.

Sweet moans spilled from beneath the shut door followed by cries of pain and pleasure.

MuMu set the gun on the table. "This nigga trippin' right? Bringing that hoe here knowing he not 'pose to."

"I'm goin' in there. She comin' in here like shit sweet, she gotta give us all some pussy, fuck dat." Lil' Zippy headed into the bedroom. Milli had her on all fours, stroking her from the back.

Releasing his penis, Lil' Zippy sat on the bed in front Deja. Under any other circumstances, she would've refused, but since she knew she was in the lion's den, she let them have fun with her. Deja took him into her mouth, giving him head.

Soon, all five youngins were running a train on her for hours. Deja was loving every second of it, her young, thriving appetite for sex being satisfied. When they finally ran dry, exhausted, Deja was kicked out and made to walk back to the hood.

Milli chuckled. "We could've called her an Uber."

"Fuck dat. She can walk. She got some good ass pussy though," Lil' Zippy said, cutting on the news.

"This is New 19, I'm Carmen Roper broadcasting live from downtown Columbia. Behind me, as you can see, several thousands have continued to march, chanting justice for Gary Jackson, a Columbia native who was gunned down by police several weeks ago. Tensions are building due to police brutality within urban communities. Protesters' demands were met when the mayor ordered the DA to charge Officer Mathew Wilks with first-degree murder. Currently, there have been no arrests made."

"In other breaking news ... Riots erupt across America this evening. In Minneapolis, videos have gone viral as officers kneel on a black man's neck for eight minutes. George Floyd is heard begging for his life, telling officers: 'I can't breathe.'"

Lil' Zippy cut the television off, disgusted.

"We needa get out there," Booby said, hyped.

Milli agreed.

"The big homie told us to get here and stay put."

"We've been in here for two whole days now and he hasn't showed up or called. There's no food in here to eat, and you can't act like you're not hungry too."

"We should go to the store, get some food, come back, go to sleep."

Lil' Zippy gave it some thought and agreed.

Exiting a local gas station with backpacks filled with stolen snacks, the group of hoodlums stopped at the gas pumps to purchase fuel. They then set off across town on foot to join the massive crowds of people revolting against systematic racism. The sight of so many unified, standing together was unforgettable. Thousands of black, brown, and even white faces were rallied. Thunderous voices traveled on for miles and miles. The energy, high voltage, waiting to destruct. Rounding one building, they instantly joined the march.

By nightfall, the youths of Kill'umbia's wicked underworld emerged from its darkness. The peaceful protesting was no more as emotions ran high. Police formed a thick line outside its federal court building. Columbia Police Department had long been overthrown and destroyed, as well as many other law agencies. As the crowds began to increase, so had its violence.

Shhh ... BOOM! Shhh ... BOOM! Concussion grenades and tear gas canisters exploded among the sea of people. The deafening explosions sent those near screaming, confused.

The crowd of angry demonstrators fought back, hurling bricks, glass bottles defiled with sand, some even lighting fire whirls that exploded behind police lines, sending them scurrying for cover as well.

"No justice!"

"No peace!" The boisterous exclaims held conviction.

Suddenly, the fight became ongoing. As police continued to set off tear gas and concussion grenades, protesters became more violent.

Lil' Zippy and his friends fell in love with the chaos. "We gotta stay close." He began pumping pressure into the fuel-filled Super Soakers. His friends did the same. A police cruiser attempted to drive through the crowd. Milli took aim, spraying gas over the cop's windshield. MuMu rushed over and set the car ablaze.

The crowd erupted into a frenzied excitement. The cop abandoned ship, jumping out, surrounded by a crowd of angry faces who instantly ripped him apart.

"Burn everything." Lil' Zippy pulled the scarf over his face. With his friends behind him, they sprayed trees, bushes, wooden light poles surrounding the courthouse, setting it all on fire. Torching parked cars and boarded up businesses, the teens unleashed a burning terror against police who began to retreat.

"This is Channel 19, breaking news. As you can see behind me, police are preparing to abandon this federal building with urgency due to the rising violence. Police are unable to control the situation. It seems as if a single group within this massive crowd of protesters has found its way behind these barricades of police, setting this entire building on fire. With streets shut off by thousands, the fire department may not reach this place in time," the reporter said. "This is Carmen Roper, and I promise to keep this city informed. Stay inside, and may God bless this city."

Lil' Zippy stuffed the toy into his backpack. "Let's get the hell up outta here!"

Booby stood motionless, staring at a man in the crowd that stared at him with confusion.

"Booby? What's wrong, nigga? Let's go, you good?" Milli snatched him away.

Though he recognized the man from somewhere, there was not enough time to place his face.

"Let's fucking go!" Lil' Zippy yelled, enraged.

Together, they hauled ass as numerous explosions were set off by police.

***

C'Lo asked, timid, "You sure you wanna go down in this mu'fucken neighborhood?"

The grave expression on Cloud's face said it all.

"I'm just checkin', cuz. It's hot as fuck out here nowadays. These PineHurst posse niggas gonna be lurking for anybody that's not supposed to be out here. This is bold and damn crazy."

Cloud jacked back the chamber of the S&W .9mm. "Nigga, if you ain't built like dat, you can get the fuck out right here and let somebody else drive," he retorted. "If not, shut the fuck up and slide down this bitch. You think I give a fuck 'bout these slob niggas, cuz? Fuck no!"

C'Lo, shaken, turned into the PineHurst community.

Instantly, the car grew eerily silent. Since the loss of his mother, daughter, and son, Cloud had given up on all of life. Misery almost forced him to take his own life, but the will to take Zoo to hell with him kept him alive and searching. The streets were jammed pack block to block, celebrating the life of Gary Jackson. To them it was one more blood they had to rival with.

"It's too many people out here. What if we get noticed?"

Cloud glanced over his shoulder. "Nigga, shut the fuck up. Pull to the stop sign."

C'Lo held on the car brakes as Cloud rolled his window down. On the corner, a group of bloods watched the car closely. Tensions were high. Cloud stuck his hand out, throwing up a blood sign. "Blat. Poppin' Blood?"

"BLAAAT! SuWuu," they answered, representing hard.

Deviously, Cloud came back. This time, his hand was gripping the 9mm firmly. He did the test to ensure he was looking at bloods, and like a thief in the night, his pistol set off to snatch souls.

CLAT-CLAT-CLAT-CLAT-CLAT!

Flames burst from the barrel.

The Locs sitting in the back seat stuck their weapons out as well, squeezing triggers relentlessly, unleashing a hail storm of hot lead. The pack of bloods had no escape. Gun smoke filled the evening. C'Lo mashed the gas, escaping PineHurst before anyone could retaliate, leaving behind men grunting and groaning.

Cloud reloaded bullets into the clip in a hurry. "Find me some more of these blood niggas."

Joining the crowds marching through downtown, explosions went off. Cloud and his crew couldn't believe the intensity. It was perfect. He planned to catch any blood or PineHurst native slipping and kill them in cold blood. If he had to, he'd kill them one by one until he reached the top of the food chain. One way or another, he was going to reach Zoo.

They covered their faces with scarves to protect themselves from tear gas and thickening smoke from burning property. Seeing fires blazing high into the midnight sky and demonstrators push back against police gave them the chills.

C'Lo got his attention, pointing at the group of misfits. "That looks like your son right there, don't it? And it looks like he's with that little dude that came to the house that day with that blood nigga, Zoo. The one that did all the talking, Milli."

"That's my son!" Cloud made eye contact. "Where's he going?"
"We gotta catch'em, they're leaving."
Cloud gave chase as the teens got lost in the crowd. They searched everywhere. "I can't find 'em."
"He didn't even recognize us."
Cloud knew something was off with his son. It was as if he was brainwashed. They continued to search.
"Cuz, we're not gonna find 'em. It's too many people out here." He pushed his way through the crowd. "Well, I ain't leaving until we do!"

***

Brick was among the large group of bandits that stormed into the nearby Walmart like wild ruffians. With his rental car parked outside still running, he hauled two sixty-six-inch flat screen televisions to his car. He then doubled back, breaking into glass counters snatching phones, video games, and systems in a rush. He filled the push cart to the max. Around him the building was being milked dry and cleared out. The entire food section was wiped clean. What little was left, stragglers came for the scraps. As Brick pushed his cart to the car, he was suddenly approached by another bandit.

The fat, black man stopped him. "Aye, my man. I need all this." He grimaced.

He looked the intimidating figure up and down, drawing his pistol, aiming the barrel at his fat, sweaty face. "Nigga, if you don't get the fuck back! I'll burn yo' fucking face off. Matter of fact, run them damn pockets. Drop it on the back seat of my car."

The man wanted to faint. "You got it. You got it. My bad, brother. Don't shoot." He emptied his pockets. Brick then made the man unload the cart into his car while keeping him at gunpoint and watching his surroundings. When the man was done, he backed away. Brick slammed his doors shut, keeping his gun aimed.

"Next time, fuck nigga, don't try me."

BLAH! He shot the man in the stomach before mashing the gas out of the lot. He was sweating profusely, struggling to keep his composure. He had run out of drugs and was desperate for a strong fix. With his money low, he couldn't pass up the opportunity to make a lick.

Looking at all the shit he had stuffed around the car, he wiped his face dry. "Who the fuck am I going to sell this shit to?" A cold chill ran down over him. The drugs had him fiening. With the pressure of the world on his shoulders, it was his only escape. Columbia had its deadly hold on him. He couldn't shake the streets like his nasty habit. With no way to get more dope, he made up his mind to get high by any means, even if the last dose of dope meant he had to lose his life for it.

Black Migo

Chapter 15

Easing off the highway, the truck rounded the bend. Its dark-tinted windows mirrored the passing destruction of cars and buildings burning. Hypnotized by the flames, mesmerized by smoke twisting into the sky, his mind drifted to the day he solidified his name as Zoo, new heir of the ghetto...

Powerhouse, fifty-six years old and a vet to the game, ran everything coming and going out of PineHurst Park. The gangsta controlled with an iron fist and for years his grip was strong without giving slack. His vicious appetite for murder and mayhem, his short fuse temper and his cold, brutal mercilessness made him one goon nobody wanted to cross paths with. But now something was disrupting the man's business.

Word was that Pierre had found his way up the ranks, now pulling in an easy 70K a week. Rule was, to sell dope in the notorious PineHurst, resident or not, came with a 31 percent tax off all profits due to Powerhouse. And so far, Pierre was guilty of tax invasion, a gesture taken as disrespect and punishable by death.

Pierre continued to drill deep in the project hoe pussy he had been highly anticipating for a while. Monica went so hard to throw it at him so he went lunatic in her box until sloppy gushy noises echoed through the apartment. Her moans could be heard outside. She wanted to be sure the whole projects was listening to her get crushed by the next up and coming chief. Thought he hated to fuck chicks in the hood since they kept drama rolling, Monica he made the exception for. Her thick thighs, fat, juicy, heavy ass cheeks clapped against his pelvis while his balls slapped against her clit. Juices from her clenched pussy spurted everywhere. AS he unleashed his thick load into the condom, orange light prancing across the window blinds got his attention. Pulling out, he squinted his sights peeking outside.

"What the fuck?" He snatched the condom off and began dressing quickly.

Monica looked confused. "What's wrong boo?"

"I'll be right back."

Rushing out into the parking lot his heart sunk deep the moment he realize his 68' Impala, drop top sitting on 30s was torched, up in fiery flames. It wasn't the car itself that had him furious, it was the two kilos of cocaine, and a half key of raw heroin locked inside burning in the flames. He had a worthy guess of the man responsible.

As he turned, Pierre noticed the crowd in the distance watching the spectacle. Amused, in the midst, Powerhouse stood rubbing his palms together with a malicious grin that struck a nerve in him instantly. In an aggressive stride he headed over to the crowd.

"Yo", Powerhouse, Let me holla at you right quick."

Powerhouse smiled, looking around his crowd of soldiers. "Who me, young blood?"

Pierre's silent response said enough.

The gangsta stepped out from the pack of killahs. His 6'6, 260-pound bulky build headed to Pierre with a cocky, arrogance and confidence in his murder game and violent reputation. "Y'all Lil' niggas stand down. What can I do for you, Pierre? Or should I call you ... Zoo?" He taunted.

"This all you right here? You taking responsibility for this?" He glance to his can

Powerhouse gazed at it with amazement. "Isn't it pretty? A little price we all have to pay when we fail to follow simple little rules. No hard feelings, young blood."

"No hard feeling, huh?"

"None at all young blood."

KRAAK!

Pierre reached back quickly that Powerhouse couldn't dodge the violent blow to the jaw. It's impact sounding off into the night. The big bulk of a machine stumbled backward off balance.

He was hot on the falling victim. He was fed up with the man's methods and tactics. The OG couldn't believe Pierre's power and fell to his side hard. He was determined to keep his throne, as long as he stayed in position the younger generation couldn't not climb and destroy the game.

Kraak-Kraak-Kraak! Pierre broke his jaw.

"Kill. This. Nigga!"

Pierre stomped his head. Snatching the strap off his waist, he growled. "Kill who, nigga? I'm Zoo, king of this mothafuckin' jungle. A mu'fucka ain't gon' do shit to me, and they don't move unless I say so!"

Ferociously, Powerhouse shouted, "I said kill this nigga!"

The young boys refused to budge. The OG's frightened facial expression said it all.

'So that's how we playin' it? I take good care of you little faggots and you betray me?"

The red beam from the Beretta .45 marked his chest. "Don't worry OG, I'ma take good care of 'em!" He squeezed ten rounds into him. Dead.

When police came to investigate, all that were present hadn't seen a thing ...

Zoo instructed Babygirl to get off the highway exit heading to one of his few downtown condos. His past still gave him the chills.

"The city doesn't even look the same." Taylor spoke softly. "Everything is closing."

He nodded his head in agreeance. Seeing the streets be shaken by recent events scared him. He hadn't lived his best life yet and wasn't prepared to give it all up.

Once parked, Taylor hauled up the TV box loaded with kilos. They all took the elevator up to the twelfth floor, entering apartment 1220. He rarely bought any one since it's where he stashed majority of his product. Taylor sat the box in the back room.

Babygirl faced him. "If you don't mind BOSS, I need to go get myself together. You know I don't like feeling dirty."

His eyes traveled down her B-cups, flat stomach landing on her camel toe. He nodded his head, sending her away. When she was gone to her apartment directly across his stash spot, he removed the Apple laptop from beneath the couch. After punching in codes, his accounts came up. There was 6.2 million combined in his offshore accounts. 1.1 million in his savings and 700 thousand in his business.

Taking a deep sigh, he rubbed his forehead staring at numbers. In two months he had lost two cousin's, 600 thousand and so many goons at this point he was concerned if things didn't sort out he'd be further in some shit.

"How the fuck am I going to launder this 1.7 mill?" He spoke aloud, thinking hard with the city on shut down due to riots, nothing was open.

And then there was ... an email from Black Elmo requesting he wire the owed money. "I ain't payin' that bitch nothin'," he gritted with utter disgust.

The ringing of his phone stole his attention. Pressing the silent button he ignored the call from G50. He couldn't trust family. No one.

Taylor returned from the bathroom. "What's on the schedule for tonight, homez?"

"Same ol' shit. Check this out though, I need you to hold the crib down until I get back."

Taylor removed the pistol from his waist. "No problem."

Zoo left the apartment heading across the hall to Babygirl's. The door opened. Seeing her hair pent up in a shower cap while holding a towel up over her breasts, soap suds covering her body, made his dick hard as steel.

She giggled, rushing away. "I gotta finish shaving my pussy."

He locked the door, stripping down following the young tender. Stepping into the steaming water he gave her the chance to finish up.

Last filled the space between them. Babygirl began washing his abs, then well denied chest. Slowly she washed him front to back. She took her time washing his back, ass and legs. She then lathered up the rag again, carefully washing up his balls. Staring deeply into his eyes. He held the rail as she catered to him. Her delicate fingers wrapped around his girth. She licked her lips in anticipation, barely able to grip his thickness while stroking him.

Passionately, he kissed her lips. She moaned, melting. With each stroke she caressed the thick probing veins of his length. The electricity between them had her pussy spasming, steaming, hypersensitive. The moment he reached down and gently caress her wild flower, sweet nectar exploded. She gripped his dick like a safety rail as her orgasm subsided. The heavy breathing turned him savage. The intense gaze hypnotized her.

Babygirl could feel another orgasm build in her soul. The inside of her thighs tremor as her finger shit. She jacked his dick rapidly to match the excitement of her thumping heart. She went harder, faster. He finger jet speed, together they come in unison, she watched in amazement as his load burst all over her stomach and legs.

She sucked the remaining seed from his dick, seductively. "We're not finished." She hurried and cleaned up. Zoo lifted her to the bed, sitting her on the edge. There was already condoms scattered about ready for use.

He gritted, sliding into her tight warmness. Too small and compact for his largeness he set out to loosen up the sugary walls.

She clasped ahold the sheets. "Ohh … shiit!"

"Don't fight it, Babygirl. I'ma have my way regardless."

"Zooo!" she bellowed. "Don't hurt me, baby. Go easy," she pled.

He ignored her cries, drilling deep burying his pipe. Her walls gripped. He touched every sensitive spot she had. Before midnight they had went at it four rounds and was now tired and exhausted.

Out of breath and cum, he flopped beside her.

After a while she spoke. "Please, don't give me no more of that dick, Zoo."

"What's wrong?"

"You! I can't keep letting you fuck me like that, hell no. It's bad enough I love you crazy," she said, "I would rather we stop since you know you're not going to make me your woman."

"You belong to me. Regardless."

She rolled her eyes. "I wanna really be your bitch. All you need. You're seventeen years older but I want you all to myself."

"We'll get back to this conversation later. I have somewhere to be in two hours."

She rolled over a top him. "You're not going anywhere until I finish giving you some head."

***

PineHurst was crawling with police and seething angry bloodz seeking revenge. Though none of the five homies got killed on the corner two days ago, all cribs would soon hope they had.

"I'm telling you Zoo, they came through here pretending to be Bloodz and aired this shit out. What you want us to do?" Tabitha's son, Savion reported.

"Go back to ya' crib, I'll let someone else know."

"Awe, mannn," the teen drawled, angrily. "I thought they was playin' when they said you was getting soft." He shot in the house.

Zoo wanted to break his neck, and would have if he didn't need to get in and out the hood. Tensions were thick. Young Bloodz were two seconds away from opening gun fire on police to run them out the hood. Dark clouds of gloom looming over haunted the streets. He moved carefully. Obviously the feds were watching.

"Hey, Zoo. Just the face a bitch needed to see." Mona surfaced. "How are my bad ass boys? I hope they're not giving you any trouble."

"I promise, they're good. I'll make sure to drop them off." He kept his eyes on his surroundings just as Taylor. "How you?"

"We can all use some groceries around here. All the stores are closing behind protesting tearing everything up. It's all bad for us."

PineHurst was his first love, his people were important to him and anything they needed, he felt obligated to assist. He sent out a text. In no time four food trucks and two ice cream trucks arrived giving away free food.

A trio of young girls yelled in unison. "Thanks uncle Zoo!"

He waved to them just as thick ass Keisha walked up. Hugging him.

"Lil' Monkey is good. I just went to see'em a few days ago. He told me the feds was trying to get him to rat you out. Of course you know his ass isn't going to crack. He knows better and I told'em not say shit."

"Let'em know I said keep his head up and stay solid. Anything he needs I got'em," he told her, leaving out the fact he'd already drop money on the boys books. Still, he took out $500.00. Send that to 'em."

"I will, Zoo. You know he loves you. We all do. I 'preciate all you've done for us out here. This hood wouldn't be shit without you."

Zoo told her goodbye and headed in G50's direction. He pulled up on his cousin looking around cautiously. "I'm gonna make this brief."

"Damn, what's goin' on?" G50 was nervous at the hostile approach.

"You can have PineHurst. It's yours. I'm falling back from this shit, from everything. I don't want no parts in it."

"The whole PineHurst, mines?"

He shook his head, yes.

"Why all of a sudden?"

"This what you wanted, you got it." He kept his attitude in check. His cousins disloyalty left a sour taste in his mouth, instead of acting off emotion he moved on instinct.

G50 slapped hands with him excited. "My nigga, I 'preciate it. What about the -"

"I ain't fuckin' wit' that anymore either. I'm calling the godfather in New York soon to let'em know I'm stepping down from this blood shit. I'm retiring my flag."

"Zoo, you're serious?"

He nodded his head. There was no need to be connected to niggas who would ultimately betray him. He wouldn't sit and wait for it to happen.

"Who you leaving the position to? It gotta be me, I'm family."

"I'll call a meeting and let everybody know."

"Let me know when and I'm there."

I bet you will be. He walked away, looking stylish for the pictures being snapped away.

Black Migo

Chapter 16

CO James spat with disgust. "Pack up your things, Ms. Wilks." She came to the cell window mean mugging with envy and hate. The hatred between Queenie and the officer was unresting and forever. Any chance the two got they locked into a heated argument filled with nasty retorts. Queenie was aware of James tactics and wasn't going to give in to it though she so badly wanted to entertain thirty extra days in the hole, finally it was her time to breathe. Trapped in a box was driving her crazy. Now the day had come to be another step closer to freedom.

Petty, she taunted CO James escorting her into population. "You miss me already don't you?"

"Little bitch, don't get you nappy head ass knocked out in this hallway fucking playing with me. I owe your ass anyway."

"You ain't built like that. You ain't tough."

"Bitch, I'm from Hyatt Park, If I catch your ass out on them streets I'ma show you exactly what I'm built like."

"And bitch I'm from Pine Hurst!" she retorted. Though it wasn't entirely true, she long ago figured since it was the community she hung out in with Gary, made money and felt at home, it was in her right to proclaim the stomping grounds. And since Pine Hurst Park was one of the most vicious, why not use it to stoke fear? "Your ass damn sure ain't coming out there 'cause you pussy, so I guess I'll have to come to you."

"Don't get this uniform confused. This is just a job, fuck you. I'll see you in traffic, thot ass hoe." She shoved Queenie into the noisy dorm.

CO James handed over the file to a much shorter, nice woman.

Queenie looked around the dorm at all the faces studying her. She wasn't nervous at all but ready to fight anybody who got out of line.

James snickered on her way out. "And don't run back to the hole when one of these bitches beat flames outta you."

Yeah, you got me fucked up bitch. I ain't running nowhere, she said inwardly.

"Okay, Ms. Wilks. I'm CO. Brown, have a seat while I find you a bunk."

Suddenly, she noticed two girls in the top right corner staring at her hard, whispering between one another. They appeared to be the youngest among the women. Queenie wondered where she'd seen the face before and would soon find out as they headed her way.

The prettiest of the duo spoke up first. "How old are you?"

"17, why?"

The second girl told the CO. "There's another empty bunk over in the corner with us. She's the same age as us too."

CO. Brown wrinkled her brow. "Ms. Wilks, that's where you'll bunk. First time y'all get into anything, I'm breaking the group up."

"We got you Ms. Brown." The first chick led the way.

Helping her make the bed, the second girl asked. "What's your name?"

"Queenie, what about y'all?"

The prettiest spoke first. "I'm LaLa. That's my best friend and like my sister, Mena."

"Where y'all from? Y'all seem so familiar." She sat on her thin cot.

"We was saying the same about you. You be in PineHurst don't you?" she answered, timid.

"I thought so," LaLa said. "That's where we're from too. Four Season's apartments."

Mena sat up straight. "You're the chick that was messing with Gary, huh? That was my mu'fucken dawg. It hurt us so much when he got killed. It hurt everybody. They say his funeral was so lit they had to call reinforcements."

"That's why we're trapped in here too."

"How's that?"

LaLa traced her lips with the cherry Chapstick. "You ain't heard?"

"I haven't." Queenie frowned.

Astonished, Mena giggled. "Now I really remember you. You're the girl, Queenie, that was on Bull Street with me. I left two weeks after you got there on my birthday. You was throwing bloody pads at all the nurses."

LaLa laughed. "This is who you were talking about?"

"Yes, this bitch is crazy. You were back there bucking in the hole too?"

Queenie answered with a smile.

"And I thought we was thuggin' when we set the news truck on fire."

"Y'all did what?" she asked, excited, instantly getting comfortable.

"Girl ... let us tell you." LaLa took an hour to tell her everything. Queenie was having a hard time taking it all in.

"All that happened for Gary?"

"And the white cop who killed 'em is on the run. He killed Gary unlawfully. The boy didn't even have a fucking gun on him. Then this George Floyd madness has the streets going crazy too."

Stomach tightening with the news, with her dad, a monster on the loose out there running wild, she'd never be chill. Her sister's safety was her worry. She still had no idea where Precious was and it messed up her head.

"When them niggas from Pine Hurst gets a hold that cracker, they gon' kill'em and everybody linked to 'em."

They betta kill'em before I do, Queenie thought.

Black Migo

Chapter 17

"Guess who the hell is calling you?" Cresha spoke with panic, bringing the phone to where ZiZi lay across bed counting money.

"Who?"

"Girl ... Zoo."

ZiZi sat upright, afraid. "For real, what he want?"

"Bitch, I don't know." Cresha tremored.

"Answer it."

"Hell no, you answer it. He's calling your phone."

She looked around the room, nervous, unable to think clearly. It had been a while since she heard from Zoo. After running off with his dope and money she tried to steer far away from him. Now all she could wonder why he was calling and why hadn't she changed her number.

Does he know we're spending ... she shook away the thought.

"Bitch, he's calling back. Don't panic and act normal. He probably just wants to put us in a new trap house."

ZiZi took the phone, answering it, petrified. "Hey, boo what's up?"

"You ain't seen me calling your ass the first time girl?" he asked playfully.

She was relieved. "I was laying on it and didn't hear it the first time, my bad. What are you up to? Staying out of trouble, I hope. I heard about your cousin, Gary, getting killed. So sorry for your loss," she told him sincerely.

"It's all good, we gon' be alright, same ole shit. Say, where your friend Cresha?"

ZiZi cut her eyes over to Cresha, who was waving her hand not to say she was there. "She right here sleep on the bed."

"Both of you pull up. I got something I need handled."

"We'll be there in about thirty minutes."

Zoo hung up.

Sighing, Cresha was not happy to be mentioned. "If we're going over there, let's at least get our story together, 'cause I don't trust 'em."

Together, they stepped out the Uber looking around cautiously. Cresha had complained the entire drive over, and her paranoia was contagious. ZiZi had to let her know. "You need to get it under control. You're making me nervous as hell, damn, act fucking normal." They surveyed the rundown apartments of Doctors Circle.

"Bitch, hard head soft ass. I don't trust this."

"Shut up." ZiZi knocked on the front door, taking another look around.

Suddenly, the back door swung open. Staring them in the face were two Glock .19 barrels and a pair of stone-face teens who showed no sympathy. Wide eyed and horrified, the two girls were snatched in.

"What the fuck, Zoo?"

"Have a seat. How y'all sexy hoes been?" He grinned.

ZiZi and Cresha exchanged nervous gazes. Zoo's demeanor was throwing them off badly. "Good, I guess. How you been?"

"I've been better. Where you living?" He kept his eyes glued to the computer screen.

Quickly, the two gun-wielding teens ran their hands all over the chicks' bodies for hidden wires. Once cleared, they started talking.

"Uh ... We've been living at my home girl Tashia house in Irmo. Ever since Dae Dae got killed, it's been hard. I'm really trying to figure it all out. I thought since that situation in Apple Valley you weren't fucking with me anymore. Were you ever able to catch them dudes?" ZiZi kept it cool.

Babygirl's icy stare was making them all uncomfortable. The fact that she tossed a hand grenade into the air, catching it over and over, enhanced the tension.

Abruptly, Zoo shut the laptop. "That shit you're talking is a bundle of bullshit, ZiZi, and I had the nerve to think we were better than that." His fiery glare threatened them both. "I think you and your girl fucked me out my shit. You ran off with my sack."

Cresha jumped to her feet defensively. "No the hell we didn't! Them crip dudes ran in the house and robbed us."

"Bruh, don't say that. I'd never do that shit. Especially not to you." She swallowed hard.

Zoo eased the baby blue .380 off Babygirl's lap, smirking. He could see them sweat. "I hate to keep getting my hands dirty, but since y'all hoes playing me like a fuck boy, I might as well, right?" He aimed at Cresha's chest.

"No, wait, we—"

BLAH!

ZiZi bolted to her fee, wailing. Instantaneously, Babygirl punched her in the mouth with so much force she put ZiZi dead on her ass.

"Y'all bitches tried him like he ain't official." She stomped ZiZi in the head repeatedly.

Cresha was slouched on the couch, staring at the ceiling wide eyed, clutching the hole in chest. Tears rolled down the corners of her face, blood gushed from the hole as she took her last breaths.

"What did you do, Zoo? Oh my god!"

He chuckled. "What it look like, bitch? Now—"

"Fuck that, let me kill this bitch!" Babygirl spat. "I don't like how she tried you."

"No, please, Zoo. Don't let 'er kill me. I didn't do nothing. I swear we didn't take nothing."

Babygirl kicked her in the stomach then the ass. "Bitch, don't fucking lie to him!"

"I'm not, I swear. Please, Zoo. I swear."

He watched on, amused.

"Bet not lie to her, she gon' fuck you up."

"But I'm not ly—"

Babygirl kicked her teeth out. ZiZi spat up blood. For another fifteen minutes, Babygirl beat down ZiZi for the truth. It finally came. Zoo was impressed. Just as he handed over the gun for her to put a bullet in the head, one of the young goons standing guard at the window turned.

"There's some guy getting out his car coming straight this way."

"MuMu, take that body and put it in the closet. Mack, take that hoe up the stairs in the back room," Zoo ordered.

In a hurry, Babygirl helped stuff the dead body into the closet.

A sequence of knocks rattled the door. Zoo sat on the couch nodding to Babygirl.

"Yes, how can I help you?" She opened the door, gun hidden behind her back.

Mack returned.

"Hi, ma'am. My name is Mark Gruttle. I'm with the city. I came days ago to forewarn this residence and a few others that we'll be performing a mass extermination of roaches by the weekend. So if you have anything of value, we ask that you put it up nice and secure. Due to the large quantity of chemicals we'll be using, it may be safer for you to avoid returning for at least 24-48 hours, starting Friday."

She smiled warmly. "Thanks for the heads up." She then locked the door, sighing a breath of relief. "Thought I was gonna have to kill'em. Now, can I finish that bitch off so we can get away from here?"

Shattering glass coming from the upstairs room stole their attention. Panic set in. By the time they reached the bedroom, the back window was broken. ZiZi was gone. Mack stuck his head out, searching below.

"She's running through the trees!" He turned and ran downstairs to chase her.

"MuMu, dump that body somewhere. Meet me at the mansion later on." He left out with Babygirl right on his heels.

They searched the area high and low to no avail. "I should've just crushed that bitch!"

Zoo shook his head, disappointed in himself. *I'm fucking up big time.*

***

ZiZi knew her days of living were over the instant Zoo figured out she had cuffed the drugs and money. Witnessing Cresha be shot dead pained her deeply. If only she would have listened to her friend, they wouldn't have come in the first place. Now she was faced with the heartbreak of losing two people she loved more than herself. Tears flooded down her face hopelessly.

Right when Babygirl was going to finish her off, the knock on the door restored her faith. She didn't know who it was but prayed it was the police there to save her life. After being rushed to an upstairs bedroom, she waited and listened. The voices in her mind told her, bitch go!

Unable to sit by and wait for death to come to collect her soul, she tried to lift the window. It wouldn't give being that it was sealed with nails. So, she looked around in desperation. She took the lamp in the corner and hurled it, shattering the window. With force, she kicked away the remaining shards. The sound of footsteps racing up the stairs got her moving. ZiZi grabbed the seal, cutting up her hands before jumping onto the garbage can below. Blood dripped from the gashes. She ran as fast as she could through the trees into a second housing development.

As she passed the first building, she ducked into bushes, allowing the boy looking for her to dash past. She took off in the opposite direction, sprinting full speed. Adrenaline pumping, her pounding heart, and burning lungs didn't stop her. Fear propelled her. ZiZi jumped into a dumpster, burying herself under mounds of trash. She could hear the boy outside the garbage unit cursing. Tires burning rubber could not be mistaken. Zoo was zipping through the streets trying to locate her. ZiZi dared not move. It stunk bad, but she fought through it, whimpering. She kept strong.

After a thirty-minute wait, she climbed out the dumpster, shivering with fear. She knew police would be somewhere around Richland Memorial Hospital, so she set out for it. Running full speed, afraid Zoo would be somewhere lurking, she rounded the building corner dashing across the street.

A black Chevy Silverado came to a screeching halt before her, cutting off her path. Before she could change course and continue the run of her life, the passenger side doors burst open. Two men jumped out with lightning speed, giving her a stroke.

"Get in!"

"No!"

ZiZi tried to fight them off, but they were just too strong. She was shoved into the back seat kicking and screaming as the truck barreled through the streets.

Chapter 18

Odd pieces of charred black wood were all that remained standing among ashes. Death lingered in the air like smoke. The once million-dollar Green Street was now anything but that. Instead, destruction and turmoil riddled the streets, sending fiends lowering in their darkest corners and residents too afraid to leave their homes.

Zoo studied the block from behind window blinds. His hawk eyes and keen observation skills kept him alert to any movements. Any potential threats, shooters were on standby ready to neutralize.

It had taken time, but with patience, in a week he was able to secure a three-bedroom house on Green Street directly across from Brick's old trap house, as well as a house on both ends. Shop was being setup. A demolition and reconstruction crew was summoned at each of the three new trap houses to install fortified, steel-reinforced doors and frames, barred bulletproof windows, escape traps, along with top-of-the-line security systems inside out so he could keep a close eye on his assets. Each trap house came with state-of-the-art police scanners to detect any activity in a three-mile radius. Any wired informants would later learn a bug fry system imported from Japan would prevent them from recording. The times were changing, and he sought out to keep the lead against rivals.

As nightfall came, he studied the screen closely. There were cameras around the strip as well to give him a view of everything coming and going. The moment he gave the order, the private contractor he had perform the immaculate job was kidnapped, killed, and never to be seen again. He couldn't take any chances.

"New era is a go," he told one of the young dealers who raced through the surrounding neighborhoods on a bicycle giving out test product.

He continued to play with the iPad's gadgets, using the front porch camera to spy on Brick's vacant house. He couldn't help but to feel as if someone was inside hiding in the darkness watching him as well.

"Maybe that scary nigga in there somewhere." Babygirl read his thoughts. He smirked. With that, he answered his ringing phone.

"Who dis?"

"Bitch ass nigga. You tryna play games with me like shit can't get real as fuck, huh?"

"What you want, Shay? I ain't letting you eat this dick no more."

"Nigga, don't fuckin' play with me. You know why I'm calling," she yelled. "You thought that shit was cool? Pressing up on my sister Venice in the mall, touching her'n shit. I bet your ass won't think it's funny when she has her husband murder you, silly ass. Matter fact, I'ma just get on some police shit and tell the police you're the one who shot up Dirty. I can buy some heels with that ten-thousand-dollar cash reward. Say I won't do it, bitch. What … You got mad I was fucking him?" Her words dripped with venom.

Anger pinched his chest. "You finished?"

"Pussy, ain't nobody scared of your ass. Fuck you! You're gonna see one day that you can be touched. I got niggas that'll hit you from long distance for a piece of this good pussy. Play wit' it." She unleashed bottled up anger held back since the moment she caught him cheating and got her ass beat because of it.

Nonchalantly, Zoo replied, "Ain't nobody stopping you, do what you do." He then blocked her number. "Kill your stupid ass."

***

Leaving the Wendy's drive-thru, Lil' Zippy was the first to spot the gold Cadillac CTS creeping along traffic behind them. Calmly, one hand gripped the steering wheel, the other holding his sandwich as he ate away. He eased the Tahoe into the far-left lane, slowing down to allow the car to pull alongside them just as he was turning through the intersection. He got a glimpse of the driver and passenger. Both were faces he remembered from the protest. They had chased them through the crowds. The Cadillac tried to switch lanes fast enough to continue pursuit to no avail. Traffic was too thick.

That wouldn't stop Lil' Zippy. After making the left turn, he got onto the right shoulder, banking a quick right on the first street.

He then sped to a stop sign, made a right, and jumped into thick traffic. Two traffic lights ahead, he spotted the Cadillac. His friends were anxious to Swiss cheese the car.

Lil' Zippy called Zoo, got the order, and followed it to the T.

At sunset, the trio of hoodlums got out on foot, walking down a side street. They weren't sure where they were or how far away from home they traveled but knew it didn't matter. They stood in the darkness, having left a friend behind with the truck.

Keeping their weapons concealed, they headed down the street toward the Caddy, making a quick survey of the house while strolling past. The porch lights were on, along with a dimly lit window. Since all windows were sealed, they couldn't get a good glance through the front side.

Making a left on the block, Lil' Zippy counted five houses. The house was silent. No lighting. Together they headed through the front yard into darkness, keeping a close eye on their surroundings. They reached the gate splitting the two back yards.

Lil' Zippy held a finger to his lips. "We gotta be real quiet. Can't let this nigga hear us coming," he said before jumping the gate.

MuMu and Booby climbed the gate like bandits. Removing their weapons, faces concealed behind black rags, the trio spread out in the darkness of the back yard. The sudden barks of the Pitbull raging behind a cage caused them to halt.

Arrgff-Arrgff-Arrgff!

On signal, MuMu jumped into the cage with the ferocious animal. The dog lurched for his forearm, and with quick hands, he pushed the animal's head aside, giving his knife space to drive. The sharp blade entered the dog's neck, killing it instantly.

The trio stood still in anticipation. Silence. No one came to check on the dog, so they continued through the yard, pressing their bodies up against the house. A few minutes passed.

Booby whispered, "All the lights off except the TV in this bedroom."

The window was too high for them to peek into easily. MuMu retrieved a water bucket, positioning it beneath the window before standing on it. The television brightened the room. Moans escaped a woman's lips.

"Quii! Baby, yes. This. Dick. Is. So. Gooodd!" She rode C'Lo in the reverse cowgirl position. "So fuckin'. Good. Baby, it's in my stomach ... everywhere."

He jumped off the bucket. "Super bad bitch in there on some porno shit."

"Shit, let me see." Booby stepped on the bucket, eyes lit up with excitement. "She going crazy on dat nigga shit," he whispered.

MuMu nudged Booby out the way. "My turn, I wanna see." He jumped up. "Damn, that pussy look like it's good as a muthafucka. You think she'll let us hit too?"

"Nigga, shut up and come on." Lil' Zippy took the bucket and placed it where he found it. "We gotta find a way inside without getting messy. They're not coming out anytime soon."

MuMu gestured toward the dog trap.

Without argument, each of the teens slithered and squeezed through the dog door until they were all inside the cold darkness of the home. Triple X-rated sex spilled from the hallway. Slowly and cautiously, the bandits did a quick sweep.

"Ohh, baby, YESSS! YESSS! That's it right there," the woman cried. They listened excitedly.

Booby tiptoed into the kitchen and opened the fridge, digging for food. He returned with a handful of grapes to see his friends quietly searching beneath furniture for any hidden weapons.

"Let me get some of them, foo'."

"Hell nah, get your own."

MuMu left and came back with the whole bag of grapes. Standing around the living room as if they belonged, they joked silently. The slapping sounds of sex ended. Swiftly, they took up hiding as the bedroom door opened. Zippy peeked around the couch from his crouched position. The woman walked naked into the kitchen, opening the fridge.

"Where in the hell is my grapes?" She searched, bending over.

Lil' Zippy wanted to fuck. He tiptoed up behind her, eyeing her curvy frame lustfully. She stood upright, and her body was tempting. Yet, the butt of his pistol crushed into her temple, sending her crumbling to the ground. He managed to catch her midway, laying her body down gently.

MuMu nodded to Booby, who turned and eased down the hallway toward the slightly ajar bedroom door. C'Lo lay sprawled across the bed on his stomach, facing the wall. Pushing the door open, they entered like ghosts. Booby glanced back over his shoulder for reassurance. It would be easy to shoot him in the head and end it. Adrenaline pumping, they did it for the thrill. Booby pushed the pistol into his waist band, removing the bundled shoe string from his pocket. He wrapped both ends around his grips.

With gentle, catlike steps across the thick carpet, he lurched onto C'Lo's broad back, straddling him. "Hey, fuck boy!" he growled. C'Lo's head shot up, staring at Booby in the headboard's glass mirror as the lace cut into his throat.

C'Lo weezed, eyes bloodshot with terror.

"Shut the fuck up, nigga," Booby gritted, tightening the lace as Uncle Jerry taught him. C'Lo struggled, gasping for air in a frenzy. "Don't fight it, bruh."

Desperate, C'Lo fought, digging at the string cutting off his air. In sixty seconds, he was exhausted, then motionless.

"That nigga dead?" Lil' Zippy asked once they returned from the bedroom. Their look said it all. He then strangled the girlfriend before heading out the way they came.

Black Migo

Chapter 19

Queenie tried to move but was yanked back into place. Her body was drenched in cold sweat, and she didn't know where she was. The cold shackles around her ankles cut skin and hurt to the bone, bringing instant discomfort and pain. Wincing, she steadied her balance but was unable to control the rapid speed of her heart. Tears sailed down her face, warm to the skin. She was surrounded with complete darkness.

"Stop, Daddy, stop!"

Distant wails sent chills up her spinal cord. Terror paralyzed her. Sniffling, she could only imagine what was going on.

"Daddy, no. Please, stop!" Precious's voice boomed. Hearing her sister in distress sent fire through her veins. She fought against the chains until they finally gave. With all her energy, she ran and ran and ran, chasing her sister's voice into darkness.

"Dadddyyy, nooo!"

Queenie ran faster. Harder. Desperate to reach her younger sister. Her knees ached, cramps crept up her calves and thighs. She wasn't sure how long she'd been running. So badly she wanted to give up, but the pain, fear, and horror in Precious's voice kept her moving frantically.

The sound of her wails turned into a globe of light surrounded by a mass of pitch-black darkness. The closer she reached for it, the more the path turned into a tunnel with light at its end. Her body was on fire. Sweating profusely, she chased it for a while more before catching it finally. There was no sky, no bright sun. Instead, she found herself beating on a glass room. Inside, Precious was strapped to a hospital bed kicking and screaming, sobbing uncontrollably.

Queenie banged on the glass. "Let her go!" Her demands went unheard. She continued until her voice was hoarse. Yet, she beat and beat and beat.

Mathew used the scapple to slice the pregnant belly down the middle. Precious's loud shrills were deafening. The sinister smile on her father's face as he enjoyed the torturing of his child made Queenie angrier. She could do nothing to make him stop.

Precious's belly opened completely, and the baby spilled out onto the floor, its wails ear piercing. Mathew glared over to Queenie. With pure hatred and evil, he stomped then kicked the baby aside as he rushed toward her. The glass fell away, the scalpel raised high, evil glistening in his gray eyes, he brought the knife down swiftly…

Queenie bolted upright in her bed, panting, drenched with sweat. Shivering to the bone, struck with fear. The rigid moves were happening frequently. Taking medication to help rest at night was useless. Wiping beads from her brow, she took slow, deep breaths to calm her drumming chest all the while looking around the quiet dorm. The overhead lights were dim, mixed with snoring of chicks. It was well after midnight. Glancing over the wall, she realized her friends were missing. She threw back the covers, surveying the dorm.

Across the dorm, LaLa and Mena were on their bellies slithering across the floor silent as a sneaky snake. The CO sat comfortably behind the computer, chin resting on his chest, asleep as the two set out toward another inmate's bunk. Big Cherry, a big, mean, gorilla-looking bull dagger that ran an in-house store where girls could purchase snacks for double back on commissary day, w was always teasing Mena with flirtatious comments. Mena wouldn't express her disgust openly but among them, she was overly offended.

As the gorilla beast woman snore up a storm, LaLa untied the net bag string that connected the bag to the bed as a homemade security system while Mena worked the string to a second bag. Slowly, quietly, Queenie watched in suspense. She hoped Big Cherry wouldn't wake up. It would be a grizzly scene. She kept watch, hoping they would not be caught. Heart pounding, ears ringing, and hands sweating, she peeked over to make sure the police did not wake up.

A five-minute heist later, the girls were sliding across the floor out of camera view. Her two friends hauled two large bags, enough to hold them all for two months.

LaLa whispered, excited, "Oh my god, you're up?"

"Watching y'all bitches' backs, of course."

Mena panted. "We gotta hurry up and split all this up before anybody wakes up. That big bitch is gonna wake up for a snack any minute, and I don't wanna be up when she do. We'll have to catch a charge then."

"She ain't gon' do shit. And if she act like she want smoke, we'll give her sum'n to choke on," Queenie said.

In minutes the two large bags were split evenly between the trio, all evidence disposed of.

That morning, the entire dorm was not only awakened by the CO announcing breakfast time, but also by the blaring rage in Big Cherry's masculine voice. "Who the fuck took my shit? I'ma beat everybody ass in this muthafucka if I don't find out who took it." All but three thought the heavyset woman was starting the morning off with a joke as she walked into the day room with panties a few sizes too small. Her voice boomed, the sleeping giant had been awaken. "Alright, nobody got shit to say. I'ma beat the shit outta whoever the fuck took my shit, watch!"

LaLa ripped open a bag of Cheetos. "Y'all want some?"

"No, thank you. This gut is getting bigger every day," Queenie said.

Mena chuckled. "Girl, please. That's just skin. I'm not gon' lie, though … you been getting thicker and thicker. Fuck 'round one of those studs gon' be tryna get some of that pussy. See how they be staring at you already as is."

They all laughed.

Queenie had to keep it serious. "I wish a bitch would."

Together, the trio chowed down on the stolen commissary, knowing tensions were rising as Big Cherry put her press game down on the weak. It wouldn't be long before someone figured it out. Neither cared. There were many suspects. Queenie sat Indian style, taking small bites of an iced honey bun, watching the dorm, amused.

CO Brown approached. "Ms. Wilks?"

"Yes?" she answered, confused.

"You have a visit in five minutes, booth four."

"Huh, are you sure it's me?"

"Yes, I'm sure. Queenie Wilks. Get yourself together, booth four."

Her puzzled facial expression matched with her friends. She was unsure what to think or who was visiting. Could it be Precious? She prayed that it was. It needed to be in order to silence the voices in her mind. She climbed the stairs to the visiting booth.

Entering the privacy of the tiny booth, she instantly felt suffocated. Her throat tightened. Anxiety climbing, she sat down looking at the small screen and the unfamiliar individual through the plexi glass. His blond hair was prickled out beneath the military veteran hat. The icy blue eyes stared at her, his gaze bone chilling. She looked back out the door, thinking maybe she had the wrong booth. Utterly uncomfortable, she was going to leave when the mysterious man tapped on the glass, pointing at the phone. He picked it up slowly, placing it to his ear, his gaze unblinking.

Queenie swallowed hard. She lifted the phone from its cradle, staring back into his eyes. "How do you know me? Why are you here?"

Grinning, he replied, "It's really nice to see you, Queenie."

"W-What?"

He looked around. "For a while I couldn't find you. I've searched high and low. But then a friend of mine told me you were in the crazy house, losing your mind. When I tried to come see you they wouldn't let me. But now that I can see you here, it's pretty nice to see you again … daughter." His sinister tone gave her goosebumps. Anger burned in her chest like acid reflux. She wanted to cry, scream, break down the glass to unleash her own evil upon him. But she couldn't. His presence paralyzed her with fear.

"Where's my sister, you sick, disgusting bitch? I'm going to tell everybody that you raped her, she's pregnant, and you're going to rot in prison for it, you freak!" she growled. "You think you're on the run now, wait until what the world learns about you. Your whole reputation will be destroyed, you fucking rapist pig."

A nervous grin hinted she struck a vein. "You'd never. Think about your sister. I can reach her no matter where I am. You won't be able to do anything about it because your cute ass is going to prison for a very long time. See how destiny works? You sit in jail while I run free." He laughed deviously.

"You won't be free for long. When you do get arrested and go to prison, guys are going to get a hold of your bitch ass, Dad. They're gonna give me a new mom," she taunted. "You think I'm gonna let you get away with what you did to Mommy, Uncle Drew, Miranda, me, Precious, and Gary?"

"You don't have a choice!" His eyes moistened, red rimmed. If he hadn't exposed his identity, the disguise would've fooled her. The contacts, wig, and costume beard. "I'll kill Gary's grandmother. I met 'er once. Everyone you ever called a friend, I'll murder them in cold blood."

Queenie glared into his eyes. "Bitch, I don't care what you do. When I do get the chance, I'm gonna kill you." She slammed the phone down in its cradle, spitting on the screen before rushing out. She couldn't privilege him with seeing her tears fall. The nerve of him to haunt her, ruining her innocence. She promised to avenge everyone she'd loved.

Enraged, she headed to the upstairs bathroom stall. Queenie was so caught up in her head that she hadn't sensed the hostility thickening in the dorm.

Cat, a recovering drug addict, approached. "Hey, Queen. Be careful, your friends are in the bathroom fighting."

She moved with haste, pushing into the bathroom, and instantly noticing Big Cherry punching both LaLa and Mena in the head with her heavy hands.

"Y'all bitches think you can just eat up all my shit? Hell no!"

Her friends were tag teaming the big gorilla-like chick, but were cornered into the stall and unable to flee. "I want all my shit back triple!"

In two long strides, Queenie was on Big Cherry. Her left hand took the strongest grip of the woman's thick, nappy hair while the right fist wound back then exploded in a vicious hail storm of blows. Built-up rage gave her tunnel vision.

"Bitch. Bitch. Bitch!" She rocked Big Cherry's face. "You think we sum'n to play wit'?" She then jerked the beastly woman away and onto the floor in a loud crash, while keeping her firm grip.

Big Cherry tried to cover her face. She had been taken by surprise and was now unable to fend off the vicious attack. Her back teeth loosened each time a blow connected with her jaw. "Shit ... wait, hold up!"

"Nah, hoe. You touch one of my bitches, I'll kill you." She continued her rampage, seeing red. Cherry's right eye swelled, then the left. Soon, her face was like a balloon. Her nose burst, blood leaked everywhere, but Queenie was unsatisfied, wanting more. She drilled in the woman's mouth until more blood leaked. The bathroom stall door opened for the entire dorm to witness. Her forehead split into a nasty gash. More blood. "Try us the fuck again and I'ma break your face next time."

"Yeah, bitch. You don't want this pressure!" LaLa stomped Big Cherry's head. Mena was in the mix, football kicking the ugly beast in the pussy and gut. Cherry wailed in pain, even called for assistance. No one moved. The officer was in the restroom, oblivious, while the entire dorm listened in utter disbelief.

By the time they finished, Big Cherry was sprawled across the floor barely conscious, bloodied, and beaten. Queenie walked out first, arms covered with blood. All eyes were on them as they went to Big Cherry's property box. She wiped the blood away on the chick's sheets before taking every other valuable.

When they finished, Cherry was left on empty. With Queenie leading the way, angry scowl and blood evidence of her viciousness, it was perfectly clear who was nothing to reckon with and now in charge.

Chapter 20

Zoo entered one of his many nightlife establishments an hour before opening. He had to be sure his manager and staff knew exactly what was expected of them. Going down the list, he made sure she had a clear understanding of her duties. As staff went about setting up, expecting a heavy crowd for the weekend, he eased out the building with Taylor beside him as they heard toward the parked Wraith.

A white-on-white BMW truck came to a slow creep. Taylor drew his twin Glocks, ready to drill, until Zoo told him, "It's cool, youngin'."

G50 and Shooter parked then climbed out. "I gotta holla at you right quick," G50 grimaced.

Zoo ignored the hostility in his cousin's voice. "Make this shit quick, 'cause I got somewhere to be, blood."

"I thought you said you was falling back from the streets?"

"Something like that. Is that why you're upset, foo'?"

"Fuckin' right, blood. You leave the hood to go set up on Green Street when that was my idea. Then you take all the fucking customers and clientele. Fuck kinda shit that is?" G50 fumed.

Shooter mumbled, "Some bitch nigga shit."

"Say what?"

"Nigga, you fuckin' heard me." Shooter swelled.

Zoo smiled, amused. "You done took enough ass whoopings, so I'ma let that fly shit slide just this one time. I know y'all in ya feelings, but it is what it is. Get over it. Y'all niggas grown."

G50 couldn't believe his big cousin was handling him. He didn't know where any of the animosity was coming from. "Say less, homie."

Shooter waved him off. "Fuck this nigga, he ain't God."

Zoo had enough lightning speed that he got up on Shooter before he could register how close he had reached him. Swiftly, he brought his massive arm around his neck, locking it in place, squeezing. "Uh-huh. See what that big mouth get you? Don't even fight this shit, boy. I'll break your fucking neck, bitch," he spoke to Shooter while he fought against the hold. When Zoo let his arm go,

Shooter crumbled to the ground, heaving wildly. It wasn't over. With his size thirteen Timberland boot, he began stomping Shooter out like something caught on fire. "See these feet, nigga?"

BOM-BOM-BOM!

He growled, "Eat these fucking boots!"

"You might as well let me crush'em now," Taylor said angrily, upset Zoo had to lift a finger.

G50 broke it up. "Chill, dawg. You made your point."

***

Vincent Taylor and Jason Bryson watched the whole scene unfold, hoping Zoo would order the kill and lock himself into federal prison for life. They had caught everything on camera, anticipating more.

"That should at least prove these guys are linked together. Conspiracy will be easy to prove," Jason said.

"Ten or twenty years isn't enough." He kept his eyes on the screen. "I don't want any bloods to ever get out of prison. Never."

Jason agreed. "And we need these promotions."

Rubbing his palms together, he said, "And we'll get them one step at a time."

***

Brick wouldn't stop itching, scratching his neck and chest like bugs were feasting on him. He stepped like he had to piss so bad he could go in his clothes any minute now. Paranoid, he looked around the store, scared the Grim Reaper would come snatch his soul.

The Arab had seen many beggars but none as aggressive as Brick. Exasperated, he asked, "How much for the damn TV, my friend?"

"I told you already, you Bin-Laden mutherfucka. I want five hundred for one TV and a thousand for all three. Not no damn scratch-off tickets or no cigarettes or no goddamn food. I want cash money," he spat, sweating profusely. The monkey was on his back and he needed to get high.

"No, no, no, my friend, that's too high. Sorry, take elsewhere."

"Fuck it, gimme six hundred for all of 'em and a pack of cigarettes" he said desperately.

The Arab nodded. "Bring them in."

Brick scurried away, hauling the stolen Walmart merchandise sitting it behind the counter. The Arab then plugged each TV in the wall to be sure they all worked. Satisfied, he counted out six hundred in twenties, handing them over. Brick's mouth was salivating as he counted and recounted before pocketing. He started to pull out his pistol and kill the Arab for negotiating him down from his number. Maybe he'd rob the man for his TVs back, he pondered, heading down the aisle. He needed something cold to drink, and as he opened the cooler, his ears twitched into eavesdrop mode.

"Yes, girl. I told you his ass was crazy," Maya bragged to her best friend, Cocoa.

"That's why I don't fuck with these niggas out here. They get too emotional."

"Ain't it?"

"They be ready to kill a bitch 'bout some pussy. I damn near don't want to even fuck nothing, scared one of these nuts might get too attached and try to cuff my shit. Hell no. Not happenin'."

"Bitch, who you tellin'." They burst into laughter. "I can't go without no dick, but I can't go being tied down either."

Cocoa teased, "I feel you, girl. I'm saving my hot box for my special someone."

"Ah shit, who now?" Maya joked.

Cocoa giggled. "Bitch, don't play. I'm talking about our fine ass brother."

"Giiiirrrl! Now you know my brother, Zoo, is the dog of all dogs, right?"

Brick's ears tingled.

"Boo-Boo ..." Cocoa sighed. "I don't even care. He can dog me out all he wants. I'm not gon' even fight it or complain none. I promise."

Maya, tickled, said, "I hear you. Matter of fact, let me call you back. I gotta call my brother and tell'em I got accepted to University of South Carolina."

"Okay, boo. Put a word in for me too."

"Bye, girl, silly self." She hung up, buying candy and snacks for her nieces and nephews. After paying, she headed out to her parked Lexus off to the side.

Brick followed her out. The red in his eyes was the glow of evil. Hearing Zoo's name made his mouth dry.

Maya smiled brightly as Zoo's voice came over the phone. "Hey, baby daddy." She giggled.

Zoo chuckled. "Girl, quit playin', funny ass, what's up?

"Nothin'," she cooed. "Headed home. What you up to, sexy?"

"You gotta quit flirting with me. You is not my thot."

Brick waited until she popped the unlock button on the key chain. She eased behind the wheel. He quickly opened the passenger side door, falling into the seat, gun aimed at her face. Maya recognized him instantly.

"Brick?"

"Shut the fuck up, take me to your brother!" he growled.

The phone fell from her hands between the seats.

Wham! He punched her in the jaw. Her head bounced off the window. He then took the car keys from her grip then turned the ignition. "If you make me, I will kill you, bitch. Drive!" He checked his surroundings and saw no one had noticed.

"Fuck you. My brother gon' kill you." She held her jaw, tears flowing. Her hands trembled violently.

He spat, "Not if I kill you. He won't know. Now fucking drive."

"Okay, okay, don't hurt me." She straightened.

The pistol pressed into her jaw. "Bitch, drive!"

Maya shifted the gear, pulling out the parking lot into traffic. It was a little after 9 p.m. and the streets were active along North Main. She was overwhelmed with emotion. She couldn't believe the same man the streets were after had found his way into her car. She didn't know what to do and couldn't imagine anyone causing her big brother any harm. She'd die for Pierre but didn't want to. Her heart hurt terribly, like it would explode. The menacing snarl made her uncomfortable.

Pulling to the red light, she contemplated.

Brick erupted into hysterical laughter. "He thought he was untouchable. It doesn't seem that way now, does it?" He gripped the pistol tighter, checking the side mirrors, anxious.

"Zoo is gon' fuck you up," she defended her big brother, easing through the green light. Maya wiped away tears, slowing down at another red light.

He scratched his chest. "Fuck your—"

Maya made her move for the gun. "Get the fuck outta my car!" She gripped the gun, shifting it away from her. He gripped her hair with his free hand, trying to pull her away. She let the patches rip away, biting into his forearm savagely. Brick screamed like a bitch.

"Heelp!" Maya shrieked. "Somebody help!" She managed to apply pressure to the horn, honking it. She fought for the gun. Refusing to let go, with the willpower to protect her brother she was determined to get away.

Brick could feel the gun loosening. He had underestimated the petite chick and took her for weak. With traffic thick and the horn blaring, the noise was likely to get someone's attention. So he snatched away his free arm, left hooking her jaw. Her grip on the gun never loosened. She bit down on his forearm. He yelled, frantic.

"Aguh, you bitch!"

Maya was not giving up nor was she letting go. She fought and wrestled, but the gun wouldn't fall.

He punched her again. Her grip loosened a small fraction too much.

Blooom! The deafening explosion pierced his eardrums. The driver side window was splattered with red. Maya slumped over into his lap, shot in the throat, dead. The Lexus slowly eased into traffic.

He stared at the blood, horrified. His chances of getting paid, out the window. Instincts kicked in. In a hurry, he pulled Maya's body out the front seat into the back, before regaining control of the wheel. Sweating profusely, he smashed the gas in search of a heroin dealer.

***

Zoo listened closely. Terrified for his sister who fought back with the perpetrator. His heart thumped rapturously in his chest, afraid of the outcome. He gripped the phone tight wishing he could get to her, but he had no idea where they were.

The gunshot was a blast through his own heart.

"Maya?" he yelled into the phone, praying for an answer. He listened intensely. All he heard was the man mumbling under his breath, cursing himself while speeding through the streets.

Tears welled in his eyes for his sister. "Maya?"

Taylor sat in the passenger seat, guns out. Tears welled in his young dangerous eyes seeing his leader visibly hurt.

Zoo hung up, pressing tears away. He sighed, shuddering. Murder raced through his veins like venom. It was time to bite down and squeeze.

Chapter 21

Krissy tossed back volumes, swallowing dry while staring at herself in the bathroom mirror. Face to face with her image, tears well in her eyes. Killing Ta'maine hadn't bothered her conscience not once since mentally chalking his death as justified. It hurt because the streets were on her chest for protecting her life. To survive in Kill'umbia, a bitch had to be ready to put in work. Now she was wondering if letting Ta'maine rob her, possibly kill her, was a better route. Let the streets say, she was supposed to die so he could live.

Disgusted with the thought, she twisted up her face, wiping her lids dry. "Fuck that pussy ass nigga."

She continued to stare into her eyes. She was still shook from her recent run in with death. The Grim Reaper stood a foot away, gun drawn, aimed at her face. She could vividly see the barrel smoking a few feet away. *Click.* The empty gun echoed in her mind. The slightest sound resembling it forced her to relive the moment over and over. The cold gaze of murder from G50 gave her the chills. "That nigga tried to kill me."

Krissy dashed her face with cold water. A knock on the front door sent her anxiety rising until the meds kicked in. She picked up her pistol from the couch before checking the door. She quickly hid the pistol behind the couch cushion. She opened the door for her grandmother-in-law. "Hey, Mrs. Avery."

They kissed and hugged. "Hey, sweety, how's everything?"

"I'm trying."

"You look good, gaining some weight."

"Yeah, well … I'm pregnant. Dirty wants me to abort because he thinks it's not his!" She held her emotions. "Don't say anything to 'em about it. I can't take any more arguing right now. That's all it leads to."

Avery frowned. "Where is he?"

As Dirty and Avery chatted, Krissy got dressed. She desperately needed to get out of the house for a while. There were things she needed handled, and although she didn't want to risk running into G50, she couldn't sit around Dirty any longer. "I'm going to get some things handled, you need anything while I'm out, Dirty?" she asked courteously.

"As a matter fact, yeah, I do. Stop at the food gallery on your way back and grab me something to eat. Call me when you get there. They'll have a special I might want."

"Be safe," Mrs. Avery said.

Two hours later, after getting a Q60 Infiniti truck and making a much-needed stop to a friend, she pulled into the soul food restaurant, dialing her man. After memorizing his order, she headed inside to place it, having to wait ten minutes.

She was in Dirty's territory, so she felt safe. The entrance bell chimed, and she jumped, startled. A short, handsome young man entered, no older than nineteen, dressed in all black, speaking on his cell phone. She became alert. Trouble was a scent in the air. Panicking, she licked her dry lips while drying her sweaty palm against her jeans. Deliberately, she eased her hand into her purse, thumbing the safety off her gun, taking a deep breath. Frazzled nerves had her jumpy. She watched him closely as he placed an order then slipped the phone into his pocket.

The cook called out, "Ticket 122? Order up."

Krissy relaxed, dropping the pistol into her bag. She noticed the boy in all black instantly as she retrieved her order. It was one of Dirty's trusted workers. A good kid who had always shown her the utmost respect. "Hey, what you been up to, Quake?"

"Shit, chillin' out the way." He gave her a friendly hug. "What about you? It's been a while since I seen yo' ass out and about."

"Yeah, I know. I'm doin' good, though, thanks for asking. Wish I could stay and chit chat, but I gotta get going. You know how Dirty is when he's hungry." She took up the meal, waving on her way out.

It felt good to see a friendly face. A cutie at that. As she made her way through the parked cars to her truck, she opened the door, sitting the meal on the back seat floor board. As she opened the driver's door, she was suddenly snatched up off the ground at the waist. She screamed loudly, "Nooo! Get off me!"

It was happening so quick, Krissy was caught completely off guard yet holding onto her purse for dear life. A second masked figure ordered, "Get that bitch in the trunk!"

"Heeelpp. No. Help!"

The blow to the back of her head nearly knocked her out. Still, she fought both attackers with all her might.

"Hit that bitch again!"

The next blow dizzied her. She was so scared, it was happening so quick. She knew if she didn't fight hard she'd be taken, even killed. She reached in her purse, drawing the pistol.

One perp said, but it was too late, "Shit, this bitch gotta gun!"

BLOOOM!

The assailant who had her by the waist hoisted into the air, screamed in agony, crumbling to the ground bringing her down with him. "She shot meee!"

Krissy aimed the angry barrel at the second man, squeezing the trigger as he took off full speed through the parking lot, weaving in and out of cars ducking shots. She bolted to her feet in a hurry, gun sizzling, snatching the mask off the wounded man's face.

"Quake?"

"Ahh, shit! Bitch, you shot me in the foot!"

Astonished, she trembled. "You tried to kidnap me? Tell me I'm fucking tripping, nigga."

He whined, holding his leg. "It wasn't my idea."

Krissy pressed the barrel against his cheek. "Y'all niggas keep tryin' me like I'm a random hoe. You already know I'm dat bitch."

"I swear, you know I wouldn't have done shit to you if the call hadn't come in. I think I'm getting cold. Don't let me die out here. Not like this, Krissy."

Sniffling, she replied, "I know who sent you. Why? To hurt me, scare me? Tell me, Quake, or I'll blow your shit back 'fore the police pull up. Tell me?!"

"To … to kill you."

A knife entered her heart. "That's what's up. If you ever come for me again, I'll kill you no hesi', understand me, nigga?"

"You got it," he whined.

"Now let me see your hand," she said calmly. "Let me see your fucking hand!"

She shot his hand. *BLOOOM.*

"Arrghh! My hand."

"Don't ever put your fucking hands on me," she spat, jumping into the driver seat, leaving him wailing. She knew soon with all the static coming her way that she'd have to turn herself in. She was on borrowed time.

Wiping away tears, she checked her mirrors as she pulled in the driveway. *I'm still dat bitch.*

***

Denise was overwhelmed with guilt. He felt extremely terrible for cold shouldering his son, Brick, but it had to be that way. His wife and business were all he had. There was no way he could allow his son to stress them out behind his foolishness. Simple as put, if the streets were where he wanted to be, it was where they would leave him. However, as he worked hard to rebuild the transmission in the quietness of his shop late into the night, he couldn't shake the regret of being so harsh. So brutal.

He continued his work relentlessly, his mission to keep and maintain a good reputation. Finally finishing up a day's work, Denise wiped his hands dry of oil. When he turned to leave, he gripped his chest, his heart. It felt like a stroke.

"What's good, old school?" The tiny terrors smiled deviously. They had been there for the last twenty minutes watching him without him knowing. "Damn, dawg. I think we might've gave this old nigga a heart attack or sum'n." One kid grinned.

He was almost struggling to breath after being frightened. "W-what do ya want? W-why are you here? What's your business?"

The leader stepped forward, his menacing scowl unlike anything Denise ever faced. "A real powerful man sent me here to handle business. We're here for your son, Brick. He's pretty hard to find and we don't like that. It took a minute to find y'all, but thanks to the internet and yellow pages, it wasn't hard. Since there's a lot of people looking for him we're hoping to catch'em first. Maybe you know where he's holed up. You're his father, you have a wife, a school teacher, right? Don't worry, we know everything, so where is he—"

"I-I don't k-know where that boy is," he answered, shaking. "I haven't seen him since he went on the run from the US government."

The trio of bandits glared. "That ain't good, OG. We need your son."

"But he's not here, and I don't know where to find him."

"Zoo ain't tryna hear that fuck shit." Milli pointed the pistol. Lil' Zippy brought over the chair, shoving him down into it. "Old head, you better tell us sum'n."

"But I—" Denise was suddenly duct taped into the seat. His mouth was gag then taped up as well. Lil' Zippy brought the monkey wrench down hard over the man's left knee. His muffled screams pierced ears, eyes wide as baseballs, the excruciating pain jolting through his body. He tried to break out the bonds to no avail.

MuMu laughed at the man, dropping a steel bolt into the slingshot deviously. He pulled back as far he could, standing across the room aiming his shot. "Five dollars I hit'em in the forehead first try?"

"Nigga, I bet that five you won't."

When he let go, the bolt barreled through the air so fast they heard it slicing through the air. Denise's head snapped back, his forehead burst open, blood gushing everywhere. He screamed over the gag.

"Yes! Nigga, pay me my five dollars," MuMu celebrated.

"Get back."

MuMu aimed a new bolt. Another direct hit. Denise raged, unable to move or wiggle free. Blood continued down his face. The massive headache made him dizzy and nauseous. He wanted to vomit. It felt like he had been in a car collision head on.

Lil' Zippy was a sore loser, but he paid up. "Let me try this stupid shit." He took the slingshot. The first dozen attempts all missed. After a while he got the hang of it, directly hitting Denise over and over until he was barely recognizable. Bored, with nothing else to do, they tortured the old man. It wasn't until Milli beat him with the pistol over the head that they killed him.

"Where we gon' hide 'em?"

They looked around, undecided. "Fuck dat, leave dat old nigga right there."

***

Shooter stared at his own murderous gaze in the bathroom mirror. The ugly gash across his forehead needed seven stitches. The badly bruised face reminded him of the head-up encounter with his high-ranking leader, Zoo. He felt cheated, as if he was sneak attacked. His heart raced outrageously as he rolled his tongue across swollen gums. Three front teeth had been kicked away, his nose broken. Each time it replayed in his head, he became furious.

He envied Zoo. His wealth. Position. Authority. He so much as wanted to kill the leader. Shooter felt out of place, as if he was with the wrong cause, movement. He second guessed being a blood. When he first joined it was a brotherhood, hanging out, partying, and fucking project bitches. When serious money came into the picture, he felt as if niggas started to believe and act better than the other.

He hated that.

Being singled out every time he made a mistake. Humiliating him, treating him less than a man. Those days were over. Looking at both black eyes of his infuriated him. His bloodshot eyes a reflection of what he thirsted for.

He wanted his get back.

Shooter listened thoroughly. His baby mother, Meka, entered yelling as usual.

"Where the fuck is yo' ass at?" She came barging into the bathroom, angry. He had made her leave work early. "What the fuck you mean come get my son 'cause you're not watching him? Bitch, that's your son too. It shouldn't be a problem for you since you ain't got shit better to do anyway!" she shouted. "I'm at fuckin' work trying to keep a roof over our heads while your sorry ass run the streets all day gang banging and selling dope. You ain't even got shit to show for it except that fucked-up face."

"Bitch, get the fuck on 'fore I fuck yo' ass up. Go spend time with your son, or I'll bury yo' ass in here."

Meka looked at him like he was crazy. "You quick to wanna beat a bitch ass, but all these niggas out here you scared to fight. You a pussy. You let Zoo beat the pissy shit outta you, got you lookin' all sad'n shit. But you ready to leave the house, you shouldn't even want to be seen, ugly nigga!"

Shooter went to knock her ass out. Meka ducked traumatically. Just as he was going to beat the breaks off her, the gunshot explosion was deafening, breathtaking. Suddenly struck with the fear of God, they scrambled out the bathroom. Their son, a two-year-old, burst out into wails having touched the gun's trigger. Shooter had left his pistol beneath the bed pillow where his son lay. A hole the size of a watermelon was in the wooden headboard.

Meka ran and scooped her son. "Oh my god, baby." She held him. Shooter was trembling. His son had almost killed himself under his supervision. He felt terrible. Rattled to his core. The boisterous screaming from his son mixed with Meka's sobbing sent his stress levels through the ceiling.

"Get the fuck out, Shooter. Get all your shit and get out!"

He smacked her hard across the face and onto the bed. "Don't fuckin' talk to me like that no more, bitch, or I swear…" He took his pistol and stormed out the house, taking her car keys with him.

Shooter drove aimlessly around the city, gripping the weapon. Everything happening in his life, he blamed Zoo for it. Arriving outside the nightclub, he flicked his hazard blinkers on, parking on the street. With purpose, he jumped out, coming around the car, gun extended. Its infrared beam luminous across the club's dark-tinted front windows. Remorseless, he opened fire on the line of people, shooting into the establishment. Pandemonium erupted. Savagely, menacing rounds shattered windows, hitting bartender, a DJ, and several partygoers. He wasn't satisfied until the club was empty.

Unfinished, he hopped inside the car pulling away while reloading a fresh extended clip. It wasn't until he had bullet riddled and destroyed three of Zoo's main businesses, causing chaos, that he felt better. Still, he wouldn't be satisfied until the score was even.

Chapter 22

Cloud scowled angrily after attempting to reach his friend C'Lo for two whole days straight. "I don't fucking understand why this nigga ain't answering the damn phone!"

Blue wearily said, "He ain't answering for me either. What you think is up?"

"We don't need to jump to conclusions. C'Lo and his girl had to get the new pipe system done today on the house. More than likely they're home. Know Stacy like to kidnap that nigga. We'll just pull up." He started the car.

Outside C'Lo's house, he noticed the gold Cadillac still parked. As they stepped out the car, a red beamer drop top arrived as well, along with a plumbing service behind them. A beautiful black woman emerged from the coup in form-fitting jeans, Timberland boots, and a long-sleeve thermal top. She came into the yard.

"Are you guys friends or family to the residents?" She smiled warmly.

"Family. Have you spoken with them recently?" Cloud watched the plumbing company unload equipment.

"Actually, I haven't. I've tried to reach them both on their cells. No response."

Cloud walked up to the front door, knocking hard. He tried to peek inside but the blinds were sealed tight. "I can't get a good look."

She took out a set of keys, stepping onto the porch. "Well, I am the landlord." She open the door and stuck her head in. "Hello, is anybody home?"

A horrendous odor hit their noses simultaneously. Cloud locked eyes with the woman, both exchanging knowing gazes. He stepped inside, cautious, anxious. The entire home reeked. There was no sign of the source. The landlord snooped around. Something wasn't right. Cloud and his friend Blue sensed the foul play. C'Lo and his girl were missing, nowhere to be found. It was unlike C'Lo to not check in.

Blue stood in the kitchen, vexed. "something ain't right with this."

Cloud agreed.

Shrilly, the woman's startled screams collected their attention. Cloud dashed down the hallway turning into the laundry room. In a slim closet almost invisible to the eye, behind the main door, was where the bodies were stuffed. The woman puked, disgusted. C'Lo and Stacy were folded into the narrow space. Their bodies pale and frigid. Both their eyes were wide open. The blue bruises around their necks pained Cloud. There was only a group of killahs ruthless enough to send such message.

"I-I have to call the police." The woman stumbled out the room, terrified.

Cloud headed to the car with Blue in tow. Neither said a word. It was as if they could read each other's thoughts. He drew his pistol, chambering a round. Blue followed suit. He navigated the Impala up Pine Hurst's back streets. His face was still fresh from his last drive-by, and a bounty was on his head with teams of goons searching to make ten thousand quick dollars. Neither of the two cared what happened to them.

After the first drive through, Blue told him, "Go back through the park area. I think I may have seen that nigga G50 standing in those apartments."

Cloud bent a few corners, hoping to keep from losing a target. Heartbeats fleeting, they spun the block a second time. The moment he set his vision on G50, his blood boiled seethingly.

"Don't pull into the apartments. It's one way in and out. Park at the entrance, I'll handle business. Give me cover if it gets ugly." Blue hit the door unlock button.

Cloud gripped his 9mm. Bending the last corner, a police cruiser eased past. The female officer locked eyes with him. He straightened the wheel, preparing for an abrupt stop outside the Four Seasons entryway.

Blue had his eyes on the side mirror. "Shit. She whipping around behind us!"

"What you wanna do?"

WOOP-WOOP! The sirens sounded off. The cruiser sped up on their bumper. The officer's voice came over the PA system. "Pull over, NOW!"

Cloud pulled along the street, easing the gun under his thigh. He parked at the Four Seasons entryway. Swiftly, he jumped out, hands in the air feining distress. "What I do, Officer? I didn't do anything. What's the problem?"

She came over. "License and registration, please?"

"What I do though?"

"You have two busted tail lights, of course. Are you two even from out here? You seem awfully suspicious." Her keen sights watched them closely.

She stepped too close to Cloud. With lightning speed, he leaned in with a stiff right jab that snapped her head back and sent her tumbling to the concrete. He pounded on her, connecting two more blows, knocking her out cold. Blue was amazed. With haste, he rushed into the treacherous apartments, pressing the trigger frantically. There was no sign of G50, so he clapped at everything. From second-story windows, automatic gunfire erupted in retaliation.

Parked cars were battered with waves of heavy assault rounds aiming for Blue, who was pinned back behind a Buick Regal. From several directions, teens opened fire in a blood-thirsty frenzy. His mission soon went from a surprise attack to a rescue mission. Blue fired recklessly, unable to get a chance to pinpoint the exact location of the shooters.

"Aye, cuz, you good?" Cloud was pressed against the corner of the concrete building.

"I'm almost out!" He cringed. Lead ricocheted off concrete and metals. If they didn't do something quick, they'd be picked off like prey. More teens spilled from the woodworks putting in work. Multiple caliber weapons ruptured, and massive tennis ball holes ate into the parked Buick.

Cloud stepped front the corner wall hitting. Empty shells from his gun flicked through the air. He gave Blue enough cover to escape the trap he was in. Together, they ran back to the car full speed, returning fire. An elderly woman stood at her doorway with a twelve-gauge Mossberg pump aimed at the Impala.

Chi-Chikk-BOOM!

From around the tree, two young girls, no older than fourteen, squeezed .22 revolvers. An old man who had been fixing a bike hurled rocks, hoping to hit home. Cloud and Blue had no time to open the doors, so they dove through the window openings. Bullets barreled through the metal frame, lodging into the interior. Desperate to escape death, Cloud backed off the street, running over the unconscious female officer.

"These mu'fuckas vicious!"

Blue reloaded his pistol as Cloud sped through back streets.

The 6 p.m. news had both Cloud and Blue's faces plastered across every channel, having their actions caught live on police dash cam.

***

Pastor Jacobs, a short, stubby, fifty-two-year-old black man, wrapped his massive arms around Mrs. Knox sorrowfully, trying his best to give spiritual and emotional support. She sobbed uncontrollably, overwhelmed with grief. All but the Lord had been snatched from her. She couldn't bear the anguish. The sound of her broken heart resembled metal scraping against metal as she wept. Tears welled in his own eyes. A woman of pure strength, faith, and resilience had been brought to her knees by grief. He could understand her pain and felt sad he could offer only kind words to console her with prayer. Even that may not be enough.

"Why, Lord, why?" she shouted. "Why me? What is it you want me to do? I have surrendered my soul to you. Worshipped and praised your name all my life. I have nothing else for you to take. Why my family, why? What did my husband do to be punished so brutally? Lord, have mercy on my soul, on the soul of my husband, my son, and those responsible." Mrs. Knox sobbed some more.

"Your husband is in heaven. The Lord has sent for him to serve beside him. There is a battle against evil and our warrior, Denise, is needed. Cry tears of joy. Have compassion for thy enemies, for they know no better. They, too, are all God's children. Open the floodgates to your heart and allow him to heal you," Pastor Jacobs's soothing voice whispered into her ear. For an hour he prayed over her until her spirit was calm. "Are you going to be alright, sista?"

Sniffling, she replied, distraught, "I will be. Thank you so much."

He led her out his office and into the church's worship area. Voices came in clearly as they entered.

"I said, Loooorrdd! Why ... do they try gangstas? When they know they ain't 'pose too?" The young boy stood at the podium talking to a congregation of only two other kids. He mockingly mimicked the voice of a reverend.

The two kids laughed, humored. "Why they do that, Pastor MuMu?"

"Beeecaauuse, they are ... STUPID. Mmhmm!" he harmonized.

Laughter ensued. "Preach on, Pastor MuMu."

Pastor Jacobs thought it was a sick joke being played. Mrs. Knox was a ghost. "Get down from there, right now. This is a place of worship. Not a Toys R' Us. Who are your parents?" His voice boomed, authoritative.

"Honestly, Pastor ..." Lil' Zippy drew the .40 off his waist. "Since you like God so much, go meet his ass."

Blah-Blah-Blah-Blah! The gun spat viciously. He walked up to the bleeding man, putting one in his face for good measure. Since he'd been molested as a baby by a pastor, he had no love for any.

Milli turned his pistol on Mrs. Knox. "How you doin', ma'am?" he asked politely. "We're hoping you can tell us where your son, Brick, is? He's wanted by the devil."

She gripped her chest, then fainted. The trio stood around her sprawled body, puzzled. Kicking her leg for a reaction, MuMu asked, "Think she's dead?"

Milli aimed the .45 at her, squeezing two thunderous rounds into her face. "Not no more."

***

The women's dorm hadn't been the same since. There was an instant shift the moment Queenie showed her fangs. She was ready and willing any time of the day to sink them into anyone stepping wrong to her. Beating fire out of Big Cherry was a show she was nothing to play with. If anything came up missing from anyone's box, it was automatically assumed she was responsible. No one dared to confront her about it.

LaLa sighed, exasperated. "This shit is starting to drive me crazy. Next plea offer they come with, I'm taking it. I'll take whatever right now."

Mena sucked her teeth. "No the hell you ain't, either. The last plea was ten."

"So they'll have to come with something lesser. Whatever it is, I'm going to take it."

"Don't. We all gonna get outta here. The longer we sit and be patient, the better," Queenie voiced. She, too, was growing impatient and irritated. Though she wasn't afraid, she dreaded the time she would spend in a women's prison. The harsh reality was tearing them down. Her two friends wanted to get out so they could go back to smoking weed and getting lost in hype. She had a different agenda. As long as she had no real validation of her sister's safety, she wouldn't rest.

"What did your lawyer say today?" LaLa said.

"That I fucked up. All them assaults on staff carry zero to five years. I can get my ass fried if I got to trial. He said he'll see what kind of plea I can get with everything included."

Mena flopped back on the mattress. "Something gotta shake for a bitch."

"Mail call! Mail call!" the CO announced. "Bring your IDs when your name is called. Rhodes Jackson. Valentine. Jones. Wilks…"

"Queenie, you got some mail, girl. That's what's up. Hurry up so we can see."

She was nervous as hell retrieving the small envelope. No name or return address. She was curious, anxious to learn the contents. Her chest rattled from her thumping heart.

"Who wrote us, girl? You look terrified." LaLa noticed.

"I'm not sure who it is. There's no name, nothing on it. It might be Precious."

"Your sister? Open it and see then."

"Here, you open it."

Mena opened it slow, suspenseful. Removing the single sheet of paper, she set the envelope aside, glancing up at Queenie, who stared intensely. LaLa unfolded the sheet. Furrowed brow, she snarled.

"It's from Krissy."

"What she want?"

"A phone number is on it. She says to call her soon as you get this." LaLa handed it over. "You gonna call?"

"I don't know."

"That's the same bitch who killed Ta'maine at club Top Floor. I'm surprised she's still alive out there. Them bloods gonna blow her damn boots away."

"I forgot y'all used to hang out. What, y'all not cool-cool no more?"

"Actually, no, we're not." She reminded herself of the last time she saw Krissy. The gun kissing the nape of her neck still gave her nightmares and chills. "She stole my money and put me out the house for no fuckin' reason."

"Are you gonna call her, at least to see what that shiesty bitch want? At least see what she gotta say. She might wanna be your friend again. I mean ... I would call her, it won't hurt nothing."

Queenie looked at the letter long and hard. She wasn't sure what the bitch wanted, but something told her not to get entangled in Krissy's web of trouble and drama. Then again, she needed to talk with her. After all, it was Krissy who called and told her about Gary's death.

Black Migo

Chapter 23

The tables vibrated, rattled wildly as the three high-powered money-counting machines blared loudly. Zoo sat on the living room couch, sullen, deep in thought as his young goonz rubber-banded up stacks as they had been for the last four excruciating hours. So much was on his mind that his attitude was etched across his face in an evil scowl. The disappearance of his sister Maya had him crushed mentally and emotionally. His core was slowly rotting. All ability to stay in control, deteriorating. Though his youngins had murdered Brick's parents, that still wasn't enough. Until he had the luxury of destroying Brick, he would hurt and stress.

His mind drifted off as he stared into space …

… At sixteen, Maya had blossomed tremendously. Her flat chest and bottomless backside spread and flourished dramatically. She had sprouted so beautifully that he wanted to lock his baby sister in the house away from the world and all those unworthy to be graced with her ambience. Her personality was spicy, her mouth slick and sharp. Though he had spoiled her coming up, he made sure to teach her to be humble. One day …

He came over to his sister Kema's house to check on them. He found Maya at the kitchen table, lip busted and eye puffy.

"What the fuck happened to you?" He became furious. The last thing they wanted was for Zoo to get involved. When no one said anything, he snapped, pulling the gun off his waist, sitting it on the table top to emphasis his seriousness. "I said, what the fuck happened to you?"

Kema sighed. Tati was scared to speak up. Tears welled in Maya's eyes.

"Y'all think I'm playin'?" he growled.

"Tell'em, Maya. Might as well," Tati said.

Maya sniffled, swallowing hard. "My boyfriend did this to me at school 'cause I broke up with him. His sister them are going to be at the school Monday to beat me up, and everybody talkin' about me, picking at me that I got beat up." She cried. It broke his heart. He figured since she was going to a district two school that she wouldn't be surrounded by the harshness he came up in. He was wrong.

"Monday is your last day going to that school, ya hear me?"

"But—"

"I said it. I ain't gon' say it no more." He left out.

Monday, the last bell sounded, and Maya headed to the car pool. Everybody knew her ex-boyfriend, Rex, would have a group of girls waiting outside to jump her. It was the rumor. She was afraid and wanted to run. She wasn't the fighting type. She hated confrontation. With her anxiety rising, she descended the three-story flight of stairs, pushing into the school courtyard.

Rex stood on the bench searching for her, which didn't take long. Behind him was a group of fire chicks in tennis shoes, sports bras, and hair in ponytails. They were there to dish a blitz. "That's that bitch right there!" he pointed out.

They waited for her. Students gathered for the spectacle. Maya was shivering with fear. "Why y'all gon' jump me, what I do?"

Rex was smiling brightly. His few senior homeboys laughed with him. "Come out here and take the 'L' since you think you so tough. "Ain't you said you'll beat my sister dem asses?" he instigated.

"No, I didn't."

"Bitch, come on and get this shit over with. It ain't gon' take long," one sister said. "Come the fuck on."

"I didn't say that though," she defended, frightful.

"Aweee, Princess Maya scared to break a nail," someone in the crowd of students taunted.

"Fuck that. Drag her ass off campus," Rex ordered. The group of five chicks headed for her.

Suddenly, an entourage of ten or more cars came revving through the school lot getting everyone's attention, a burgundy Wraith leading the way. On the drop of a dime, all the doors burst open. Zoo led the way into the courtyard with twenty girls and ten guys with him, reach ready to brawl.

"Yo, Maya, who the fuck out here fucking with you?"

Maya rushed to her brother, relieved. "Let's just go home. I don't wanna be here."

"Hell nah, who put their hands on my lil' sister?" He glared.

A student pointed. "Rex. And he was going to have them girls jump your sister just now."

Zoo laid eyes on him. Rex thought he was tough. He had no idea. The five chicks with him were nervous.

"Get'em!" was all he had to say. A riot erupted. He had brought Pine Hurst's top head bussas to a suburban school district. Each guy with Rex got demolished. The five chicks didn't stand a chance against the project bitches who threw down ruthlessly. Students stood around amazed, entertained thoroughly.

Rex stumbled toward Zoo on wobbly legs, having been beaten down by a goon twice his size.

"This the nigga who put his hands on you?" He glared.

Maya nodded her head yes.

Zoo grabbed him by the collar, smacking blood off his lips then standing him up straight. "Punch this nigga back."

"Bruh, no. Let's just go!"

"I said punch'em in the fuckin' mouth!"

Students stared.

Maya cocked back, popping him in the mouth with all her mouth, bursting both lips. The crowd erupted with excitement. She felt better.

"Hit his ass again!"

She jacked her hand back and punched Rex twice in both eyes. Zoo kicked him in the ass when he fell on his face.

"Next time my sister tell me a muthafucka fucked with her, we'll be back, and next time, it'll be worse."

Zoo snapped out his reverie.

"Big homie ... Big homie?"

He shook away his daze. "What's good?"

"Four hundred thousand dollars total."

"Duffle bag it up. Get ready to move it." He sat back, rubbing his hand over his face. Babygirl sat on the opposite end of the couch, eyes glued to the screen, focused on cameras.

She asked, "Are you gonna answer your phone?"

"What's up, Kema? I don't feel like arguing with y'all. This shit wasn't my damn fault."

She sobbed uncontrollably. "Turn on the news."

His stomach sank deep.

"Twenty-five-year-old Maya Montana went missing nearly two weeks ago. Investigators say she was abducted from outside a North Main gas station. At this moment, she has been pronounced dead. Investigators were able to track her cell phone signal to this massive storage facility behind me. Her body was stuffed in the trunk of her car after being shot …"

Zoo went mute, hanging his head. "Let me call you back." He hung up, clenching his jaw tightly. His grief was unlike any emotion he'd ever felt before.

A text message from Kema popped on his phone.

I already told police that guy Brick did it. Don't want you getting in trouble.

His teeth grinded violently. Silence was his only refuge. He had to keep control of his emotions. Anger could make him act irrational. Babygirl watched him, fearful. His fuse was shortening, getting smaller and smaller. His heavy breathing made them all nervous. He was seconds away from destructing. He couldn't stop the tears from flowing. A better half of him was destroyed. The half that made him human. He loved all his sisters to death, but Maya … She was like his daughter. He was her first love and the only father figure she knew. A man she could depend on, rely on. Still, he slipped up and let the enemy get her. He would never forgive himself for failing to protect his dearest jewel.

Wiping away his tears, unashamed, he stood. "Load that money in the Hummer. Babygirl, follow me."

As the boys hurried out his way, she followed him timidly into the bedroom. Zoo had to release some stress, so he vented by thrashing her love box before heading out to move his money.

***

Taylor held his breath as he crept into the backyard of Brick's old trap house. He wasn't sure why Zoo hadn't burned it down with the rest of the houses but didn't voice his thoughts. His heart beat rapidly, anticipating a confrontation. If he could kill Brick, Zoo would give him the most praise. Having the boss man happy with each of them for doing good was one thing. To get praise was another. With a target on the menu, he agreed to break into the haunted house. Alone.

The midnight sky made it hard to get a good look inside. There was no sound, no visual of any movement. Bravely, he pushed the back door in. Stepping inside, he kept the gun aimed ahead of him. The red beam was luminous against the darkness. Taylor was sharp. His keen senses hypersensitive. He could feel Brick's presence. Somewhere inside the darkness, he knew Brick was lurking. He was unintimidated.

Standing in the pitch-black bedroom, he thought he'd heard something. A breath, maybe a ruffle of clothes. He didn't flinch. When his phone rang, he answered coolly. "Yeah?"

"Anything?"

"That scary ass nigga ain't in here. I was hoping so. I would've shot shit out his ass." He chuckled.

"Say less. Get up outta there." Zoo hung up.

"Yeah. We can bring some bitches in here and go crazy," he joked, slipping the phone back into his pocket. He heard creaking wood sounds. This time it seemed extremely close. Without panic, he picked up the bed sheet and men's clothes off the floor before heading out the way he'd come. There was no doubt in his mind something, someone was home.

A grin spread his lips as he left the yard heading down the block. "Stupid ass nigga. Don't even know who you fuckin' wit'."

***

The black-on-black Hummer weaved through the streets. It was late into the night, the wee hours of the morning. Zoo had eyes and ears on every street corner searching for Brick and his whereabouts.

His patience was running thin. Brick had managed to shoot up three of his clubs, and this made him all the more anxious to get a hold of him.

Zoo ignored the incoming calls spilling in about PineHurst. He was aware of the shootout with Cloud and Blue. It was all over the news. Same as every other murder his youngins committed. His focus was homed in on one man and one man only. Brick.

Babygirl glanced over to him after answering her phone. "Lil' Zippy dem say they need us to pull up in Ames Manor. It's important!"

He nodded his head.

The sun had begun rising from behind violent gray storm clouds, casting an eerie blanket of gloom over the streets. They rode in silence, suspense, entering Ames Manor projects. At the far back of the lot in front of one of the rundown buildings, Lil' Zippy waved the truck over.

Zoo asked in a grisly tone, "Do you have Brick?"

"Big homie, we on that boy trail, we—"

"Then why the fuck you call me out here for then?" he snapped.

"We got a nigga in the back of this building say he was serving Brick dope."

Hastily, he was out the truck, walking into the back where MuMu and Milli had a skinny drug dealer hugging a wide tree trunk with his hands tied, mouth gagged, pants down at the ankles, ass exposed. He was standing on a large red ant pile, stepping in pain.

"What the fuck is this?"

MuMu laughed. "This nigga can dance, ain't it?"

Zoo snatched the gag away.

"Please, man. I don't know nothing," the guy pled.

"Brick. How can I find'em?"

"I don't know that nigga like that at all. Like I told them gits, he came through here tryna cop some dope. I served 'em a gram. He got high in the stairwell. He bought more from me and shot it all up. When he ran out of money, he robbed me for everything, dawg. I gave it all up'n took off. That's the god's honest truth. That was midnight." He winced. Ants were chewing on his dick, ass, and legs. "Please, man. I'm being real. I'm just a petty nigga."

Zoo ordered, "Let 'em go."

"Hell no, bruh. This nigga seen our faces. If we let'em go, he'll put our business in the streets," Milli gritted.

It was a test. The youngin' answered correctly. Lil' Zippy came back with the rope. Gagging the man's mouth again, MuMu placed the noose around the man's neck, throwing it up over a branch. Lil' Zippy and MuMu caught it, pulling down with all their body weight as Zoo cut loose the guy's bound wrists.

Instantly, he ascended into the air, legs kicking and groaning over the gag. His fingers gnawed at the neck tie, desperate for air. He fought, struggled to no avail.

Zoo stared emotionless, until the man stopped kicking, twitching dead.

By noon the body was discovered by children playing. Until he caught his man, many more would suffer.

Black Migo

Chapter 24

Krissy checked her appearance one last time in the mirror after parking her rental truck behind her home. She swiped away tears that sailed down her face. Though she refused to continue to cry, it kept coming. It was due to her hurt feelings. Grabbing the bag of food from the passenger seat, she proceeded inside. Mrs. Avery had left, leaving her and Dirty all alone. Without announcement, she entered the bedroom.

Dirty gaze up from his cell phone, surprised.

"I'm home, and here's your food, baby."

"I didn't even hear you come in." He studied her with suspicion.

Krissy ignored his gaze while taking out the Styrofoam tray from the bag. She then sat it on the food stand. "What's wrong, you're not hungry?"

"Nah, yeah. I mean, I'm just ..."

"Yeah, I know. Enjoy your meal, I'm going to take me a bath." She grabbed a few items then headed into the guest bedroom. She ran a steaming hot tub of water, sitting her pistol on the toilet seat for close access. She knew after today, she'd never be able to trust a man. He couldn't trust her either.

Sitting in the scorching hot water, she couldn't help but to wonder why she hadn't received the call she'd been waiting for. She closed her eyes, rubbing her tummy. "What am I going to do?" she whispered as tears cascaded off her face.

Suddenly, her phone vibrated. The restricted incoming call made her nervous. "Hello, who this?"

"You have a prepaid call from ... Queenie. An inmate at Alvin S. Glenn Detention Center, to accept these charges press #1, to ignore press—"

Krissy hurried and tap the #1.

"Your phone call will be recorded and monitored. Thank you for using Global Tel, you may begin speaking now."

Silence.

"You there, Queenie?"

"What you want, Krissy? I already told you that I don't fuck wit' you like dat."

"Boo, listen. I know you're still in your feelings about that incident, but I promise ... I didn't put you out. Nor did I tell Dirty to do some foul shit like that. I thought we already established that?"

"Whatever, Krissy, what you want?"

"You ain't got no solid reason not to fuck with me. I'm a real bitch. Me and you were better than that, I thought. If I didn't care about you, I wouldn't have went out my way to reach you and make sure you good."

Queenie sucked her teeth. "I hear you, Krissy."

"Do you remember that night at Top Floor, when that boy got killed?"

"Duh, Krissy. I was there, remember? I watched him fall," Queenie replied with sarcasm.

"I mean ... I know that. How you feel about it?"

"He got what he deserved. How else I'm 'pose to feel? He pointed a gun at my damn face."

Krissy agreed. Swallowing hard, she asked, "Do you still have the gun."

"No, why?"

"Just asking. So how have you been holding up back there? You need money? You know a bitch got it."

"It's been rough to say the least. Driving me crazy. I'm good though, thanks."

"I can't even imagine."

"You have sixty seconds remaining," the operator interjected.

"But don't worry, lil' mama. I'ma make sure you good. Real bitches do real shit."

Queenie sighed. "I hear you, home girl."

"Call me back though." Krissy managed to say before the phone hung up. She sat the phone on the edge of the toilet seat, having saved the recorded call. So much was going through her mind that she couldn't focus on one topic. After finishing up the bath, she entered the bedroom where Dirty sat up in bed watching her closely. Ignoring his curious gaze, she went about oiling up her body.

"Shit crazy. You heard about that shit happening to Quake? Nigga got shot up at the food gallery." He broke the silence.

"Damn, that's too bad. I wonder why, what he do?" she asked, feigning concern. She took up his trash, leaving out. *Lord, he better be lucky I'm pregnant. I'd body 'em playin' wit' me.*

***

Queenie walked back to her bunk area after speaking with Krissy. She couldn't shake the funny feeling she had afterward. She had said too much. Flapping on her bed, LaLa and Mena sat on their own beds playing cards.

LaLa shuffled the deck. "What that hoe want?"

"Shit. Asking me if I'm alright. How I been holdin' up. Not to worry, she gon' make sure I'm good. A bunch of bullshit basically."

"That's it? She ain't finna send no money?" Mena asked.

They laughed. That's all Mena ever cared about. Queenie answered, "She needs to. She told me to call back though."

"Are you?"

"Fuck no, fuck her."

The sound of the dorm's entry door opening got each of their attention. Four new chicks holding bed rolls walked in with a CO escort. All but one stood out. She was the prettiest, thickest, and clearly out of place. Queenie recognized her the moment she came in. How could she ever forget such a face?

"New pussy on the tier!" someone yelled. The dorm erupted into chatter and noise. Some whistled while others stood on their beds like savages thirsting for fresh meat.

LaLa said, "I think I know that light-skin bitch."

"That hoe does look super familiar," Mena added.

"She used to fuck with my man. That bitch name is Tempest."

LaLa and Mena exchanged gazes. "Fuck it, let's beat this bitch up."

"She doesn't know I'm here. I'll pull up tomorrow."

Tempest surveyed the room for familiar faces. She hadn't recognized anyone as of yet. She was uncomfortable being out of place in jail. She controlled her nervousness as she headed to her assigned bunk downstairs. She began making her bed. The few women sharing the neighboring cubicles leaned over the belly high walls built to divide every two bunk areas.

"Hey, new girl. I'm Big Cherry. What's your name?"

She glanced up at the swollen face, big bull dyke. Damn, bitch, who fucked you up? My name is Tempest."

"Okay, Tempest. That's a cute name. Where you from, if you don't mind me asking?"

"PineHurst."

Big Cherry swallowed her disgust, having remembered the ass whooping she just received. "Oh, so you know LaLa, Mena, and the girl Queenie, huh?"

One name put a sour look on her face. "I don't know them other girls, but I do know that bitch Queenie. The same bitch ass I beat 'cause she was fucking my man, Gary. The same bitch that shot and killed Ta'maine at club Top Floor." She babbled on, expressing the pure hatred she had for Queenie, who stole her man. She always thought about how he tossed her out just to have a lame chick.

"Word?" Big Cherry was astounded.

Tempest frowned, trying to make herself a friend. "Do I look like I tell lies, homegirl?"

"Them some heavy words. I hope not." The dyke walked away. By morning, Tempest's words had spread around the dorm like wildfire, and she hadn't the slightest clue.

Queenie was furious when she heard of the rumor Tempest spread. She managed to avoid seeing the girl all morning, and her friends didn't like it. She had a reputation to keep.

LaLa put her shoes on. "So what you gonna do?"

Queenie tightened her ponytail then added Vaseline to her face. "Just watch, you and everybody else gon' see."

"All those interested in church service, go ahead into the service room quietly, please. You have five minutes before the chaplain arrives," the CO announced.

Patiently, she stalked Tempest from a distance. By now, she had learned Queenie was also present in the dorm. She regretted ever opening her mouth to Big Cherry.

Tempest surveyed the room. She couldn't spot Queenie. As the chaplain entered, she faced front, nervous, anticipating confrontation.

"How is everyone?" the chaplain, a short white man in his 60s, began.

"Good and you?" they asked in unison.

"I'm great. Bow your heads, let's begin," he instructed. "Lord, we come to you today from this prison asking you to—"

"Bitch, you running 'round here talkin' 'bout you beat my ass?" Queenie snuck up on her victim like a cat.

Startled, Tempest shrieked, "What?"

"Hoe, you heard me! You tellin' lies when you know I dogged your ass. What, you still mad Gary kicked your ass to the curb?"

"He ain't kick me to no curb, that's a lie."

The chaplain watched in disbelief. "Ladies, it's—"

"Shut the fuck up!" She glared at him. "And you got the nerve to say I killed Ta'maine?"

"That's what I heard." Tempest saw how everyone was smirking at how she was being handled. Unable to accept it, she swelled with animosity. "Bitch, you're just mad I'm pregnant by Gary and that you're not. Sit the fuck down somewhere 'fore I give you another motherfuckin' ass—"

BAM! Queenie's fist landed in Tempest's mouth, drawing blood instantly. She stumbled backward against two girls who immediately shoved her toward a right hook. Queenie tried to break her face on impact. Jolting pains shot up her arm, but she didn't care. She viciously punished Tempest in front of the congregation like she was taken by the Holy Spirit. Just as she was going to unleash more, her two friends jumped in, and together they mopped the floor with her like a rag doll. Officers rushed into the room, breaking it up. Tempest was beaten into a bloody pulp. Queenie spat as cuffs secured her wrists, "Stupid bitch. Now you know again, I'm Queen."

Black Migo

***

Shooter examined the new set of dentures in his mouth. His body warmed with anger. Niggas were laughing at him in the streets. Even his own homeboys thought it comical that he got what his big, slick mouth asked for.

Meka drove. "Let me see how it looks. It actually looks better."

"Daddy new teef?" their terrible two-year-old son asked from his car seat, excited. "New teef, Daddy?"

"Yes, Daddy new teef," she answered. "So, are we still going to your mother's?"

Shooter shut the visor up. "Head there now, matter fact."

The drive to Woodfield Park was a short one. As Meka stopped in the Decker Blvd median preparing to make a left turn, Shooter spotted the black-on-black Hummer turning into a shopping plaza. His veins were swelling with vengeance. Instinctively, he drew his pistol, jacking the slide back.

"I'll be right back, don't fuckin' pull off."

Meka shouted, "Shooter, no, are you serious?"

"Leave me and I'll blow your face off." He reached back, took his son's shirt, and pulled it across his face as a mask, then jumped out, racing across the busy intersection. The black Hummer came to a stop. He knew it from anywhere. The front tag read PHP.

He wasn't sure who was driving and without regard, he stood five feet away, squeezing. The thunderous explosions were followed by slugs smashing through the Hummer's thick exterior. Fire spat from the barrel a foot long. Murder filled the air thick as gun smoke. He tried to fire at the vehicle from all directions. It didn't take long before his thirty-round magazine ran empty. Frantically, he sprinted full speed to his girl's car. His son was wailing, and Meka was shaking tremendously.

"Drive this muthafucka!" He pointed the empty pistol. She hurried and mashed the gas into the neighborhood parking lot behind Shooter's mother's house.

Reloading his still smoking pistol, he prayed it was all bad and man down for Zoo.

Black Migo

Chapter 25

CO James was the first face she saw enter lock up, frowning with utter disgust. "Stank pussy bitch, back with us, huh?"

"Keep on playin' with me, bitch." Queenie glared. She was shoved into an empty shower stall alongside her friends, awaiting a cell within the special housing unit. Tempest had to be rushed to an outside hospital.

Mena asked, "Think they're gonna charge us?"

"Fuck'em!" she answered. As they waited, two male guards walked into the dorm. Soon they were coming directly for her. She knew it was probably to get her ass beat, maced, tazed, then strapped into a physical restraint seat for a week straight. She was ready to turn the fuck up and go off on everybody.

The grimace on CO James's face hyped her emotions.

"Y'all already know it's finna get ugly. I'm not going into no fucking cell. Go ahead and call your reinforcements, 'cause you're gonna need it, on god." She cracked her knuckles, ready to thump.

The first male asked, "Queenie Wilks?"

"Fuck you gon' ask me some stupid shit like that? You know I'm Queenie, you big pussy ass nigga, looking like a punk boy," she spat. "What the fuck you want? I'm tellin' y'all now, this shit going to get ugly. Matter fact, fuck y'all pussy police, this my jail now!"

LaLa and Mena stared at her, shocked she was going so hard. The look on her face showed she was a whole different chick. A beast. Even the officers seemed nervous.

"Are you done?" he asked.

Silence.

"If you're Ms. Wilks, you're ATW (all the way). Your bond has been paid."

Queenie looked over to her friends, disbelieving what she heard. The hatred deeply etched into CO James's face hinted it was true. She was going home. As they opened the shower gates without cuffing her, she stepped out, mean mugging James. She flinched, and the CO liked to fell on her ass. The two male officers laughed.

"Let's go, Ms. Wilks."

"Queenie, don't forget 'bout us, boo," LaLa said from behind the bars, her gaze saddened. They all had gotten so close that she was literally on the verge of refusing to leave without her friends.

"Yes, boo-boo, don't forget about us," Mena pouted. "We love you, girl."

"I promise I'm not gon' forget. I love y'all too," she said, following the officers down the flight of stairs onto the first floor, passing the cells housing women locked away, some forgotten to all. She couldn't help but to feel the pain and hurt they endured. She had firsthand experience of what those four walls and steel doors could do. She had gotten to know a lot of them on many nights of yelling into vents and under doorways.

"Where you going, Queenie?" White Girl Charlie, accused of killing her husband and sister for sleeping together behind her back, yelled through her cell door crack. She noticed all the doorways were filled with faces.

"I'm going home. Somebody paid my bond."

Charlie banged on the door loudly. "That's right, girl. Go out there and give'em hell," she screamed obnoxiously. A smile spread across her lips. Her heart warmed. She never felt this much love before. The entire lock up erupted into celebratory farewells of beating, banging, and kicking on the doors.

"We love you, Queenie!" some cheered.

"You're really famous in jail, huh?" one of the escorts asked.

"I'm not famous. Just a real bitch from the bottom that doesn't give a fuck 'bout no police," she replied proudly.

Having to leave the jail in nothing but a hospital gown had Queenie livid. She had lost her phone, her clothes, her money, and the gun. Every day she wondered where the hell it went to. If the police and ambulance found her on the scene damn near dead, there was no way she wasn't supposed to be charged with a weapon. It kept her puzzled. She was going to figure that out. Her main concern now was who the hell paid her bond. As she neared the jail's front exit, her heart beat rapidly. It was a dream come true to walk out a place she thought she'd never leave.

"Hey, sexy," the familiar voice spoke. "These are for you." Krissy removed the big shades from her face. "I thought you'd need something fresh and fly to leave in."

"You paid my bond?"

"Are you upset that I did?"

"Uh … no. I actually really appreciate it all." She fought back emotions. "I thought I'd never see the light of day. At least not anytime soon."

"Put this on in the restroom. We can talk in the car."

Queenie was overwhelmed with excitement. Her eyes were all over the place. "Everything looks so … different."

"I know. Wait 'til you see downtown. Them protesters fucked everything up and then some."

The drive to Krissy's house was short and quiet. Stepping inside, she locked the door up and set her bag on the couch. Queenie stood, taking in the decor all over again. It was the same as she last saw it, with the same cozy vibe that could make a stranger feel right at home.

"We need to have a nice long talk, Queenie. A lot has happened since, like I told you, Dirty got shot up really bad, and I'm still on the run for murder with all kinds of people coming at my throat. Just recently, your brother-in-law, G50 dem, chased me in a car and shot up my rental so bad it was a total loss. That nigga looked me in my eyes and pulled the fucking trigger. Luckily, he ran the hell outta bullets." She fanned her face, temperature rising reliving a traumatic moment.

"That's crazy."

"That's not even all of it. In a week I have to turn myself in. I'll be getting right back out though. I have a really good lawyer who's already guaranteed me a bond and a lesser charge to plea to. The sooner I can get this behind me, the better. I hate looking over my shoulder, losing sleep, feel me?"

Queenie nodded sympathetically.

"And that's why I need you. I had to pay twelve thousand to get you out. If you help me and, of course, Dirty, you can make a lot of money in the process, get back on your feet, and do your own thing."

"I ain't doin' shit unless you or Dirty give me back that money taken out my bag. I worked hard for it and it's mine. I had to live in the fuckin' woods, almost got ate by a bird and raped and killed. Again. That shit almost destroyed my life some more, and I don't appreciate it." She twisted her face up.

"Know what ... you're right, and I feel you a hundred percent. Come into the bedroom so you can press'em yourself." Krissy led the way, and Queenie gladly followed.

***

Blue drove the forest green Expedition through the traffic light. To his left, Olympia Boarding School was letting out students for the day. His heart fluttered. "I know I ain't trippin'," he said aloud, looking back over his shoulder at the teenager clad in school uniform.

Milli was excited when the call came from Zippy that they needed his assistance in putting in more work. He jumped eager at the call of duty. Leaving school, he held onto his backpack strapped with a .44 snub nose. He would never go anywhere without the heat and always paid close attention to his surroundings. He headed up the sidewalk, picking up the pace as his phone rang.

"Damn, nigga, where you at?"

He lit up a cigarette. "I'm three blocks away, dang. I'm walking fast as I can, nigga."

"Aight, man. Well, hurry up, we ain't got all day."

Milli hung up, walking faster.

"Aye, my man, can I bum a light off your cigarette?" the man leaning against the Expedition asked, as if he'd been dying to smoke all day.

He started to lie, but his friends were only a block away and a few seconds wouldn't hurt. He came over close enough for Blue to smack him in the head with the gun, knocking him out cold.

Milli opened his eyes, having a dream he was standing under a shower head with warm water beating down his face. That was until he batted his eyes open to find a man holding his dick, relieving his bladder all over his face. "Ah shit, bro, what the fuck?" He tried to turn his face away from the hot yellow stream to no avail. He realized he had been stripped naked completely and duck taped to a kitchen chair.

"Wake yo' ass the fuck up, nigga." Cloud shook his dick dry in front of the boy's face.

"Why you got your dick in my face? I'm a dude."

"If you don't tell me what I want to know, lil' dude, I'ma put this dick in your mouth, understand?" Cloud glared maliciously.

Milli was nervous. He looked around the kitchen and noticed the stove eye on high with an ice pick laid across glaring red. "I don't know shit!"

"Lil' dude, right now ain't the time to play tough. This ain't no school recess with you pumping up your chest acting all tough. You the same little fucker that came up on our grass in Apple Valley talking that super G shit, 'bout you ain't gon' repeat yourself twice. So now YOU listen up," Blue said. "You tell this nigga what he wanna know, or he gonna violate your little tight ass in the worst way."

Cloud smacked Milli so hard across the face his back teeth loosened. "Where the fuck is my son? Lie and this hot pick goin' in your face."

"I don't know shit!"

He grabbed the ice pick by the handle and stabbed him in the thigh as the smell of burnt flesh filled the room along with his screams of agony. At that exact moment, Cloud plunged his pistol into the boy's mouth without remorse, muffling his cries.

"I'ma ask you this shit again, little nigga. Tell me what the fuck I need to know, or you're gonna be here all night until this Glock catch a nut. I ain't no mu'fucking minute man either. Like the fuck I asked, where the fuck is my son?"

"I don't fucking—"

Cloud poked him again then stuffed the strap down his face. This went on for hours until blood spurt everywhere. The room was filled with the smell of blood and charred flesh. Milli had thrown up all over himself. His body had been stabbed over two hundred times. He could take no more.

"Ple-please, man. I don't know nothing," Milli said, weak.

The boy's strength and resilience angered him. He despised young niggas. The new generation was unruly. Untamed and savage. Milli proved him wrong. He expected the boy to cave in hours ago. He hadn't, and now Cloud was fed up. Taking the ice pick off the red eye, he stabbed the boy repeatedly in the stomach.

Milli had no energy to scream anymore. He could feel the life in his body escaping slowly. He'd protect Zoo to the end. Nothing would make him fold. Nothing. But at this time, he couldn't withstand any more torture. His body shook violently, his teeth rattled. Covered in sweat, he shivered, freezing cold. Tears sailed down his swollen, bloody face.

"Just kill this little nigga and get it over with," Blue said.

Cloud was in a wicked daze. He removed the ice pick from the burning hot eye.

"W ... ait," Milli whispered.

"What you got to say before I kill you, boy?"

Before taking his last breath, he whispered his revenge.

Chapter 26

Zoo winced, massaging his shoulder. Though he had only been grazed by bullets, the pain still fucked with him. He and Babygirl had been ambushed and nearly killed. It was a miracle they made it out the rubble with only a few wounds. They hadn't seen the assailants but knew it was someone wanting him dead, for sure.

The loss of Maya had emotions burning in his chest. As he moved through his ghetto mansion, he fed TiTi and Boo-Boo. He had neglected them for too many days and he hated himself for it. "Do y'all mis me?" he asked lovingly, allowing his parrot to pick fruit from his palm. The monkey bounced on his shoulder, lips peeled, showing off its teeth excitedly. He had trained them to understand him, to respond on command. "I miss you lil' babies too." He rubbed them down. "I gotta handle some things here in a few. I gotta leave you two with my keeper, so be good."

The parrot bobbed its head. The monkey bounced on its pamper. Zoo sent them away, heading into his office. Taking his time, he placed the clear box container over the top of the large case. He tapped on the container. The large spider hurried into new territory, fangs erect and ready to puncture flesh. Once he had the violent, aggressive creature secured into a thick black sack, he left the room after locking it up.

Climbing the stairs to the third level, he tapped on the door.

"Yes?" the angelic voice answered.

"Do me a favor, keep my animals fed, will you?"

The latches unlocked. The gorgeous woman stood before him gracefully, her vibrant glow warming his cool skin. The fine hairs all over his body stood erect, connecting with her powerful ambience. She oozed energy. "What's wrong, love?" she asked, sensing his vibe. The intensity in her gaze was hypnotizing.

The same as it had been the first time he met her over ten years prior. She was exotic. Erotic. Mysterious. And also his therapist. She had a gift that he utilized. A secret. She was a goddess. One of many abilities.

"I have to handle a few things. I trust you."

She stared into his brown eyes, searching. "I know you're going to do something dangerous maybe. Be safe, love." She leaned down from the top stair and kissed his forehead. The moment her lips connected to his forehead, electricity rippled through every fiber of him. The drumming of his heart slowed tremendously. Time stood still. Her breathtaking beauty was mesmerizing. "Handle your business."

"I will. Peace." He stepped away.

Inside his burnt orange Bentley truck, he set the black box on the passenger side floor board. He stood out and whistled loudly. "Sheba, Solomon. Let's go!"

In the blink of an eye, both wolves came racing from the tree line. As they neared, he opened the back door. "Get in. Have a seat."

The vicious pets jumped in obediently and excitedly. As he whipped out the massive compound he had built from the ground up, his mind could only focus on his uncertain future.

***

Keisha jumped up and down to squeeze her luscious figure made up of super-thick thighs and ghetto fat booty into a pair of size too small leggings. Her friend, Mona, hogged up the mirror touching up her makeup. The two had gotten up early so they could make it to a club early for free admission and drinks.

"Girl ... I ain't tell you Zoo did something to my damn sons?" Mona spread a thick layer of lip gloss.

"For real? Like what?"

"I don't even know, honey. Those little fuckers act like they're soldiers. They all respectful now, going to summer school. They're being good and all."

Keisha frowned. "What's the problem then?"

"I miss them acting the hell up. I'm so used to yelling'n shit that now they don't give me a reason to. I'm bored as hell now."

They laughed.

"These young boys these days are super loyal and ride or die for gangstas." She thought about her son, Lil' Monkey. She stepped out the room to make a call.

"Agent Vincent Taylor speaking."

"Hi, Mr. Taylor. It's Keisha, Lil' Monkey's mother. I was wondering if maybe you guys could try and get me back up there to speak with my son? I think I can get a confession out him now," she said, thinking only of the thousand dollars they'd give for effort. Money was low and another boost would do justice.

"I'll give you a call, Ms. Keisha. Thanks for your cooperation."

"No problem." She hung up, her stomach tightened. The scheme to free her son and make money in the process was stalling. She loved Zoo, but she loved her son more.

***

Babygirl eased into the front seat of the Bentley truck, her mini dress showing off her smooth, succulent legs. "What's this black box thingy?"

"Better leave it alone. Don't kick it open either or that's your ass."

She folded her legs under her in the plush leather seat. In the back seat, two wolves stared at her hungrily, licking their snouts. On command, they'd eat the delicious-smelling woman down to her bones.

"You're up to something, what is it?" she asked.

Grrrr ... Both dogs growled low and dangerously the moment she touched his forearm with affection, their large fangs displayed to intimidate her. She looked at them in the eyes, glaring back.

Zoo pulled into a local gas station. He then took his phone, made a call, and quickly hung up. His gaze cast over Babygirl, who was googly eyed for him. "Go in the store, get some rubbers and duct tape."

She climbed out. Zoo pushed the Glock on his waist, stepping out as well. At the pump beside his Bentley, a black Navigator parked and rolled down its window.

"What the lick read?" Lil' Zippy asked.
"Where the hell is Milli?"
"We searched everywhere. He was supposed to meet us after summer school class, but he never came. I was on the phone wit'em. I got a bad feeling. It's not like him to not check in or answer his phone."

Zoo rubbed his chin. A tingling sensation ran across the back of his neck. He was being watched. As Babygirl climbed in the Bentley, he spoke, "Let's get outta here, spin the block and watch my tail."

***

His mouth watered anticipating the antidote to his dope cravings. Sweating profusely, Brick patted his arm for the big vein, searching desperately for a landing zone. "Shit!" he spat angrily.

Removing the rubber band, he pulled his pants down, digging out his semi-erect penis. He shook life into it, getting the blood flowing. Taking aim at the main vein, he pushed the dope into his bloodstream, allowing the euphoric sensation to wash over him in a warm wave. Instantly, his body reacted, passing gas, nodding over so far into his lap that he was headbutting his own sausage.

Fifteen minutes into the high, his senses returned. He leaned up slowly, pulling up his jeans and rolling down the window to get a circulation of fresh air into the hot, humid car. The cool air kissed his sweaty skin. Looking over the dashboard, he realized he was still at the gas station parked at a pump. The moment his dreary view set on Zoo exiting the burnt orange Bentley truck, envy, jealousy, and pure hatred pumped in his chest. He slouched down in the seat, grabbing the .40 cal off the seat with four bullets remaining.

"Fuck, shit!" he mumbled, holding his breath. Peeking over the dashboard, the Navigator peeled out the lot first. Zoo rounded his truck, coolly climbing in. Brick started to pounce on the man but knew this was the lick he needed and couldn't risk fucking up moving recklessly.

The Bentley truck eased out the lot. Brick gave it a second to get ahead. He snorted two large lines of molly and meth mixed. Murder and greed glistened in his vision as he sped out the lot to find the Bentley.

***

Vincent gripped his partner's shoulder tightly in suspense. "Well, ain't this something?" he asked, amused and thoroughly entertained.

He and his partner thought they lost Zoo in traffic but were excited to catch up to him and also find Brick hot on his trail. Their hearts pounded spastically watching each second pass. They did their best to keep the PT cruiser inconspicuous, trailing both parties at a reasonable distance.

Jason was hype as the thriller unfolded. "Brick is going to kill'em. Should we stop'em, arrest them both right now? We have indictments."

"Brother, don't spoil the movie. It's getting good. I got a hundred dollars Pierre 'Zoo' Montana gets gunned down first."

Jason pounded his fist. "It's a bet."

"Besides, whoever kills who has to shoulder more weight when the hammer of justice comes down on'em. We get promotions regardless."

***

Zippy and his team followed instructions. In the process, they became excited spotting a car trailing Zoo. MuMu clicked the safety off the AR-15. He was anxious to empty the hundred-round drum on something. Anything posing a threat to the camp.

"We getting some rec' or what?" Booby licked his lips. He was young and ambitious, eager for more drama.

Lil' Zippy said, "We'll see …"

Zoo pulled the Bentley truck out front of one of the new trap houses on Green Street. The Nissan eased onto a second street, parking.

The trio of wild youngins parked seven houses down keeping their eyes glued, watching Brick step out cautiously. He looked around like a thief scheming on a plot. In the blink of an eye, he vanished into darkness.

"Where the fuck that country nigga go?" MuMu tried to spot him.

Booby was on alert. "That dude move like a fiend, right?"

"I'm ready for blood. We should hunt that nigga down. Gut'em like a deer."

Lil' Zippy checked the hunting knife on his waist. "Hold me down right quick. I'll be right back." He jumped out.

Walking up the block, he removed the blade slowly, smoothly. Circling the Nissan, he tried each door to see if it was unlocked or if anyone would come to its defense. He hoped Brick came rushing back. The driver's door was unlocked. Easing the door open, he slid in checking everywhere for weapons. Instead, all he found was drug paraphernalia.

Reaching beneath the steering wheel, he yanked wires down, using the sharp edge of the knife to sever them. He then made sure each door was locked before getting out and slashing each tire.

Casually, he walked back to the truck dialing Zoo. When he answered, he said, "That nigga Brick in the area on foot. He's all yours."

Zoo hung up.

Chapter 27

Taylor handed over the plastic bag filled with clothing he'd retrieved days ago from Brick's old trap house.

Zoo removed the contents right there in the middle of the yard. Sheba and Solomon sat loyal and obedient waiting for his command. They watched him closely, panting, licking their snouts hungrily.

He gripped them by the back collar, rubbing their noses in the scented clothes. They whined, frenzied, thirsting for blood.

"Smell it. Smell it," he taunted them until they started biting and chewing on the clothes vigorously. He growled at his two killing machines. "Now go get'em for me!"

Ferociously, both animals leaped over the five-foot steel gate with ease, dashing off through the streets in a frenetic search.

***

Brick snatched the pistol off his waistband. So badly he wanted to take another dose of the dope in his sock, but his thirst for Zoo was so strong he could literally smell the man's expensive cologne lingering with the breeze.

Blended perfectly with the shadows, he peeked around the abandoned house, laying his sights on the powerful boss who stood against his luxury SUV, oblivious. "Stay your ass right there, rich nigga. I'ma take everything, even your fuckin' life, BITCH!" He cocked the pistol.

The hairs on his neck stood up. The low growls got his attention. Slowly, he turned, frightened by what he may find. "What the hell?"

Two sets of icy blue eyes glistened under the moonlight. They sneered evilly, their razor-sharp teeth shining like silver. He trembled. "Wolves?" he said, confused. They licked their snouts hungrily, growling fiercely. "Ah, damn."

Brick pressed his body up against the house. Piss trickled down his leg, fear surged through his core, paralyzing him. He had nowhere to run. Desperate, he fired his weapon recklessly. *BOOM-BOOM-BOOM!* The pistol screamed. All misses. The wolves were unfazed. The closest wolf lurched into the air, its thick, long fangs snapping down on the gun like it was flesh. Brick let go and with haste, ran for dear life.

There was a neighboring yard fenced in. He sprang from the ground, hopping over easily. He ran hard, hopping another. Brick took one peek back to notice both dogs were right on his heels. They were hunting him, chasing him into exhaustion.

Brick jumped another gate. He then jumped onto a shed, sweating heavily. Winded, he prayed the big ungodly animals wouldn't reach him. They jumped the gate, charging at the shed. They couldn't reach him, so he burst into a sinister fit of laughter. "Fuck wrong with you stupid shits? You can't get me, bitches!"

The wolves hounded.

One looked around. There was a crate in which Brick used to get atop the tool shed. The wolf jumped onto it then onto the shed easily. Brick, terrified, couldn't believe what he was seeing. As the beast neared him, its teeth visible ready to sink in him, Brick stood on the edge. At the bottom, the second animal was on its hind legs waiting for its partner to force its prey off the ledge. Hungry teeth were waiting.

The wolf lurched forward. Brick dashed to the side, jumping to the left as the animal fell from the shed. He rolled, getting back to his feet, running top speed through a backyard. He was too afraid to look back but unable to stop himself. He dashed through the narrow driveway. The wolves were over the privacy fence heading his way rapidly. Suddenly, he tripped off a sprinkler system.

"Shit!" He got to his feet running up the street. He could hear the animals' paws pounding the ground, gaining speed. His entire body ached. Out of breath, he ran in and out of cars. Hidden behind a house, he sucked in air, desperate to sooth his burning lungs.

And then they came charging into the yard. Screaming for help as he ran, Brick hauled ass until he was back at square one. His old trap house. Bursting inside using the backdoor, he locked the dogs out, pressing his weight against the door while they barked and scratched. He chuckled at himself having escaped them again. He couldn't believe how massive they were, and frightening. He couldn't imagine them biting him. "Where the fuck them shits come from?" he wheezed.

When his breathing became better, he stood, no longer worried about some dumb dogs. His body craved to get high. He needed to feel the addiction. Brick rounded the corner of the bedroom. The house was pitch black, the way he loved it. But something was off. Before he could bolt and throw his body out the window to elude the immediate danger lurking along the walls, he was struck across the head.

Brick woke up, mouth gagged and taped, the pissy, shitty toilet water splashed across his face.

"That's right. Wake your ass up. We don't want you to miss a thing," the cute chick said. Brick could see up her dress.

He then realized he was in a small bathroom, hands cuffed to a thick toilet pipe. He had been stripped down to his pissy underwear. *Let me go!* he tried to yell, but couldn't. He laid across the wet, tiled bathroom floor at the mercy of …

The chick stepped aside, and then his heart broke. Zoo entered the doorway, towering over him. The murder in his eyes gave Brick the chills. *He can't know it was me that killed his sister*, he thought.

"I almost thought you were better than me, nigga. You was hitting my spots, my peoples, you killed my sister."

Brick yelled and kicked to deny.

"I'm here to get my licks back. I don't get over, never. I get even, boy." Zoo kicked him in the gut, and Brick groaned in agony. "Sheba. Solomon."

Wide eyed, Brick tried to crawl behind the toilet and away from the same two savage beasts that chased him. They were a part of Zoo's army as well, and now he regretted never taking anything from the man. Both wolves came into the bathroom appearing harmless. They sniffed at his feet, growling. They knew that scent. It was food. Both animals sat watching their master, cutting their eyes to Brick, who couldn't believe what was going on. He pass out, overwhelmed with fear and anxiety.

Zoo glared, red fury burning in his vision malevolently.

The hungry wolves licked their snouts, whining. They watched him.

Zoo pointed to Brick, who was waking up. He gave the word, "Eat'em."

Feverishly, razor-sharp teeth sank into flesh. In a frenzy, they ripped muscle, crushing down on ankles and knees. Brick yelled until his throat was swollen. As the wolves devoured him alive, Zoo and his crew watched unfazed and emotionless. Sheba ripped testicles away. Solomon bit into the chest for the heart. They chowed down on every inch, snatching his throat away.

In minutes, all that was left of Brick was what the wolves were uninterested in. They licked bones, their snouts. Sitting on filled bellies, they stared up at him. He could only imagine what they were thinking. *Who next?*

***

Executing an arrest warrant, the US Marshals breached the drug house in the wee hours of a Sunday morning. The horrendous smell of death pushed the team back out.

When they were finally able to enter, Agent Vincent Taylor and his partner, Jason Bryson, frowned.

When they discovered Brick in the bathroom bound to the toilet dead, it was hard to identify his cause of death.

"What the fuck happened in here?"

Jason kept his face covered. "Lord."

Vincent laid the toilet seat down, throwing down the indictment. "You have the right to remain silent …" he began.

Chapter 28

Keisha stumbled into her apartment around 3 a.m., drunk and extremely horny. She pulled the young boy in with her by the shirt then pushed him up against the wall. She locked the door hurriedly before kicking her high heels off. The shoulder straps to her dress came off first, then she wiggled out the tight fabric, exposing her desirous figure.

Lustfully, she asked, "Aren't you my son's friend?" She stood taller than the teen by two inches. She knew he was young, but that was what she craved nowadays. A fetish that flourished every time she looked around and noticed it was the young boys who were feared, heartless savages getting all the money. If she put the pussy on the right one, she'd never have to worry about another dollar. "Aren't you?" She kissed his handsome face.

"You know I am."

Keisha was turned the fuck on. If the boy was friends with Lil' Monkey, it meant he had to be getting money with Zoo. She stepped out the thong, then undid her bra, sucking his neck. "How old are you?"

"Fourteen."

"You know how to fuck a grown pussy?"

"Nah."

"You gon' learn today." She kissed his face hungrily, prying loose his belt. "You better not tell my son nothing."

"I won't," he moaned.

Keisha had his pants down. Her salivating mouth was overfilled. A moan escaped her lips as she gripped his dick and balls with both hands. She had to take a step back to get a good look at him and his joint. "You're fourteen?"

He nodded, grinning.

It's something in the mu'fucking water 'round this bitch, she thought, getting down on her knees. Sloppily, she wrapped her sexy, moist lips around his dick. Feverishly, she gave him the best head a project bitch could perform. She ate his dick off the bone, and his young excitement stood tall like a black Statue of Liberty. She devoured it as if her freedom depended on it. It did. The moment a throaty sigh left his lips while he held her head deep down on his pole, she knew her goal was accomplished. She took all his seeds down her face. He shuddered in total ecstasy. Unlike any head he encountered and if he didn't know any better, he'd handcuff her ass.

Keisha stood. "Get that dick back up." She headed into the kitchen, taking the bottle of Hennessy out the cabinet. She guzzled it down, swallowing like a champ.

The boy was in the center of her living room, dick in hand, ready to stab something to death. She smiled, drunk. He sat on the couch stroking it, putting a condom on. She headed to him. "Lord, forgive me. I'm finna fuck this lil' boy head up."

She mounted his dick, and the wetness of her pussy splashed across his lap the moment she eased down the length of him. He was larger inside her pussy than expected. Keisha started riding his dick, pushing her breasts into his face.

"Suu, ooh, boy. Suck them nipples. Suck'em hard! Bite the fuck out'em." She gyrated her hips, getting his dick to hit hard to reach places. He smacked both ass cheeks viciously. It stung, and she loved it.

"That's right, boy, fuck this grown pussy with your dick. Smack my ass! Harder. Harder!" she yelled, busting a nut. She rubbed her clit, increasing the power of her orgasm. Soon, she was shivering like a hoe in the cold, a second nut punching through her system like a battering ram. "Uhhh … fuck me!" She convulsed, releasing a strong nut. The room spun around in her head. He smacked her ass forcefully, sucking her nipples, biting roughly.

The front door came open. She heard it but didn't care who the fuck it was. She hadn't cum this hard in two years and didn't want it to stop. A third orgasm was building, causing her to grind into his dick harder as his young meaty head rubbed the G spot.

"Oh my goddd …" She quivered violently. Her pussy was having spasms. She was on the brink of another. The room was spinning out of control. Her mind was drifting into space. The pussy made noisy, gushy sounds. Her walls tightened around his joint.

"Ooh, damn, this dick is so good, lil' boy," she screamed out in lust. The orgasm gave her chills. Her heart pounded so hard it threatened to explode. While she came all over him, hands rubbed all over her body, some squeezing her super fat ass. She loved it more. Hands were all over her.

She looked back at her ass as it bounced in his lap. She went into a daze, putting on a show. Three teens stood behind her with dicks out. More of Lil' Monkey's friends. The boy she rode like a Harley pulled her into him. Her hips poked out, ass on display while her pussy rose and fell on his dick.

Suddenly, dick was running up in her ass. She came instantly, though it hurt like hell. She welcomed it. The liquor had her loose. One dick hit her stomach, while the other in her ass intensified the sensation. Double penetration had never felt so great.

"Shit. Shit. Shit. Fuck me!" she grimaced, wincing as her derriere got ravished. "Damn, pull it out. I can't take both." she cried as the dick hit too hard, too deep. "I'm going to shit on myself."

Soon, her hair was being gripped. She had a dick on both sides of her face. The devious expressions on the faces turned her on more. Seeing their dicks, she knew something was definitely in the water. Keisha sucked all their dicks. She was also passed around and slaughtered by the band of thugs. Hours later, she was sprawled across the couch, exhausted and unable to move. Her pussy was sore, ass swollen, jaws aching. She drifted off to sleep.

Dressed, the young boys stood around laughing and slapping hands. They took Keisha through the mud. Lil' Zippy removed the black cloth off the large plastic box container. The spider hissed aggressively, agitated.

"Man, hurry up." MuMu smiled, anxious.

He set the box on her big ass, sliding the lid back. The creature scurried out, sinking its fangs into Keisha's lower back. She moaned. The spider went up her spine, sinking its fangs. She continued to moan, groan, and grunt. Before long, she was marked with over a dozen bites. Her flawless shape had begun swelling tremendously. As venom set to turn muscle into liquid, the spider began its feast, having been starved.

Lil' Zippy collected all evidence. What Keisha had not known was that her son, Lil' Monkey, had gotten word to Zoo that his mother was becoming an informant. The young boy sent his blessing, wanting his mother out the world. And as promised, she wouldn't be done harsh, brutally. He had given her the easy route out.

***

Shooter massaged his jaw with ice. It still ached and hurt to eat. His tongue ran across his dentures, anger quickly filling his chest. Zoo hadn't died and this was unacceptable. He still felt humiliated, embarrassed. Revenge was priority number one.

G50 passed him the blunt of synthetic weed, spice. "Damn, my nigga, you good?"

"Fuck nah, I ain't good. Your bitch ass cousin got me over this mufucker fucked up. Do I look good?" he retorted, taking the blunt with attitude.

Chuckling, G50 replied, "I'm just checkin' on you, nigga."

"Ain't shit funny though, homes." He glared. "You know just like I know that nigga was dead ass wrong."

G50 kept quiet, nodding in agreeance.

"On BLOOD, if it wasn't for you, I would've been killed that fuck ass boy!"

"I fucks with you tight, homie, love you like a brother, but Zoo family. I don't agree with him at times, but if you ever thought about hurting him, we'll have to go our ways, Gee."

His tone made Shooter mad. "Nigga, you sound like you rocking hard with that clown, dawg."

G50 ignored his emotional friend as he pulled into a parking spot outside his baby mother's crib in Ashley Apartments. "You trippin', homes. Sit tight, I'll be right back."

Shooter inhaled, exhaled hard and sharp, watching his friend run inside. They had been friends since kids, a friendship of fifteen years, like family. Both shared aspirations of becoming major figures in the streets, but Zoo kept them from reaching. Tensions were growing. Soldiers dropping like flies. Bullets hitting too close to home. As G50 came back from giving his baby mother a load of cash, he prayed.

"Mannn," G50 drawled. "Zoo wants us to pull up on'em. I know you ain't really feeling bruh right now, though, so do you wanna get drop off?"

"Where he at?"

G50 began rolling another blunt of spice. "At a duck-off spot over in West Columbia. The Ramada Inn." He dug his pinky nail into his nose, irritated with a load of snot he quickly flicked out the window, wiping the remnants on his True Religion jeans. "You goin' with me or what?" He continued to roll.

Before he could light the blunt, the barrel of the Glock .17 was pressed against his jaw bones. "Don't be surprised, nigga. You know I'm bloody Shooter. SUWU!"

"B-brah?"

"B-brah, hell. I'm sick of you fucking fake wanna-be blood niggas. You and that fuck boy, Zoo, don't deserve to have PineHurst. I do! And to make sure I get it, y'all bitches gotta go. All of ya."

BOOM! The blast was bright and deafening. G50's head bust the driver side window. Blood and gristle splattered everywhere.

Shooter looked around the parking lot, panicking. No one seemed to be coming with haste. He rummaged through his friend's pockets removing money and his cell phone. Leaning over his bloody friend, he opened the driver's door completely. Without sympathy or remorse, he forcefully kicked his body out the truck into bushes. "Fuck ass nigga. Gang!"

He climbed behind the wheel, fishtailing out the lot.

***

Babygirl bit into the pillow, overwhelmed with ecstasy. Her sweet moans a melody to the ears as her stomach tightened. Her body tensed and shivered uncontrollably. The orgasm was aggressive as it surged through her body like the aftershocks of an earthquake. She groaned deeply and throaty, gripping the sheets while throwing her ass back while he ate it like groceries. The sensation was new to her. Obsessive, she didn't want it to ever end. Warm tears welled as each flick of his hot tongue entered her spread butthole. The strings to her heart were stuck perfectly, making her cry against her will.

"Zoo ... P-pleazzz don't-stop-daddy. Please, don't, baby." She shuddered. "I'm cummiinngg out my azzz," she shrilled as a second extracted orgasm washed over her. "I'm cummiinngg agaaainnn ..."

He spread her ass forcefully with brute strength in attempt to have his tongue reach two inches deep. The only way to keep his mind preoccupied was to fuck and suck. Babygirl was the only chick he could trust at the moment.

Her body collapsed across the bed, exhausted. He mounted her with a donkey dick. Applying KY jelly, he massaged his dick then her ass crack. Pressing his helmet against her asshole, he eased in. She yelped, and her head snapped up from the pillow. Before she could turn away, he gripped her tiny waist with his big hands.

"Chill, you can handle it, ight."

She whined, "Nooo, baby. It hurts already, it's too big." She quivered.

But her pleas fell on deaf ears. He continued to push his lumber into her bottom. She cried and moaned, fighting and biting the bed. After a while, he had the young stallion broken in. Babygirl was taking it like a champ. He dug her out until he, too, was spent. He collapsed beside her, panting.

"Dat ... was ... GOOD!" she confessed. "You took my virginity twice." She pouted playfully. "Now my booty hole is hurting so BAD!"

They laughed. "My bad, Babygirl. I need that pressure though."

She kissed his chiseled chest. "Don't apologize, baby. You know you can do whatever you wanna do to me. I'm down, I'm yours, even though it ain't official," she teased.

Though tired, he couldn't help but to admire her tight, soft, tender young body that always got a reaction. "I'm thirsty, you want something from the vending machine?"

"I'm good. Matter fact, I'ma go. I gotta get my phone and G50 dem on the way." He sat up, getting dressed.

Babygirl couldn't control herself. As he left out, she began to play with her love box, anticipating his return.

"Lord …" She tremored as the orgasm subsided. "Where is he? I'm gon' eat his ass this time …"

A loud thud got her attention. Alert, she grabbed her baby blue .380 and tiptoed to the door.

***

Zoo dug his hand into the vending machine slot retrieving drinks in a hurry to get back to his hotel room. Killing Brick rewarded him with a breath of fresh air. It wouldn't bring back Maya, but at least her killer would not be living. He had to start preparing funeral arrangements. It was no doubt he had to send her off with style.

There was so much to do in such little time. Everyone was blowing up his phone to check on his well-being. He wasn't open to having any conversation. In fact, the only person he wanted to speak with was a travel adviser. The city was in an uproar. Protesters had the streets on lock with the defund the police movement. It was as if everything was changing right before his eyes, and as a survivor, he had to adapt.

As he stood, a barrel of cold steel kissed the nape of his neck. His stomach tightened instantaneously. The urge to shit his pants was strong. *Ain't this 'bout a bitch*, he cursed himself mentally.

"Straighten yo' ass up, boy!" The frigid tone gave him the chills.

"Who the fuck—"

The pistol dug deep into his neck. "Shut the fuck up, nigga, 'fore I shoot the shit outta you. Now put your hands on the machine."

He did so, timid. It was over for him. He had been caught slipping and silently, he regretted dismissing his youngins for the night so he could relax.

The assailant's hand roamed over his waist quickly. Hope was lost when his pistol was removed. *Who got me down bad?*

"You ain't gon' need this."

"Yo, bruh. Get what you gon' take and keep it pushin'."

A sinister chuckle gave him goosebumps. "Bitch boy, you ain't tough. Matter fact, what room did you just come out of?" Two pistols were now pressed in his neck. "I ain't gonna ask again!"

"Two nineteen, dawg." He glared at the reflection in the machine's glass. "Shooter?"

BAM! The blow landed behind Zoo's head. "Yeah, it's me, nigga. Your worst fucking nightmare." Shooter shoved him.

Holding the lump in his head, Zoo began the short walk. All odds were against him. He stopped outside the room door. Shooter shoved him harder. "Bitch, go 'head open it before I dap your shit back."

The first thing he noticed entering the room … Babygirl was gone. He realized it was all a set up. "So what you want, nigga?"

Shooter kicked the door shut. "Pull your phone out, call the godfather."

"For what?" he snarled.

"Fuck boy, do it!"

"To say what, dawg?"

"That you want to transfer power. You're stepping down and giving me the 'HIGH' position."

"You know he ain't goin' for it. Not like this anyway."

"Bitch, do it!" Shooter aimed both pistols at his face.

Zoo took a step back, then another. Making the call, he paced it on speaker. Voicemail.

"Call again!"

He took another step backward. "Ight, dawg, chill."

As the phone rang, his sights landed on a pair of cute toes. Voicemail, again.

Shooter was livid. "Call again. You better hope he answer."

Babygirl tried desperately to control her panting and drumming heart. She stood behind the open bathroom door. If something was to happen to Zoo, she'd lose it. She heard his voice but couldn't see him. Not until he finally stepped back into view.

She gripped the .380 tightly, sucking in a deep breath.

"He still ain't answering, dawg."

BLAH! The shot startled her. Zoo fell backward.

Babygirl burst from behind the door, distracting Shooter in time to throw off his aim as the gun exploded, its hot lead burying itself beside Zoo's head. She aimed the .380 at his chest, squeezing the trigger, never flinching.

Pap-Pap-Pap!

"You tried the wrong bitch, nigga!" She glared. "Fuck is wrong with you." She started to give him the whole clip, but Zoo was groaning, holding the wound in his left arm.

"Get me to a hospital. We gotta get outta here," he grunted, sitting up. She helped him to his feet, then rushed around the room to collect everything linking them to the room.

***

Someone had heard the shots and dialed the police. Stepping out onto the outdoor walkway, she headed toward the room. With the door left wide open, she saw the body sprawled across the floor.

Panicking, she dialed police again, rolling him over.

"9-1-1 operator, what's your emergency?"

"Oh my god. There's a man shot in a motel room," she yelled.

"Ma'am, calm down. What's his condition? Can you tell me?"

"He's ... alive ... barely."

"Stay with him, help is on the way."

***

Zoo sat up on the hospital bed while the nurse rewrapped the wound, preparing him for discharge. The pain pills helped tremendously. He shook away the near-death experience. Lately, he found himself escaping death by inches. It was beginning to give him PTSD. He wasn't sure if he could afford to keep getting shot at and hit. Again, someone was saving him. Was it God sparing him? He couldn't be sure. One thing for sure, he needed a vacation and would be planning one in the days to come.

"There, that should be good enough. Try not to get it wet when you shower, and have your bandage changed every twenty-four hours. Also, take these antibiotics twice a day as well. The doctor has filled you an order of Percocets for seven days that should keep you out of pain." The nurse smiled then left.

Babygirl entered the room. The look on her face filled his gut with an uncanny feeling. "What's wrong?" he asked.

"We need to get out of here."

"What?"

"Shooter is alive. He didn't die," she answered gravely.

Fuck, he thought. He took out his phone to dial his youngins. Eliminating Shooter could easily be done.

"Wait. Don't call nobody. There's something else, the feds just came to his room. I think he's indicted. We should leave."

That was all he needed to hear ...

Chapter 29

Queenie swallowed her psych medications dry, needing relief from the evil thoughts of harming someone, anyone. Frustrated and hurt, so much of her time had been in confinement while her sister Precious was out there somewhere. She couldn't fathom what her sister was experiencing or if she was even alive. Now that she was free, she needed the ball in motion to find Precious and Mathew immediately.

"I told you I was going to help you, but right now I need you to help me as well." She slapped the sun visor closed, riding in the passenger seat.

Krissy asked, cutting her eyes, "Anything, what's up, boo?"

"I wanna kill my father. Take me to his house."

"You sure 'bout that?"

She stared, fervent. It was her answer. She was dead ass serious. Krissy straightened in her seat. "Okay, where to?"

The noon sun was high and bright in the cloudless blue sky. Queenie instructed Krissy to park two houses down. She climbed out with Krissy glued to her thigh. The knife on her hip was cool against the skin. If she ran into Mathew Wilks, there would be no hesitation.

As they entered the front yard to where she grew up, they noticed the windows were bare. From the street, anyone could see that no one was living there. Everything was gone. Queenie turned the doorknob, locked. She then went around back. Locked as well. She then tried to lift a window. She didn't want to believe her dad was gone. She could feel his presence still as goosebumps covered her skin.

"Nobody is here, boo." Krissy held her hand to the window, taking a good peek inside.

Queenie still tried to push up each window.

"Where else could he be?"

"I don't know, but let's go." She stormed away heatedly.

A few minutes into the drive and after leaving her friend Miranda's parents' home, getting no answer, she wanted to ball up somewhere and cry herself to sleep. Every day in jail she dreamed of the day she got released and approached her dad. She could almost smell his blood as she stabbed him over and over, repeatedly, in her mind. She clenched her jaw at the thought.

Krissy broke the silence. "You good, boo?"

"In my head."

"Hold on, let me take this call. It's my lawyer," she said. "Hey, Mrs. Johnson?"

"Ms. Burress, I spoke to the lead investigator, and they're expecting you to be turning yourself in by the end of this week."

Sighing, she said, "Mrs. Johnson, no lie, I'm going to need you to push it back one more week. I'm getting all my stuff in order. Can you please do it for me, please?"

"I do not like going back on my word to anyone. I like to keep my credibility official. But since you're a business woman and have a lot going for yourself, I'm going to ask for one more week. The sooner you get this part of the process out the way, the better. Right now, it's hindering you from moving forward."

"Okay, I got you, thank you. I 'preciate all that you've done, Mrs. Johnson. Let me know what date and we'll go from there."

"Will do, girl. Be safe and I'll be in touch." The attorney hung up.

Krissy cast her gaze at Queenie. "We gotta stop downtown to get some gas."

A few minutes later, she was coming off the highway ramp into Elm Street gas station.

"Gimme the money. I'll pay, you pump. I have to get some stamps and put money on this phone," she said, thinking of LaLa and Mena.

As she paid the twenty on pump two, got minutes and stamps, she headed up the aisle for a box of envelopes. Turning on the balls of her feet, an unexpected face was heading directly her way.

***

Panic set in, his phone was ringing off the chain. Calls were coming from those closest to him.

"Babygirl, take this money across the hall. Don't open the door for anybody."

"What about you?" she asked, worried, and for the first time in a long time, afraid for him. "Don't even think about leaving me behind."

He glared. "Go. I'll send for you."

She shouldered the duffle bag loaded with half-million cash, leaving apartment 1220, going to her own across the hall.

Zoo answered the call.

"Bruh?"

"Yeah, what's good, Zippy?"

"Dawg, get somewhere and lay. The feds just hit every apartment in the hood, locking everybody up," he spoke urgently, then hung up abruptly.

Zoo pulled the laptop out. In a hurry, he dialed his attorney, Todd Rutherwood, while punching in codes to his bank accounts.

"Yes?"

"Todd, what's the issue?" he asked.

"The feds are coming down on everything. You should—" *BOOOM!* The explosion coming from the attorney's end was ear piercing. He listened. "FBI. Get down!" His heart sank into his gut. "Todd Rutherwood, you have the—"

Zoo hung up. He tried to wire money from his few accounts but was unable to. The feds froze his accounts. His offshore accounts were still active. He slammed the laptop shut. "Lil' Pooh-Butt," he called over his youngest goon, an eleven-year-old. "Smash this up real good and burn it on the patio."

In a rush, he took the brick of heroin off the counter. Worrisome, the youngin' stood around watching him carefully. "Let's go, we're leaving town." Booby and Taylor followed him out the apartment, leaving Lil' Pooh-Butt behind. He wanted to have Babygirl come but decided against it.

Instead of the elevator, they took the stairs down twelve flights.

***

Agent Jason Bryson and his partner, Vincent Taylor, took up each side of Apt B4. State and local law enforcement aided US Marshals and the fugitive task force in apprehending wanted suspect, Keisha Durham, charged with conspiracy.

Simultaneously, apartment doors were knocked off hinges.

On three counts, the battering ram crashed the door, splintering wood bursting into the air. "Move. Move. Move. FBI, get down!"

"FBI!"

"Get—"

Agents were met with a horrendous stench of death. Jason Bryson gagged. The agents rushed past the body into rooms, securing the premises.

"House all clear."

"What in the hell is this?" Vincent holstered his weapon, covering his nose and mouth, hoping to not smell or taste the air.

Keisha Durham was sprawled across the couch swollen, leaking thick puss. She was three times her normal size. Her body was purple, blue, and green. She was expanded like a balloon, toxins brewing within.

Jason had his flashlight and pistol on her corpse, stepping in for a better inspection. Something was feasting on her, something large. Just as he inched closer, it scurried onto her ass, hissing. A Brazilian spider, one good, long, six ounces heavy.

Jason fell, startled, caught completely by surprise. The eight-legged critter plunged to the floor, landing in a thud, protecting its meal and territory.

Agents yelled in fear, most bolting out the door in a stampede. None wanted anything to do with the massive spider as it chased toward Jason.

"Kill this son of a bitch!" he yelped in terror. He had dropped his own weapon.

Vincent took aim, tapping the trigger twice before the critter could sink its fangs into his partner's boot. Bloody guts splattered everywhere. He holstered his smoking pistol, disgusted.

"Someone collect it as evidence. We'll lock its ass up too."

Jason hurried to his feet. "That thing almost ate me!"

Vincent laughed. "Don't worry, partner, you're safe now."

They looked around the room, refusing to move from where they stood. If anything else was hiding, they would not be the ones searching.

"Sir, we have your primary suspect's whereabouts." Another agent emerged in the doorway.

Both agents bolted out the door. Zoo could not escape the wrath of the federal government.

***

Landing on the twelfth floor, the elevator doors slid open. Blue stepped off first, then Cloud. The two hoped Milli had given them the proper whereabouts to kill Zoo, before he died.

"What apartment number that faggot, bitch ass little boy say again?" Cloud gritted.

"It's 1220. We're almost there."

Cloud removed two twin Desert Eagle .44s from his waistband. Blue flung the trench raincoat open, exposing an AR-15 with a fifty-round drum.

The instant they found 1220, Cloud aimed both pistols at the locks, erupting loudly. *BLOOOM-BLOOOM!*

Blue kicked the rest of the door off its hinges. Cloud flanked him. The teen jumped to his feet, startled from the forced entry. He lurched for the AK-47 on the coffee table.

BLA-LAT! Two AR rounds struck the dashing teen in the legs, sending him crashing to the floor screaming in agony. "Where you goin?" Blue yelled.

Cloud aimed the barrel at this head. "Where the fuck is my son?"

"Arrgghh … Shit. Fuck!" he yelled. "I'm hit."

"Nah, bitch. You gon' die if you don't tell me where my son Booby is."

The teen cried in agony. "Shit! He-he-he just left with Zoo, man!"

"Where they going?"

When the rest of the words left the teen's lips, Cloud planted two bullets in his face before storming out.

***

Gunshots ringing about gave him the chills. Together, Zoo, Taylor, and Booby descended the flight of stairs quickly. On the first level, he stopped to catch his breath. Taylor stuck his head out the door to check the coast. Panting, he answered his phone.

"What the hell was that, Babygirl?"

"Where are you. Are you leaving me?" she asked, frantic.

"Stay put. Now what was that?"

"Some niggas rushed the spot. They killed Lil' Pooh-Butt," she panted, near anxiety attack. "Should I hit the kill switch on'em?" She gripped the grenade. "Wait. They're leaving. They're coming your way ... They're gone. No ... I think the fuckin' feds are rushing that spot." Her voice went hush as she watch frightfully through the peephole. "What should I do, baby?"

Zoo wanted to go back up to face the gangsters that murdered one of his goons, but he couldn't be stupid. The fear in Babygirl's voice made him weak. It would finish him if anything were to happen to her. She was his responsibility. "Listen, stay put. I'll send for you."

"I love you." She hung up.

He shoved the phone into his pocket. Taylor stepped back. "It don't look right, but there are too many cars."

Zoo took a deep breath. "Fuck it. We can't stay."

***

Jason Bryson chambered a round, straightening the vest across his chest. As they sat in the unmarked bread truck preparing to raid, the radio chimed with action.

Queen of the Zoo 2

"Shots fired. I repeat, shots fired!"

"Team one, move in!"

Vincent Taylor was amped waiting for the next call. He and his partner were a part of the second team.

"Team two, move. Move. Move!" the radio blared.

"No! Wait!" Vincent shouted. "Team two, hold your positions!"

Suddenly, Zoo's face came into view. Two teens walked beside him on high alert, guns out. Their menacing glares screamed trouble.

"Two suspects are exiting the front entrance from the elevators. They're leaving the building," the radio blared. "Suspects armed and dangerous."

Jason spat, "It's Cloud."

"And his son is walking with Zoo. This could get ugly. All units, hold your positions. We do not need casualties."

"This is a conviction on the line. We need suspects alive," Vincent said, highly anticipating the drama. Each agent watched in fear of a deadly confrontation. Tensions were so thick in the air everything moved in slow motion. "I say we let them leave and pounce in traffic."

"All units standby, prepare for pursuit."

***

Taylor was ready to get shit popping. He gripped the .45 ready to go live wire in order to protect Zoo. "It's undercover cops behind us, bruh. They're following us. What's up, what you wanna do? I'm wit' da shits."

"I'm itching to kill' sum'n too," Booby added.

Zoo glanced back nervously. The warning put fear in his heart. The brick of heroin in the glove compartment wasn't anything shorter than a life sentence, not including the guns. Suddenly, his life began flashing before his eyes. He checked over his shoulder once more. He spotted them easily.

"Fuck!"

"Let me out, I'll hold them off," Booby said.

"I can lose them if you want me to." Taylor gripped the steering wheel, easing smoothly through traffic, ready to stomp the gas. His brown gaze was full of determination, fearlessness.

Zoo was amazed his youngins were ready to go all out. He checked the side mirror once more. He had to be smart. "Fuck, nah. Pull into that gas station."

***

Her bladder gave, wetting her panties in horror the moment Zoo exited the Bentley truck in a hostile stride, heading directly for her. Krissy burst into tears. There was no escaping him. He had caught her slipping. She shuddered with fear. Her body convulsing, she thought she was going to have an early baby or a miscarriage. The anger in his eyes was traumatizing. "Lord, don't let'em kill me, please," she cried.

It was over for her. The queen bitch was finally meeting the Grim Reaper. He had come to collect her soul.

Zoo glanced over his shoulder, walking past Krissy's car and into the gas station. The feds were pulling into the large parking lot. A loyal goon followed behind him to aide in his getaway.

Queenie couldn't control the wild rumbling of her heart as he spotted her and rushed her way. The world seemed to stop on its axis. Time slowed to an abrupt halt as her stomach filled with butterflies. She watched him with googly eyes. Every night in jail, she wondered about the infamous Zoo.

"Queenie, right?" He checked over his shoulder.

Mesmerized in his handsomeness, she answered, "Yes?"

"Take this, hurry up, leave." He handed her the brick, a large set of keys, a cell phone, and a heavy pistol.

"Huh, wait, what?"

"Go. Please. Hurry, before the feds come in." He grabbed her arm. "And don't trust that chick, Krissy." He pushed her away.

By then, she could see what his urgency was about. Unmarked vehicles swarmed the front entrance. Taking everything, she raced to the side door before police could spot her. No one saw her stash the load into the bushes off camera. She went to the store window. She had gotten away in time.

The front entrance door opened.

Zoo looked around, and Queenie was out of sight.

Booby clutched his concealed pistol. "Homie, we're trapped. What you wanna do?" The teen was hyper.

"Don't worry, we're—"

Wham! "Uh-huh. I finally caught you, bitch ass!" The pistol smacked the back of his head. Cloud had snuck up from behind Zoo, having come through the side door. It didn't matter if police had that bitch surrounded. He was gangsta. Wouldn't shit stop him from getting his man. "Where the fuck you think you going, nigga? No motherfucking where!" he roared.

Booby stumbled out the way, confused. Zoo held the leaking gash on his head. "What the fuck, dawg?" He couldn't believe he'd been caught down bad again. This time, he was certain he wouldn't make it out alive. Babygirl was not there.

BLAH! The blast tore through his right shoulder, lifting and spinning him into the air. Zoo's body slapped the floor, twisted up.

"Ahhgghh! Fuck!"

"Take this shit to your grave, bitch." Cloud aimed at his stomach.

Queenie watched in horror.

BLAH! The gun erupted.

Zoo bellowed, gripping his stomach. It burned, his guts felt like they were being ripped away. Blood spurt onto the floor in a puddle, gurgling.

"You killed my daughter. My mother, my homies, my …" Cloud's gaze shifted to his son, who was staring at the scene wide eyed.

Outside, agents were breaching.

"Booby, get over here! Booby? Booby, come the fuck on," Cloud barked. Booby was in a daze but went to stand behind his father. It was as if he didn't know where he was.

Cloud aimed the pistol to finish off what he started as police sirens and lights blared behind them, surrounding the store.

Zoo winced in pain, holding the hole in his stomach. He could see the tempered round, the barrel ready to explode. It was over for him. He had reigned for years. If his destiny was to die like this … He had accepted his fate. If it was his times up, so be it.

"You tryna say sum'n before I send your ass to hell, pussy?"

He coughed up blood, chuckling sinisterly. "Booby …"

"Booby what?" Cloud glared.

"Booby … kill'em," Zoo whispered.

Cloud turned. Tears were streaming down his son's youthful face. He was confused. He didn't want to kill his daddy, but Zoo's words were like the voice of God that ordered his mind and heart to respond. It did. He raised the barrel, possessed, aiming at his father's face.

"Son? Boy … Put that shit—"

BLAH-BLAH- BLAHHH! A three piece crashed into his chest. His eyes were big as saucers. Fear and hot tears fell. He landed on the ground, dead.

Zoo felt himself getting sleepy. "Go, Booby, run," he whispered. But as he turned to make a run, the store was bum rushed with federal agents. Tens of barrels were pointed at the teen.

"FBI. Lay the weapon on the ground!"

Booby halted. Blue lights danced across tears imbued across his face.

"Weapon down, last warning."

His dad was dead by his hand. Zoo, his leader, was bleeding out. All hope was lost. He went to lay the gun down slowly. The same agent he shot on Green Street glared at him. This time it was him, Agent Jason Bryson, who had the luxury of shooting first.

Bullets spat from the service pistol the moment he let the gun fall. Slugs filled Booby. Blood spurted into mists. He fell backward, his watery eyes staring at Zoo's. Like a fish out of water, he took hollow breaths, then none.

Agents roped off the scene "Mr. Pierre 'Zoo' Montana. You're under arrest." Vincent Taylor dropped the thick indictment on his chest. It landed like a phone book.

Zoo closed his eyes, sleepy, whispering, "Dammmn ..."

Queenie watched everything unfold. Seeing Zoo get wheeled away, she couldn't help but to hear her own heart break for him. "I hope you make it, boo."

To Be Continued...
Queen of the Zoo 3
Coming Soon

Lock Down Publications and Ca$h Presents assisted publishing packages.

BASIC PACKAGE $499
Editing
Cover Design
Formatting

UPGRADED PACKAGE $800
Typing
Editing
Cover Design
Formatting

ADVANCE PACKAGE $1,200
Typing
Editing
Cover Design
Formatting
Copyright registration
Proofreading
Upload book to Amazon

LDP SUPREME PACKAGE $1,500
Typing
Editing
Cover Design
Formatting
Copyright registration
Proofreading
Set up Amazon account
Upload book to Amazon
Advertise on LDP Amazon and Facebook page

***Other services available upon request. Additional charges may apply
Lock Down Publications
P.O. Box 944
Stockbridge, GA 30281-9998
Phone # 470 303-9761

Submission Guideline

Submit the first three chapters of your completed manuscript to ldpsubmissions@gmail.com, subject line: Your book's title. The manuscript must be in a .doc file and sent as an attachment. Document should be in Times New Roman, double spaced and in size 12 font. Also, provide your synopsis and full contact information. If sending multiple submissions, they must each be in a separate email.

Have a story but no way to send it electronically? You can still submit to LDP/Ca$h Presents. Send in the first three chapters, written or typed, of your completed manuscript to:

LDP: Submissions Dept
Po Box 944
Stockbridge, Ga 30281

DO NOT send original manuscript. Must be a duplicate.

Provide your synopsis and a cover letter containing your full contact information.

Thanks for considering LDP and Ca$h Presents.

NEW RELEASES

ANGEL 3 by ANTHONY FIELDS
CLASSIC CITY by CHRIS GREEN
TIL DEATH by ARYANNA
IT'S JUST ME AND YOU by AH'MILLION
QUEEN OF THE ZOO 2 by BLACK MIGO

Black Migo

Coming Soon from Lock Down Publications/Ca$h Presents
BLOOD OF A BOSS **VI**
SHADOWS OF THE GAME II
TRAP BASTARD II
By **Askari**
LOYAL TO THE GAME **IV**
By **T.J. & Jelissa**
TRUE SAVAGE **VIII**
MIDNIGHT CARTEL IV
DOPE BOY MAGIC IV
CITY OF KINGZ III
NIGHTMARE ON SILENT AVE II
THE PLUG OF LIL MEXICO II
CLASSIC CITY II
By **Chris Green**
BLAST FOR ME **III**
A SAVAGE DOPEBOY III
CUTTHROAT MAFIA III
DUFFLE BAG CARTEL VII
HEARTLESS GOON VI
By **Ghost**
A HUSTLER'S DECEIT III
KILL ZONE II
BAE BELONGS TO ME III
TIL DEATH II
By **Aryanna**
KING OF THE TRAP III
By **T.J. Edwards**
GORILLAZ IN THE BAY V
3X KRAZY III

Queen of the Zoo 2

STRAIGHT BEAST MODE III
De'Kari
KINGPIN KILLAZ IV
STREET KINGS III
PAID IN BLOOD III
CARTEL KILLAZ IV
DOPE GODS III
Hood Rich
SINS OF A HUSTLA II
ASAD
RICH $AVAGE II
By Martell Troublesome Bolden
YAYO V
Bred In The Game 2
S. Allen
CREAM III
THE STREETS WILL TALK II
By Yolanda Moore
SON OF A DOPE FIEND III
HEAVEN GOT A GHETTO II
By Renta
LOYALTY AIN'T PROMISED III
By Keith Williams
I'M NOTHING WITHOUT HIS LOVE II
SINS OF A THUG II
TO THE THUG I LOVED BEFORE II
IN A HUSTLER I TRUST II
By Monet Dragun
QUIET MONEY IV
EXTENDED CLIP III

Black Migo

THUG LIFE IV
By **Trai'Quan**
THE STREETS MADE ME IV
By **Larry D. Wright**
IF YOU CROSS ME ONCE II
ANGEL IV
By **Anthony Fields**
THE STREETS WILL NEVER CLOSE IV
By K'ajji
HARD AND RUTHLESS III
KILLA KOUNTY III
By Khufu
MONEY GAME III
By Smoove Dolla
JACK BOYS VS DOPE BOYS II
A GANGSTA'S QUR'AN V
COKE GIRLZ II
By Romell Tukes
MURDA WAS THE CASE II
Elijah R. Freeman
THE STREETS NEVER LET GO II
By Robert Baptiste
AN UNFORESEEN LOVE III
By **Meesha**
KING OF THE TRENCHES III
by **GHOST & TRANAY ADAMS**

MONEY MAFIA II
LOYAL TO THE SOIL III
By **Jibril Williams**
QUEEN OF THE ZOO III

Queen of the Zoo 2

By **Black Migo**
VICIOUS LOYALTY III
By Kingpen
A GANGSTA'S PAIN III
By J-Blunt
CONFESSIONS OF A JACKBOY III
By Nicholas Lock
GRIMEY WAYS II
By Ray Vinci
KING KILLA II
By Vincent "Vitto" Holloway
BETRAYAL OF A THUG II
By Fre$h
THE MURDER QUEENS II
By Michael Gallon
THE BIRTH OF A GANGSTER II
By Delmont Player
TREAL LOVE II
By Le'Monica Jackson
FOR THE LOVE OF BLOOD II
By Jamel Mitchell
RAN OFF ON DA PLUG II
By Paper Boi Rari
HOOD CONSIGLIERE II
By Keese
PRETTY GIRLS DO NASTY THINGS II
By Nicole Goosby
PROTÉGÉ OF A LEGEND II
By Corey Robinson
IT'S JUST ME AND YOU II

Black Migo

By Ah'Million

Available Now

RESTRAINING ORDER **I & II**
By **CA$H & Coffee**
LOVE KNOWS NO BOUNDARIES **I II & III**
By **Coffee**
RAISED AS A GOON I, II, III & IV
BRED BY THE SLUMS I, II, III
BLAST FOR ME I & II
ROTTEN TO THE CORE I II III
A BRONX TALE I, II, III
DUFFLE BAG CARTEL I II III IV V VI
HEARTLESS GOON I II III IV V
A SAVAGE DOPEBOY I II
DRUG LORDS I II III
CUTTHROAT MAFIA I II
KING OF THE TRENCHES
By **Ghost**
LAY IT DOWN **I & II**
LAST OF A DYING BREED I II
BLOOD STAINS OF A SHOTTA I & II III
By **Jamaica**
LOYAL TO THE GAME I II III
LIFE OF SIN I, II III
By **TJ & Jelissa**

Queen of the Zoo 2

BLOODY COMMAS I & II
SKI MASK CARTEL I II & III
KING OF NEW YORK I II,III IV V
RISE TO POWER I II III
COKE KINGS I II III IV V
BORN HEARTLESS I II III IV
KING OF THE TRAP I II

By T.J. Edwards

IF LOVING HIM IS WRONG…I & II
LOVE ME EVEN WHEN IT HURTS I II III

By **Jelissa**

WHEN THE STREETS CLAP BACK I & II III
THE HEART OF A SAVAGE I II III
MONEY MAFIA
LOYAL TO THE SOIL I II

By **Jibril Williams**

A DISTINGUISHED THUG STOLE MY HEART I II & III
LOVE SHOULDN'T HURT I II III IV
RENEGADE BOYS I II III IV
PAID IN KARMA I II III
SAVAGE STORMS I II III
AN UNFORESEEN LOVE I II

By **Meesha**

A GANGSTER'S CODE I &, II III
A GANGSTER'S SYN I II III
THE SAVAGE LIFE I II III
CHAINED TO THE STREETS I II III
BLOOD ON THE MONEY I II III
A GANGSTA'S PAIN I II

By J-Blunt

Black Migo

PUSH IT TO THE LIMIT
By **Bre' Hayes**
BLOOD OF A BOSS **I, II, III, IV, V**
SHADOWS OF THE GAME
TRAP BASTARD
By **Askari**
THE STREETS BLEED MURDER **I, II & III**
THE HEART OF A GANGSTA I II& III
By **Jerry Jackson**
CUM FOR ME I II III IV V VI VII VIII
An **LDP Erotica Collaboration**
BRIDE OF A HUSTLA **I II & II**
THE FETTI GIRLS **I, II& III**
CORRUPTED BY A GANGSTA I, II III, IV
BLINDED BY HIS LOVE
THE PRICE YOU PAY FOR LOVE I, II ,III
DOPE GIRL MAGIC I II III
By **Destiny Skai**
WHEN A GOOD GIRL GOES BAD
By **Adrienne**
THE COST OF LOYALTY I II III
By Kweli
A GANGSTER'S REVENGE **I II III & IV**
THE BOSS MAN'S DAUGHTERS I II III IV V
A SAVAGE LOVE **I & II**
BAE BELONGS TO ME I II
A HUSTLER'S DECEIT I, II, III
WHAT BAD BITCHES DO I, II, III
SOUL OF A MONSTER I II III
KILL ZONE

Queen of the Zoo 2

A DOPE BOY'S QUEEN I II III

TIL DEATH

By **Aryanna**

A KINGPIN'S AMBITON

A KINGPIN'S AMBITION **II**

I MURDER FOR THE DOUGH

By **Ambitious**

TRUE SAVAGE I II III IV V VI VII

DOPE BOY MAGIC I, II, III

MIDNIGHT CARTEL I II III

CITY OF KINGZ I II

NIGHTMARE ON SILENT AVE

THE PLUG OF LIL MEXICO II

CLASSIC CITY

By **Chris Green**

A DOPEBOY'S PRAYER

By **Eddie "Wolf" Lee**

THE KING CARTEL **I, II & III**

By **Frank Gresham**

THESE NIGGAS AIN'T LOYAL **I, II & III**

By **Nikki Tee**

GANGSTA SHYT **I II &III**

By **CATO**

THE ULTIMATE BETRAYAL

By **Phoenix**

BOSS'N UP **I , II & III**

By **Royal Nicole**

I LOVE YOU TO DEATH

By **Destiny J**

I RIDE FOR MY HITTA

Black Migo

I STILL RIDE FOR MY HITTA
By **Misty Holt**
LOVE & CHASIN' PAPER
By **Qay Crockett**
TO DIE IN VAIN
SINS OF A HUSTLA
By **ASAD**
BROOKLYN HUSTLAZ
By **Boogsy Morina**
BROOKLYN ON LOCK I & II
By **Sonovia**
GANGSTA CITY
By **Teddy Duke**
A DRUG KING AND HIS DIAMOND I & II III
A DOPEMAN'S RICHES
HER MAN, MINE'S TOO I, II
CASH MONEY HO'S
THE WIFEY I USED TO BE I II
PRETTY GIRLS DO NASTY THINGS
By Nicole Goosby
TRAPHOUSE KING **I II & III**
KINGPIN KILLAZ I II III
STREET KINGS I II
PAID IN BLOOD **I II**
CARTEL KILLAZ I II III
DOPE GODS I II
By **Hood Rich**
LIPSTICK KILLAH **I, II, III**
CRIME OF PASSION I II & III
FRIEND OR FOE I II III

Queen of the Zoo 2

By **Mimi**
STEADY MOBBN' **I, II, III**
THE STREETS STAINED MY SOUL I II III
By **Marcellus Allen**
WHO SHOT YA **I, II, III**
SON OF A DOPE FIEND I II
HEAVEN GOT A GHETTO
Renta
GORILLAZ IN THE BAY **I II III IV**
TEARS OF A GANGSTA I II
3X KRAZY I II
STRAIGHT BEAST MODE I II
DE'KARI
TRIGGADALE I II III
MURDAROBER WAS THE CASE
Elijah R. Freeman
GOD BLESS THE TRAPPERS I, II, III
THESE SCANDALOUS STREETS I, II, III
FEAR MY GANGSTA I, II, III IV, V
THESE STREETS DON'T LOVE NOBODY I, II
BURY ME A G I, II, III, IV, V
A GANGSTA'S EMPIRE I, II, III, IV
THE DOPEMAN'S BODYGAURD I II
THE REALEST KILLAZ I II III
THE LAST OF THE OGS I II III
Tranay Adams
THE STREETS ARE CALLING
Duquie Wilson
MARRIED TO A BOSS I II III
By Destiny Skai & Chris Green

Black Migo

KINGZ OF THE GAME I II III IV V VI
Playa Ray
SLAUGHTER GANG I II III
RUTHLESS HEART I II III
By Willie Slaughter
FUK SHYT
By Blakk Diamond
DON'T F#CK WITH MY HEART I II
By Linnea
ADDICTED TO THE DRAMA I II III
IN THE ARM OF HIS BOSS II
By Jamila
YAYO I II III IV
A SHOOTER'S AMBITION I II
BRED IN THE GAME
By S. Allen
TRAP GOD I II III
RICH $AVAGE
MONEY IN THE GRAVE I II III
By Martell Troublesome Bolden
FOREVER GANGSTA
GLOCKS ON SATIN SHEETS I II
By Adrian Dulan
TOE TAGZ I II III IV
LEVELS TO THIS SHYT I II
IT'S JUST ME AND YOU
By Ah'Million
KINGPIN DREAMS I II III
RAN OFF ON DA PLUG
By Paper Boi Rari

Queen of the Zoo 2

CONFESSIONS OF A GANGSTA I II III IV
CONFESSIONS OF A JACKBOY I II
By Nicholas Lock
I'M NOTHING WITHOUT HIS LOVE
SINS OF A THUG
TO THE THUG I LOVED BEFORE
A GANGSTA SAVED XMAS
IN A HUSTLER I TRUST
By Monet Dragun
CAUGHT UP IN THE LIFE I II III
THE STREETS NEVER LET GO
By Robert Baptiste
NEW TO THE GAME I II III
MONEY, MURDER & MEMORIES I II III
By **Malik D. Rice**
LIFE OF A SAVAGE I II III
A GANGSTA'S QUR'AN I II III IV
MURDA SEASON I II III
GANGLAND CARTEL I II III
CHI'RAQ GANGSTAS I II III
KILLERS ON ELM STREET I II III
JACK BOYZ N DA BRONX I II III
A DOPEBOY'S DREAM I II III
JACK BOYS VS DOPE BOYS
COKE GIRLZ
By Romell Tukes
LOYALTY AIN'T PROMISED I II
By Keith Williams
QUIET MONEY I II III
THUG LIFE I II III

Black Migo

EXTENDED CLIP I II
By **Trai'Quan**
THE STREETS MADE ME I II III
By **Larry D. Wright**
THE ULTIMATE SACRIFICE I, II, III, IV, V, VI
KHADIFI
IF YOU CROSS ME ONCE
ANGEL I II III
IN THE BLINK OF AN EYE
By **Anthony Fields**
THE LIFE OF A HOOD STAR
By Ca$h & Rashia Wilson
THE STREETS WILL NEVER CLOSE I II III
By K'ajji
CREAM I II
THE STREETS WILL TALK
By Yolanda Moore
NIGHTMARES OF A HUSTLA I II III
By King Dream
CONCRETE KILLA I II III
VICIOUS LOYALTY I II
By Kingpen
HARD AND RUTHLESS I II
MOB TOWN 251
THE BILLIONAIRE BENTLEYS I II III
By Von Diesel
GHOST MOB
Stilloan Robinson
MOB TIES I II III IV V VI
By SayNoMore

Queen of the Zoo 2

BODYMORE MURDERLAND I II III

THE BIRTH OF A GANGSTER

By Delmont Player

FOR THE LOVE OF A BOSS

By C. D. Blue

MOBBED UP I II III IV

THE BRICK MAN I II III IV

THE COCAINE PRINCESS I II III IV V

By King Rio

KILLA KOUNTY I II III

By Khufu

MONEY GAME I II

By Smoove Dolla

A GANGSTA'S KARMA I II

By FLAME

KING OF THE TRENCHES I II

by **GHOST & TRANAY ADAMS**

QUEEN OF THE ZOO I II

By **Black Migo**

GRIMEY WAYS

By Ray Vinci

XMAS WITH AN ATL SHOOTER

By Ca$h & Destiny Skai

KING KILLA

By Vincent "Vitto" Holloway

BETRAYAL OF A THUG

By Fre$h

THE MURDER QUEENS

By Michael Gallon

TREAL LOVE

Black Migo

By Le'Monica Jackson

FOR THE LOVE OF BLOOD

By Jamel Mitchell

HOOD CONSIGLIERE

By Keese

PROTÉGÉ OF A LEGEND

By Corey Robinson

BOOKS BY LDP'S CEO, CA$H

TRUST IN NO MAN
TRUST IN NO MAN 2
TRUST IN NO MAN 3
BONDED BY BLOOD
SHORTY GOT A THUG
THUGS CRY
THUGS CRY 2
THUGS CRY 3
TRUST NO BITCH
TRUST NO BITCH 2
TRUST NO BITCH 3
TIL MY CASKET DROPS
RESTRAINING ORDER
RESTRAINING ORDER 2
IN LOVE WITH A CONVICT
LIFE OF A HOOD STAR
XMAS WITH AN ATL SHOOTER

Black Migo

CPSIA information can be obtained
at www.ICGtesting.com
Printed in the USA
LVHW081100290822
727089LV00007B/95